Vantage Points

To Lucretia Page,

Hope you enjoy this.

Ken Libbey

July 2001

Vantage Points

A Novel of Men and Women in World War II

Ken Libbey

Writers Club Press
San Jose New York Lincoln Shanghai

Vantage Points
A Novel of Men and Women
in World War II

Writers Club Press
an imprint of iUniverse.com, Inc.

For information address:
iUniverse.com, Inc.
5220 S 16th, Ste. 200
Lincoln, NE 68512
www.iuniverse.com

Cover Design by Steve Libbey

ISBN: 0-595-16848-5

Printed in the United States of America

This book is dedicated to my sons,
Stephen and Clark Libbey

I would like to thank my mother, Jean Libbey, son Clark, and friends Carol Addlestone and Michele Gill for the feedback they gave me on the manuscript. I am indebted to my son Stephen for the cover design.

List of Abbreviations

WAFS	Women's Auxiliary Flying Squadron
WASP	Women's Airforce Service Pilots
AAF	Army Air Forces
AAFB	Army Air Forces Base
ATC	Air Transport Command
CINCPAC	Commander-in-Chief, Pacific
CO	Commanding Officer
BOQ	Base Officers' Quarters
CPT	Civilian Pilot Training
PT	Primary Trainer
BT	Basic Trainer
AT	Advanced Trainer
APO	Army Post Office

Vantage Points

A Novel of Men and Women in World War II

Except for known historical figures, the characters in this book are fictitious, and any resemblance to persons living or dead is purely coincidental. Every effort was made to accurately portray the historical figures, but the scenes in which they appear are fictitious.

The Philippines

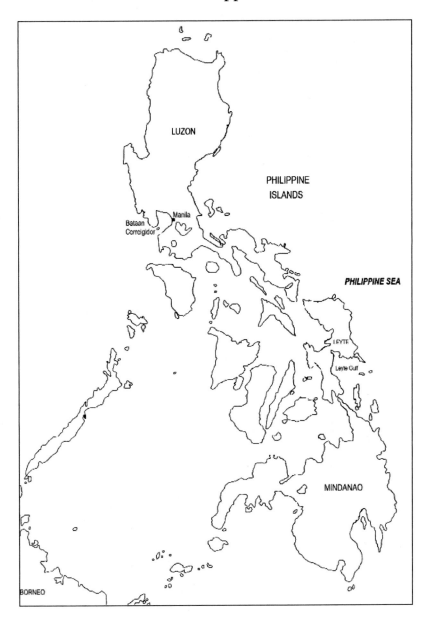

The Pacific

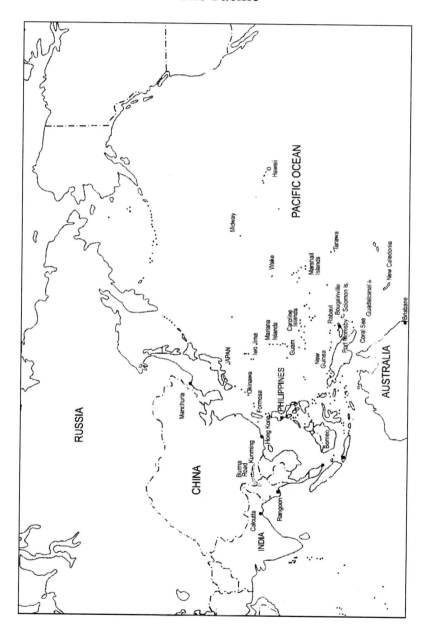

Sicily and Italy

I

Sioux City, Iowa
June 1940

It was Thursday afternoon, and Louise Mitchell had the rest of the day off from her job at the Cornelius Real Estate Agency in Sioux City. She did not earn much as a clerk-typist at the agency, but the job had an incalculable benefit for her. She managed her own workload, and as long as papers were ready when an agent needed them, she could come and go as she pleased. Whenever she could clear a half-day or more in good weather, she was on her bicycle covering the 12 miles to Schroeder Field in Merrill. Having made this trip countless times in the past 10 years, Louise had legs of steel.

Mr. Schroeder had sacrificed a cornfield to indulge his love of flying. He had even spent the money to pave the runway, something unusual for a small country field. Today Louise arrived just after 2 p.m. It was a beautiful day for flying, but there were no signs of life at the sleepy little airstrip. She rode to the entrance of the maintenance hangar, one of two small buildings at the field, and looked in.

"Anybody home?" There was no answer. The Stinson was parked nearby, and beyond were a couple of Piper Cubs. Louise rode past the fuel tank with its long, coiled hose and parked her bike outside a building with two signs mounted next to the door. One said, "Service/snacks," and the other, "Crane's Flying School/Lessons, Rides."

She took off her sunglasses and pushed her baseball cap back as she went inside. To her left were a few tables and chairs, a cupboard, an icebox, and a small counter with boxes of candy bars and a licorice jar. A coffeepot sat on an electric hot plate. Mrs. Schroeder kept a few sandwiches in the icebox on weekdays, in case any pilots stopped by for fuel and lunch. On weekends, she came out and ran a little canteen service.

The other side of the room was cut by a partition that created an office. The door was several inches open, and Louise pushed it quietly to look in. Sam Crane had his feet on the desk and his head on his chest. A bottle of bourbon and a shot glass were on the small table beside him. Behind him on the wall was the faded banner of the 94th Aero Squadron.

Louise stood and smiled. Sam Crane had taught her to fly in 1930, when she was nineteen. On a dare from one of her friends, she had gone up with him for her first plane ride. As she left the field that day, she could not decide if she was more infatuated with flying or with Sam. He was a decorated pilot of World War I and had done some barnstorming shows in the 1920s before settling at Schroeder Field. He ran the refueling and mechanical service, gave a few flying lessons, and took people up for rides. When things were quiet, he might have a shot of bourbon too many.

She heard the sound of a car and went out the front door. "Hi there," she said to a man who had just gotten out of the driver's seat.

"Hello. We saw the sign out by the road. Can we take a plane ride here?"

"Sure, it's ten dollars for half an hour."

"OK, I've got my son and daughter in the car. They've never been in a plane."

"It's a perfect day for their first ride. Let's go around back."

A boy about six and a girl about five bounded out of the car, and they all followed Louise toward the hangar.

"You can wait by the Stinson over there," she said. "I'll be right with you."

"You're the pilot?" asked the man with an air of apprehension.

"I am today. I'm Louise Mitchell."

She offered her hand, and he shook it somewhat reluctantly. He glanced at his kids, who were already heading for the plane, and decided to follow them. Louise went in the hangar to get the keys, then joined them at the plane and looked in to check the fuel gauge. "Plenty of gas, let me help you in."

She helped the kids into the back seats and buckled them in. Their father slid across to the front passenger seat while Louise unhooked the tie-down cords. The Stinson Model 74 was Sam's pride and joy, and he struggled to keep up the bank payments on it. It had ample room, so he had installed the two back seats to allow him to carry three passengers. It was too big for beginning lessons, though, so he borrowed Mr. Schroeder's Piper for those.

Louise started it up and checked the controls, then taxied out toward the runway. As she passed the terminal, she saw Sam leaning sleepily in the doorway, waving nonchalantly. At the head of the runway, she revved the 295 horsepower Lycoming engine for a few minutes, then idled down and looked back at the kids.

"You ready for some fun?"

The kids were gripping their seats and looking very serious. They nodded without smiling. Louise released the brakes and pushed the throttle forward. The plane picked up speed, lifted off the tail wheel, and soon began leave the earth behind. She climbed to 3,000 feet and banked west toward the Missouri River. At 4,000, she leveled off and smiled back at the kids.

"You can look now."

First the little girl and then her older brother looked cautiously out the side of the cockpit. They were immediately fascinated by the brown and green squares, the string-like roads, and tiny houses. "It looks like toys," said the girl. Their eyes widened and they forgot their fear.

Louise took them to the Missouri and followed it northwest for a few minutes. They could see a grain barge making its way downstream, and Louise pointed out the little towns that were visible. "Where's your house?" she asked the father.

"It's in Akron, on the east side of town."

"We'll swing over it." She dropped down to 3,000 feet and flew over Akron, a small town on the Sioux River.

"There it is," he said, "with the red tile roof. Can you see it, kids?"

"I see it!" said the boy. "Wow!"

"Hi, mommy," said the girl, smiling.

Louise headed back along the road to Merrill and set the Stinson down gently at Schroeder Field. She taxied back to the hangar and stopped near the fuel tank. As she helped the kids out, the little girl gave her a big hug.

"I want to be like you when I grow up."

"I'm sure you can," said Louise.

Their father handed Louise twelve dollars. "It was worth it and then some," he said. "Thank you, Miss Mitchell."

"Thank you, sir. Come back and take your wife for a ride."

"Maybe she'll do it now, once the kids get after her."

"Goodbye."

As the family headed for the car, Louise pulled out the hose and began refilling the tank. Sam wandered over and leaned against the plane. "Well, you bailed me out again. I don't know what I'd do without you."

"You'd lose some business, I guess," said Louise with a smile.

Together they took the tail of the plane, pulled it back into its parking space, and tied it down. Back at the office, Sam returned his feet to their original position. As she had done many times, Louise entered the flying time in Sam's logbook.

"You really should put that in your own book," said Sam. "Nobody's ever going to inspect my books."

"No sense taking chances. I'm only here on weekends, remember? Anyway, what difference does it make any more?" She pulled up the other chair and put her feet on the desk across from him.

"I wish you wouldn't talk like that, Louise. You're still young. You can do something in aviation."

"In Sioux City, with my money? I don't think so, Sam. No, I think this is my flying career right here. Besides, I like hanging around with you, you old goat."

"I'll never know why. The world has passed me by, Louise."

"Well, you're not going to find it in that bottle."

He looked away. "I know. A man needs a little companionship out here in the country."

"Sometimes I think I could use a little of that companionship."

He looked back at her. "Why don't you go somewhere? Just pick up and go. Nothing's ever going to happen out here."

"Go where? The only relatives I have are back in Pennsylvania, living in small towns."

"Go to Chicago. Go to the airport and get a job there. Take some real flying lessons."

"You make it sound so easy. What if I didn't get a job? I haven't got the money to just go bum around in Chicago. Besides, I don't know if I'm that adventurous."

"Louise, for God's sake, how many women pilots do you think there are in this country? How adventurous do you have to be?"

"Well, maybe I should think about it." Louise paused, looking at the old banner. "You got anything for me to do?"

"I've got a tune-up on one of those Pipers. Want to help me?"

"You bet. Let's go."

As dinnertime approached, Louise cleaned up and went to her bike.

"You coming out Saturday?" asked Sam.

"Around noon. I'll bring you a roast beef sandwich."

"You're an angel."

2

On Friday evening, Louise finished putting away the dishes and took a glass of wine to join Jennie on the porch. Along with their sister Rose, they had inherited the big house on Third Street when their mother died in 1938. Their parents had married back in Pennsylvania and emigrated to South Dakota before the turn of the century, but the harsh conditions drove them south to Sioux City. Louise was born there in 1911, youngest of the three by a full ten years. Rose now had her own small house, having bought it when she turned thirty unmarried. As a schoolteacher, she had been able to hang on to it throughout the Depression.

As she approached the front door, Louise paused to glance at the framed photographs on the mahogany library table. Jennie's was a profile, almost unsmiling, showing an intelligent face with smooth features. Her wavy hair was neatly pinned back, well above the modest fur collar of her coat. She could have been twenty or forty. Louise thought her sister was beautiful, but it seemed that Jennie never thought of herself as beautiful.

She picked up her own picture for a moment. It was a candid shot taken more than ten years ago, when she was getting ready for a New Year's Eve dance. She was leaning back and looking into a hand mirror, her laughing eyes inspecting the hair and makeup of the late 1920s. With a sigh, she put the picture back and went to sit with Jennie.

The humid air was seasoned with the scent of freshly cut grass from the house next door, and the sounds of children floated down the street. A teenage couple walked by holding hands, heading toward downtown. They sat quietly for a while, then Louise said wistfully, "How did we get here, Jennie? Is there something wrong with us?"

"Why?" The tone of Jennie's voice suggested that she did not care much for the question.

"Almost everybody I went to school with is married, or has been. Most of the men I know think I'm weird because I fly planes. The only ones I can talk to are pilots, and they just come and go."

Jennie did not offer an answer. She was Louise's senior by 14 years. An accomplished stenotypist, she had lived her great adventure in life when America entered World War I. She had taken a train to Washington and quickly found work in the Navy Department. Among her souvenirs was a promotion memo initialed by Franklin D. Roosevelt, who was then Assistant Secretary of the Navy. Before contracting polio, FDR had been tall, aristocratic, and charming. Although Jennie's family was traditionally Republican, she had a miniature bound edition of his inaugural speeches, kept carefully in its original envelope.

Louise sipped her wine. "It's not like I haven't tried. I probably should have married Freddie."

"Freddie? I don't remember him."

"He used to be my dance partner. We knew all the dances from the twenties. Everybody said we looked great together."

"What happened to him?"

"I don't know. I kept waiting for him to get romantic, but it seemed like he was more interested in the dances than he was in me. Then I started my flying lessons, and he went off to New York. I never heard from him again."

After a pause, Jennie ventured, "You know, I liked the school-teacher."

"Warren? He was nice, I guess."

"Why didn't that work out?"

"Oh, it just didn't."

Jennie was a lot like their mother, and there were some things that Louise did not feel comfortable talking to her about. They were quiet for a while. A neighbor walked by and waved.

The mention of Warren started Louise thinking about the one serious relationship she had had, which began when Rose introduced her to a young teacher at her school. Louise enjoyed his company, and he even let her take him up twice in the Stinson. He became very amorous, and after about three months, Louise got herself a diaphragm and gave him the green light. The first time, he became passionately aroused so quickly that she could not respond. To her chagrin, the pattern continued. She tried relaxing him with wine and dancing to the radio; she tried prolonging their petting before getting into bed. Nothing worked.

As they walked home from a movie one Friday evening, Louise gathered her courage. "Warren, I want to talk about our lovemaking."

"Talk about it? Why? I think it's wonderful."

"Maybe for you, but it's not for me. It's over too fast."

Warren stopped and glared at her. "What do you mean, too fast?" he said with growing irritation. "Look, if you're not making it, maybe it's your problem."

"It's not my problem, Warren."

"I don't want to talk about this. I'm going home. You decide if you're coming or not."

Louise stood for a while under a gaslight. Maybe she should not have brought it up, she thought. Maybe she was expecting too much. She felt suddenly alone as she looked into the darkness where he had disappeared. "No," she said aloud, "I'm not going to live that way." She turned the other direction and headed home.

Some children ran by and brought Louise back to the warm summer evening.

"Sam thinks I should go somewhere."

"So you can meet a man?"

Louise laughed. "No, so I can fly big planes."

"Where does he think you should go?"

"Chicago."

She expected a negative reaction, but after a moment, Jennie replied, "Well, he might be right."

Louise finished her wine and looked at her sister. "Remember when you came back from Washington? I was only about ten, I think, but I remember you seemed so sad. What happened?"

Jennie shifted uncomfortably in her seat. "Nothing happened. I don't remember being sad. I was probably just worried about getting a job."

Louise thought she saw a little tear in Jennie's eye, and she did not want to push her too far. "I'm sorry. I guess I was too young to know what was going on."

3

Louise turned into the dirt driveway at Schroeder Field and noticed several cars around the little terminal. Riding around to the back, she was surprised to see a light blue, twin-engine plane parked near the hangar. She went inside and found Sam sitting at a table with three men, one of whom was wearing a Stetson and cowboy boots. She recognized the others as joint owners of one of the Pipers at the field. Mr. and Mrs. Schroeder were behind the counter.

"OK," said Sam, "we can have lunch now. Mine has arrived."

"Hi everyone," said Louise.

"Louise, I want to meet Zach Lawson from Colorado. He owns the Anson out there. Zach, this is Louise Mitchell, the young woman I told you about."

"Pleased to meet you, Miss Mitchell."

They shared a firm handshake. "What has Sam been telling you, Mr. Lawson?"

"That you're a fine pilot, and a big help to him."

"Good. I pay him well for these compliments."

Everybody laughed. Louise put some paper plates on the table and took two sandwiches out of her canvas bag. The other men went to the counter and paid Mrs. Schroeder for some ham and cheese sandwiches to go with their coffee. Louise poured some lemonade for her and Sam and pulled a chair up to the corner of the table.

"What brings you here, Mr. Lawson?"

"Just out touring. I saw the field and thought I'd see if I could get some lunch."

"You live in Colorado?"

"I have a ranch in the northeast corner, near Sterling."

Louise was wondering how old Zach was. He was broad-shouldered but not heavy. His face was chiseled and well tanned, with creases in his brow and crows feet running away from his eyes. She thought he was rather handsome, even in older age.

"I've never seen an Anson," she said. "Where does it come from?"

"It's made by Avro, a British company. I got it in Canada."

"How long have you had it?"

"Six months. I fly it around for fun, but I also use it to pick up supplies and keep track of my herd."

"It sure looks nice. Is that the biggest plane we've had here, Sam?"

"Nine hundred horses, that's the most we've had."

"We can all go up after lunch," said Zach. "Then I'll have to head back."

When their food had settled, the five of them piled into Zach's plane with Sam as copilot. For the next hour, Sam and Zach took turns putting the Anson through its paces over the Iowa and Nebraska countryside. As they headed back toward Merrill, Zach looked back at Louise and asked, "You want to steer it?"

"Do I ever!"

Sam got out and let Louise into the right-hand seat. Zach gave her a brief orientation to the cockpit and said, "It's all yours."

She flew straight for a few minutes, then banked gently left and back to the right. She went into a climb, leveled off, banked left, and did a wide descending circle before picking up the landmarks and setting a course for home. "I love it. I want to watch you take it in."

Louise watched closely as Zach eased the plane onto the little airstrip and brought it to a stop. She wished there had been more time for her to fly it. "Thank you, Mr. Lawson," she said as they stopped at the fuel pump, "that was a lot of fun."

"My pleasure, ma'am."

"We're going to chip in for your gas," said one of the men.

They filled the tank, and after a round of good-byes, Zach was off and heading for Colorado. Louise stood watching him take off and climb before wandering back into the office to join Sam.

"Do you know him?" she asked.

"Not before today."

"I wonder how old he is."

Sam raised an eyebrow. "Older than me. Maybe fifty."

"Well, I'm glad he stopped here. That was exciting."

She sat down across from Sam. "Any lessons today?"

"One coming in at 4:30. First landing. Better have our fire truck out there."

Louise laughed. "Sure. Where have you been hiding it?"

While Sam and his student were up in the Piper, a young couple in an old Ford stopped and asked about a ride. "It's our first anniversary," said the woman.

"What a nice way to celebrate," said Louise. "I'll give you the anniversary special, eight dollars."

The man insisted that his wife sit next to Louise, and she noticed that the young woman watched her intently as she guided the Stinson through the tour. "Ever thought about flying?" asked Louise as they turned toward home.

"No, I haven't," said the woman with a note of surprise in her voice. "How long have you been flying?"

"About 10 years. I started right here."

The young woman glanced back at her husband.

"Maybe we'll learn someday," he said.

As she watched the couple walk hand-in-hand back to their car, Louise felt a twinge. She was reasonably attractive, although at five-feet seven, she was one of the taller women in town. She had a slightly round face and kept her hair bobbed like it was at the end of the 1920s. Maybe it was a mistake to start flying, she thought. She had set herself apart, and few men had been willing to approach her as a woman. Her dreams of flying in the big races had never come close to realization, and she spent most of her spare time at this dusty little field, with a man who no longer dreamed.

A few weeks later, Louise was pumping gas into a visitor's tank when she noticed a large plane approaching the field. As it touched down, she realized it was Zach's Anson. I wonder what he's doing back here, she thought.

"Hello again," said Louise.

"Hello, Miss Mitchell, I'm glad you're here."

"Oh? Well, I'm here most Saturdays."

"You know, Miss Mitchell, I kept thinking about how much you enjoyed flying that Anson, and I thought maybe you'd like to go up again."

Louise smiled, but she was not sure what to say. He was right that she wanted to go up again, but had he flown all the way from Colorado just to give her a ride? "Mr. Lawson, that's so nice of you."

"My pleasure. Do you have any coffee inside?"

"Sure."

They went in and found Sam sitting with a cup. "Zach, you're back."

"I told you I like to fly around. Can you spare this lady for a little while?"

Sam glanced at Louise, and she smiled. "Yeah, it's not like I'm overwhelmed here."

Zach had coffee and a candy bar, and then he and Louise headed out to the plane. "Here, let me show you how to put this on," he said as he took out a parachute. "I carry two of them, just in case."

After giving her instruction, he put the chute in a back seat and they climbed in. Zach went over the preflight checks with her, giving her as much information about the plane as he could. He had a nice manner, calm and deliberate but not patronizing. Louise liked him.

Zach narrated as he took off and climbed to 5,000 feet. "Time for the copilot to take over," he announced. Louise assumed the controls and banked south to fly over Sioux City. She followed the river for a while until Omaha was in view in the distance. "Take it up to 10,000," said Zach, "you'll see how cool it is up there."

Louise climbed and leveled off over Omaha, gradually banking west and north to head back upriver. "You're right, I'd have to dress warmer for this."

She descended gradually and turned east toward Merrill. "You're going to take it in, I hope," she said.

"I think you could do it. Let me talk you down."

"Are you sure?" Louise could feel the adrenaline flowing.

"I'll take it if I think we're in trouble," said Zach.

There was no trouble. Hanging on Zach's every word, Louise brought them in for a smooth landing and taxied to a stop. "Boy, that was fun!" she blurted out.

Zach reached over to shake her hand. "Well done, Louise."

She grinned back at him. "Thank you, Zach."

4

As June ended, Louise found herself wondering if Zach would come back again. She had had a good feeling when they were flying together, but she thought it was probably just the comradeship of pilots. After all, he must be several years older than Sam.

One evening, the phone rang on Third Street. "Louise, it's for you," said Jennie.

"Hello, this is Louise."

"Louise, this is Zach."

"Why, hello. Are you in Iowa?"

"No, I'm in Colorado. I was just wondering if you had plans for the Fourth."

"Oh, just helping Sam at the field. It's usually a busy day."

"Do you think he could let you take a little trip?"

Louise hesitated. She was not sure she wanted to cross this bridge. "Maybe, what did you have in mind?"

"Have you ever been to Wind Cave?"

"In South Dakota? No, I haven't."

"There's a little strip at Hot Springs that I can get in and out of. We could make it in about two hours."

"Really? That would be a lot of flying for you in one day."

"I thought I might fly over on the third and stay up at Merrill overnight."

Louise was feeling a little flustered. "Well, I guess it would be OK."

"You seem reluctant."

"No, I'd like to do it. Look, Zach, there isn't any place to stay in Merrill. Why don't you fly into Sioux City and stay here. My sister and I have a guest room."

"Are you sure?"

"Yes. The manager of the airport knows me. His name is Harry. I'll let him know you're coming. We can get an early start the next morning."

"What's your address?"

"970 Third Street. It's a short taxi ride."

"OK, I should be there by seven."

"We'll be watching for you."

"Goodbye, Louise."

"Goodbye, Zach."

Louise leaned against the wall and took a deep breath. She could hardly believe that she had just invited a man to stay at their house. Louise was not shy around men, but she had never taken the initiative like that. She went to break the news to Jennie, as diplomatically as she could.

A little after 7 p.m. on the eve of Independence Day, Zach got out of a cab and Louise came out on the porch. "Welcome to Sioux City."

She led him inside and introduced him to Jennie, who was clearly surprised at Zach's age. She was gracious, however, and soon they sat down to dinner.

"This is delicious, ladies. I'm very grateful."

"How large is your ranch, Mr. Lawson?" asked Jennie.

"I own a few thousand acres," said Zach. "But I have grazing rights on some BLM land."

"You must have a lot of cattle."

"Somewhere around 800 head, give or take."

"My goodness, how do you keep track of them all."

"It's a big job. I've got five hands who try to keep the herd together. We bring in the young ones for branding twice a year. As I told Louise, I've started using my plane to look for strays."

"Do you have any family?"

Jennie was a real inquisitor. Louise rather liked being able to sit quietly and learn so much about Zach.

"I have a son. He's my foreman now. Gives me a little free time."

They finished eating and Jennie suggested they have sherry and dessert on the porch. As twilight gave in slowly to darkness, fireflies appeared in the lawn and the sound of firecrackers came from random directions. Louise was a little high from the wine and was thoroughly enjoying the evening.

Zach looked at Jennie. "Do you like to fly, Miss Mitchell?"

"Louise talked me into it once. I was pretty scared."

"I'll bet you'd be comfortable in my Anson. Would you like to go with us to Wind Cave?"

Louise was not ready for this turn of the conversation. Was Zach just being polite? Although she had always believed that her sister was beautiful, Jennie had never cultivated her appearance and never encouraged men.

"That's very kind of you, Mr. Lawson, but I promised my sister Rose I'd go to the church picnic with her. Perhaps another time I can ride in your plane."

Louise quickly cut in, "Would you like to take a walk, Zach?"

"Sure. Can I help with the dishes first?"

"No, let me do that," said Jennie. "You two take a little walk."

Louise and Zach walked slowly down Third Street and back along Fourth. "I love walking at night," said Louise. "I love seeing the light through the stained-glass windows."

"They are beautiful. Nothing like that where I live."

"Can you walk at night on your ranch?"

"It's pretty dark. You can see a million stars. I keep pretty early hours out there, though."

"How long have you lived there?"

"Thirty years, I guess. I was the foreman for a while, then I had a chance to buy the spread. The bank took a chance on me, for some reason."

"What's your son's name?"

"Tony."

Louise could not resist any longer. "What happened to your wife, Zach?"

"She died three years ago. Influenza."

"I'm sorry."

"It's all right, I'm over it now."

They went back in and found Jennie putting away the last of the dishes.

"Did you have a nice walk?"

"Lovely, it's a nice area," said Zach.

"We're going to put you in Rose's old room. She has her own house now."

Zach picked up his bag and Louise showed him upstairs to his room. "Do you want me to knock in the morning?" she asked.

"Don't worry, I'll be awake at five. I'll be all cleaned up when you get up."

"Good night, Zach."

"Good night."

Louise went back to say good night to Jennie.

"He seems like a good man, Louise, but isn't he awfully old for you?"

"Of course he is. I'm just going out to Wind Cave with him. I've never flown cross-county."

"Well, be careful. It seems odd to me."

"Jennie, he likes flying around in his plane, and he'd like some company. He's not expecting anything."

Jennie did not say anything more. Louise went up and got ready for bed. It was still very warm, and she stretched out on the bed in her cotton nightgown. In spite of her best efforts, she fell asleep wondering what it would be like to make love to Zach.

The next day, they had an early breakfast and called a taxi to go to the airport. With Zach coaching her, Louise put the Anson into the air and headed slightly northwest. She felt exhilarated as the Missouri trailed away behind them and Zach pointed out landmarks on his charts. After an hour, she was ready for him to take over, and he kept it the rest of the way to Hot Springs. By 10 a.m., they had rented a pickup truck from the owner of the airfield and were driving through stands of Ponderosa pine in the Black Hills.

It was only seven miles to Wind Cave, but they saw several elk and deer on the way. As they came into some open grassland near the cave, they were a hundred yards from a small bison herd. Soon they were leaving the 80-degree July weather for the 53 degrees of the cave.

The caverns were spectacular, with massive honeycombs of calcite and seemingly endless tunnels heading off into darkness. They wandered slowly, pausing beside the underground pools of water. After two hours underground, they emerged for lunch at a pavilion built recently by the Civilian Conservation Corps. Although he did not say a lot, Louise was finding Zach's company very pleasant.

Back at the airport, he purchased fuel and turned to her, "Take us home, lady."

She took off and this time kept the stick all the way to the terminal at Sioux City. As they stood outside in the late afternoon sun, Louise offered Zach her hand. "That was a wonderful trip. Thank you so much, Zach."

"You did most of the work, Louise. I just enjoyed the ride."

"I hope you'll be all right flying back."

"Yeah, I've got at least three hours of daylight left."

"Well, you better get started."

"Maybe I'll be back sometime. Take it easy, Louise."

"Goodbye."

She watched him taxi out and disappear into the western sky. It had been an amazing day, a real event in her life. She saw Harry getting ready to leave and bummed a ride from him.

"Nice looking plane," said Harry. "You say your friend is from Colorado?"

"He's a rancher."

"You fixin' to go to Colorado?"

Louise laughed. "Goodness no, Harry. No, I'll probably stay right here in Sioux City."

5

The late July heat radiated from the pavement as Louise sweated out another ride home from Merrill. She was thinking very little about Zach now and more about what she was going to do with her life. Flying had been her anchor, but she was approaching thirty with no prospects other than these bike rides and Sam's friendship. Maybe she should take his advice and just leave Sioux City. Maybe she should have done it long ago.

At home, she drew a bath in the big porcelain tub and sprinkled in some bubble soap. She sat and nearly dozed off as the water became tepid.

"Louise," called Jennie from the stairs, "you have a call. It's Mr. Lawson."

Louise quickly dried and wrapped the towel around her.

"Hello?"

"How are you, Louise?"

"OK, about the same. How are you?"

"I've been busy as a cat on a tin roof. I haven't been in my plane in two weeks."

"Oh."

"Louise, would you like to see my ranch?"

"You're ranch?" She tried to stall, wondering if she wanted to let this go any further. "Uh, when?"

"I could pick you up Saturday morning and bring you back Sunday."

Three days away. Her mind was racing, trying to weigh the situation between sentences. If she said yes, what was she saying yes to?

"This weekend, let's see."

If she said no, that would probably be the end of it. She would have to say no eventually, best to do it now.

"Louise?"

She hesitated. "OK. I can come."

"Great. Wear your jeans. By the way, what's your shoe size?"

"My shoe size?" She was too confused to ask why he wanted to know. "I'm an eight."

"I'll be in Sioux City by ten. Can you meet me at the airport?"

"OK. Goodbye."

Louise stood there in a daze, holding the towel in front of her with one hand.

"What now?" asked Jennie.

"He wants me to visit his ranch."

"Well, Louise, I hope you know what you're doing."

She stared at Jennie and tried to suppress a laugh. Pulling the towel around her, she laughed her way upstairs.

Saturday morning, Louise took a taxi to the airport wearing her jeans, a black and white plaid cotton shirt, and her gardening shoes. Zach got out of his plane carrying a paper bag and a dark gray Stetson.

"Mornin', Louise, try this on."

He put the Stetson on her head. "It fits perfectly," she said with a big smile. "How do I look?"

"Like a million bucks."

"What's in the bag?"

"Here, I picked these up in Sterling." He produced a shiny new pair of cowboy boots, black with silver scrollwork."

"Wow! Zach, you shouldn't have done that."

"If you're going to ride with us, you'll need them."

"Ride a horse?"

"Just like driving a plane, let her know you're in charge."

"Well, let's go inside so I can put them on."

Louise pulled her jeans down over her new boots and went into the ladies room to check herself out. She liked what she saw. "OK," she said with a laugh, "I'm ready for Colorado."

As they climbed aboard the Anson, Zach handed Louise the wool-lined denim vest she had worn on the last trip. She piloted for the first hour, with Zach showing her the charts as they went along. Then he took over, and a lull ensued in the conversation. Louise gazed out the window and began to take stock of the situation. She was going to stay overnight at Zach's ranch. Did he expect her to sleep with him? How was she going to deal with it? She glanced his way. His face was bony and weathered but kindly. His body looked hard and well proportioned. It was the right time of the month; maybe she would just go along.

Louise began daydreaming about her previous encounters. She felt she had a normal sexual appetite, but her chances had been few and mostly disappointing. She wondered if it was her fault.

"You see those rivers coming together down there? That's the Platte and the North Platte."

"Huh? Oh, yeah."

"It's a good landmark. We're two-thirds there."

Louise smiled at Zach. "Sorry, I guess I dozed off a little. Would you like some coffee?" She poured them each some coffee from her thermos.

"Are we going to land at your ranch?"

"Yes, ma'am. I hired a bulldozer to smooth out a nice long strip. Built a shelter for Betsy here, put in a fuel tank."

"You call her Betsy?"

"Actually, I call her a lot of things. Guess I ought to settle on a name."

"How long have you been flying, Zach?"

"A few years. I took it up after my wife died."

"Really, I thought you had flown a long time."

"That's a compliment, coming from you, Louise."

Louise looked out her window for a few minutes. "What do you think about this war, Zach?"

"War? I don't think anything about it. It's none of our business."

"You don't think we'll get into it?"

"I certainly hope not. Those people have been killing each other for centuries. We all came over here to get away from it."

"Were you in the last war?"

"Nah, I was too old."

Louise wondered how old he had been. Let's see, she thought, we entered the war in 1917. Sam was 22.

"It's hard to imagine what it must be like for those people, being taken over by the Nazis. I think I'd be terrified."

"Well, I've got enough to worry about without that," said Zach.

6

Zach was starting his descent into Colorado. As they swung in over the brown prairie, Louise saw a collection of cream-colored buildings in the distance. Getting closer, she could make out an adobe hacienda and several smaller buildings nearby. The place had a distinctively Mexican look.

He brought the Anson down on a dirt strip and taxied back to a shelter that he could pull into from one side and out the other. Louise noticed some men doing something around the stables about 50 yards away. Zach picked up her suitcase and led her into the house, which was built around a small courtyard. It was neatly kept and attractively decorated, with southwestern wall hangings and pottery. A large oak table was set for lunch. He proceeded down a hall to a corner of the house.

"This is your room," he said.

Louise went in and glanced around. "It's lovely."

"When you're settled, join us for lunch."

She surveyed the room. It was bright and cheerful, with windows on two sides. There was a twin bed with a colorful quilt, a dresser, and a rocking chair. A mahogany-framed full-length mirror stood in one corner. On the dresser, a hand mirror and brush lay on a white linen cloth that was decorated with bright red needlepoint.

Louise guessed that this had been Zach's wife's room. Well, she thought, so much for speculating about sleeping arrangements.

Lunch was served by a Mexican woman, assisted by a man who seemed to be her husband. "Miguel is our blacksmith and caretaker," said Zach. "Ah, here's my son."

Louise looked around to see a dark-haired, dark-eyed young man wearing a black leather vest over a denim shirt. He smiled faintly. "Pleased to meet you, ma'am."

They sat down to a lunch of sautéed vegetables, corn bread, and refried beans. Louise felt a little uncomfortable, but she tried to relax. "I hear you're the foreman," she said to Tony.

"Yes, ma'am."

"How many men work with you?"

Tony glanced at her without smiling. "Five, ma'am."

He was uncommonly handsome, thought Louise, but something mysterious was lurking behind those eyes. She felt a little shiver down her spine.

"Where are all the cattle?" she asked, looking at Zach.

"On the range. There's no food or water for them near the house. We pick out 30 or so head every month and drive 'em up to the UP, about 40 miles. Then they get on a train to Omaha. We're gonna take you out for a look."

"You know, I've never been on a horse."

"Don't worry. We've got a gentle mare that my wife used to ride. We'll give you some good lessons."

His wife's room, his wife's horse, thought Louise. I wonder if I've been wearing his wife's hat? She finished eating in silence.

"OK," said Zach, "let's see what we can do."

One of the ranchhands, also with a Mexican look, had a horse ready for her in the corral. "Always stand on her left," said Zach. "Never behind her. Here, you can pet her a little. Get to know her. Her name's Chiquita."

Louise patted the mare's head. "Chiquita, are you going to take care of me?"

"Now just relax. Put your left foot in the stirrup and take the saddlehorn." Zach gave her a lift, and Louise nearly went off the other side. "You'll get the hang of it. Now let me show you how to use the reins."

Chiquita seemed to know she was teaching someone, and before long, Louise was feeling more confident. In half an hour, they had progressed from walking around the corral to a gentle trot.

"You're a natural," said Zach. "Let's go for a ride."

Tony and two of the men joined them, and they rode out into open country. About two miles out, they began to see cattle grazing leisurely in the hot sun. They rode to a stream, where a number of cattle were wading and drinking. "This runs into the Platte," said Zach. "It's spring fed, doesn't dry up."

They arrived back at the stables late in the afternoon, and Zach showed Louise how to take off the saddle and bridle and give Chiquita her dinner. Then they went to the house and sat on the veranda for a while. The Mexican woman brought them tall citrus drinks with something strong in them.

"Thanks for teaching me to ride, Zach. I loved Chiquita."

"She must have liked you too, as careful as she was being. She's used to these roughnecks getting on her."

"Do the men stay here all the time?"

"They live here. They go into town once in a while."

"Aren't any of them married?"

"The two Mexicans are married. They go home twice a year to visit."

"That seems like a hard way to live."

"They consider themselves lucky. They can provide a decent living for their families. Excuse me a minute, I need to speak with Miguel."

As Louise sat alone with her drink, Tony appeared.

"Evening, ma'am."

"Hello, Tony. How did I do today?"

"You did fine, ma'am." He stopped near the door and looked over at her. "I understand you're a pilot."

His eyes were piercing. She guessed he was close to her age. She could feel her heartbeat picking up. "Yes, I am."

"That's unusual."

"Yes, I guess it is."

"Why do you do that?"

Louise was startled by the question. She looked out toward the range, then glanced back at him. "I just love to fly."

Tony pondered the response for a moment and then reached for the screen door. "Excuse me, ma'am."

Louise took a drink and tried to settle herself. What am I getting into, she thought? She realized that Zach's wife must have been Mexican. Now Miguel's wife seemed to be the only woman on the ranch.

Zach reappeared. "We'll be having dinner about 7:30. Miguel is heating some water so you can have a bath. I'm going to rinse the dust off, too."

A little later, Louise was standing in a wooden tub in a small room, washing as best she could. Back in her room, she took out the long floral print dress she had brought and inspected it for wrinkles. She had rolled it carefully for the trip and hung it up on arrival, so it was in good shape. It was light green, with white lace on the neckline and sleeves. She held it up to herself in front of the mirror, thinking that she would look just like a pioneer lady.

They sat down to a wonderful Mexican dinner with red wine. One of the men who had ridden with them appeared with a guitar and began to play quietly at the side of the room. "Do you always have music with dinner?" asked Louise.

"No, this is a special occasion," said Zach. "The men usually play outside the bunkhouse. I listen to them from the veranda."

Louise was seated at the side of the table with the men at each end, and she was doing her best to avoid looking at Tony. He seemed to be doing the same. "Have you always lived in Colorado, Zach?"

"No, I grew up in west Texas. Near El Paso."

"Is that where you met your wife?"

"Yes."

Louise sensed that Zach did not want to continue this line of questioning. She took a sip of wine. "The music is beautiful," she said, and they listened quietly.

After dinner, they returned to the veranda and Tony disappeared. "It's very peaceful here," said Louise after a little while.

"Peaceful and lonely. That's why I like to get out in my plane."

"Are there any other ranches nearby?"

"I'd say my closest neighbors are about twenty miles away."

Louise was running out of questions, and Zach did not seem inclined to quiz her. As music began to drift up from the bunkhouse, she suspected he was thinking about his next move. Darkness fell, and they stepped out to look at the stars.

"There's the Milky Way," said Louise. "We can't see that in Sioux City, too many lights."

"It's one of our attractions. But you can see why we go to bed early."

Louise wondered if this was an invitation. She had to make up her mind quickly. They went inside and Zach turned off two of the oil lamps in the front room. It was her first realization that there was no electricity at the ranch. He picked up the remaining lamp and led her toward the hall. Would they go to his room?

"I'll leave you this," he said outside her door. "I'll be up front in that first room if you need me. Sleep well."

"Good night, Zach." She noticed a glow coming from a room in the back hall. It must be Tony, she thought. Why is his door open?

Louise made her way to the bathroom. It had no running water, so she washed with the pitcher and basin. She returned and closed her door, then put on the pretty cotton nightgown she had brought. In the dim light of the lamp, she looked in the mirror and felt a little let down. She climbed into bed and thought about her day. It had been a real adventure, but it was not turning out as she expected.

She was wide awake and wondering if she would be able to sleep in this room. Why did Zach leave her alone tonight? Was he concerned about what his son would think? Maybe he brought her out here to meet Tony. She thought about the dark-eyed young man so close in the room at the back. He frightened her. He seemed to look right through her. What if Tony came to her room? She would not dare to speak, for fear Zach would hear. She would have to let him have his way. She listened for the sound of footsteps. She could hear the crickets and, in the distance, something that sounded like a dog howling.

Louise suddenly realized that she was stroking her thighs. She got up and sat on the side of the bed. God, she thought, it's been so long. Silently, she went to the door and opened it gently, peering in both directions. The glow was gone from Tony's room, but she could not tell if his door was closed. She leaned against the doorframe and breathed deeply. Could she do it? She stood for a moment with her heart pounding, then closed the door and crept back to bed.

She lay there thinking about the situation. She had almost gone to Zach's room, almost given in to desire. She wished he had just taken her to his room and made love to her. She would have been glad to have sex with him. Instead, he seemed to be courting her, and that was more serious. Eventually, fatigue caught up and she drifted off to sleep.

By the time she awoke, the others had been busy for a while, but Zach had waited on her for breakfast. Afterward, he took her for a morning ride on Chiquita, including a brief gallop. They had another delicious lunch, and then Louise packed her things and headed out to join Zach at the airstrip. She met Tony in front of the house.

"May I carry your case, ma'am?"

Louise handed it to him and walked nervously to the plane. He put the suitcase inside the cabin and turned to look at her. With a slight smile, he took her hand and kissed it gently.

"Goodbye, ma'am."

She felt as if he had sent a charge of electricity through her. "Goodbye, Tony."

Soon Zach was taking off and banking east. They were quiet for a while, and Louise wondered what he was thinking. She began trying to assess her own feelings. She had enjoyed seeing the ranch and riding Chiquita, but she had not been comfortable there. She was not enamored of the primitive living conditions or the feeling of isolation. Most of all, Tony disturbed her. What would happen if she went back? Would he want her? Would she want him?

How did she feel about Zach? How old was he, anyway? How long could they have sex? Could they have a child? She glanced at him and wondered what it would have been like if she had gone to his room. Then she thought about how much fun it would be to fly this plane around. It suddenly dawned on her that she was getting ahead of herself. Nobody had asked her to live in Colorado.

"Want to take over?"

"Sure."

As Louise took the controls, Zach poured them some coffee. "What did you think of the ranch?"

"It's nice. Different from living in the city."

"I'm hoping we'll get an electric line before long. Then we can pump water from the well and put in some plumbing."

"Where did you call me from?"

"From the saloon in Sterling."

"Do you go there very often?"

"I go once in a while with the rest of the crew."

"What goes on there?"

"Drinking, mostly, a little poker. There's some music on Saturdays."

"Dancing?"

"A little."

They did not say much the rest of the way, and Louise brought the Anson in for a landing at the Sioux City airport. Zach carried her suitcase into the terminal.

"When do you think you'll be back?" asked Louise.

"Before too long."

"Come see us at Merrill. These are busy weekends for Sam."

"I'll do that."

He was ready to leave. Louise put her hand on his shoulder, thinking he might want to kiss her. "Goodbye, Zach."

"So long, pardner."

7

July became August, and Louise went on with her life of working, caring for the garden, and helping Sam. The familiarity of it was rather comforting after her recent adventures. She began to think that Zach was not coming back. Maybe he realized that she was too young for him. Maybe he sensed the tension with Tony. She decided not to worry about it.

With temperatures hitting 90 most days, she set out early on her Saturday ride to Merrill. Sam was puttering with the Stinson when she arrived, and she went over to help.

"Gonna be another warm one," he said. "Be nice to stay up at 5,000 feet."

"Maybe we'll be lucky. Can we use the Cub today?"

"Yep. You get the odds and ends."

"Thanks a lot."

"I need to spend some time in this thing. I've been working on it."

Customers began showing up before ten, and soon both of them were in the air. As Louise brought her second tour in, she saw a familiar plane parked near the terminal. Oh, oh, she thought, here we go again. She taxied over and collected from her customer. Then she went inside with a feeling of apprehension.

"Hello, Zach."

"Hello, Louise. I see you're out here making Sam's living for him again."

"Oh, I make some nice change here." She touched his hand and sat down. "How are things at the ranch?"

"Busy. Hot. Dusty."

"Well, you've got no monopoly on hot."

"You look busy here. You gonna be able to take a ride today?"

"When Sam gets back I probably can, for an hour or so. That reminds me, I filled out my logbook for our trips. I need you to sign the entries."

Louise got her book and found the places for Zach to sign. "Sounds like Sam is back," he said.

They went out and saw Sam helping a couple out of his plane. As he came over, he shook Zach's hand. "Hello, Zach."

"Mind if I take a spin in the Anson?" asked Louise.

"Anybody waiting now?"

"No such luck."

"Go ahead, I can keep up with them."

They went over to Zach's plane. "Take my seat this time," he said. "We're logging you in as the pilot."

Louise took off and picked up the Sioux River, a tributary of the Missouri. She followed it north to Sioux Falls, circled the city, and headed back to Merrill. As she approached the field, she saw Sam taking off. Arriving at the terminal, she cut the engines and glanced at Zach. "Thanks again, Zach. I really love flying this plane."

"You coming to the ranch again, Louise?"

She hesitated. "Maybe. Why don't you visit us in Sioux City again? Could you come on a Friday afternoon?"

"Well, I guess I could."

Zach hung around while Sam had lunch and Louise took two women up for a ride in the Stinson. Then she walked him back to the plane.

"Thanks for coming, Zach. It was great."

"You're welcome, Louise."

They stood out of sight and looked at each other. Suddenly, she put her hand on his shoulder and kissed his cheek. She drew back slightly, then kissed him softly on the lips. He smiled and returned the kiss.

"So long, pardner."

"Goodbye, Zach."

Louise stood watching the plane taxi away and pondered what she had done. It was unlike her to be so spontaneous, but she had enjoyed it. She was aware, however, that she was now in uncharted territory.

Not long after that, Zach called Louise on a Thursday.

"Thought I might come over tomorrow."

"Good. We can go to a movie."

"You sure your sister won't mind?"

"I'll talk to her. I'm sure it's all right."

"OK, pardner, see you tomorrow afternoon."

She went back to working on the salad. Jennie waited, but Louise was thinking about what she wanted to say.

"Was that Mr. Lawson?"

"Yes. He's coming to visit tomorrow."

"Well, we'd better think about dinner."

"I'll get off early and do some shopping."

"I don't mind helping. It's nice to have company."

Louise waited a few more minutes, then tried to choose her words carefully.

"Jennie, there's something we need to talk about."

"You want to sleep with Mr. Lawson."

Louise stopped tossing the salad and looked at her sister with a startled expression. "I'm not planning on it. But just in case it happens?"

Jennie shrugged her shoulders. "The house is as much yours as it is mine. You don't need my permission."

"I don't want you to feel uncomfortable."

"I'm not your mother, Louise. If this is what you want, you don't need to worry about me."

Louise went back to poking the salad. "I don't know what I want."

Jennie was very engaging at dinner, more than Louise had ever seen her. It was a relief to have someone else carry the conversation.

"I would like to hear you play the piano, Miss Mitchell. Do we have time Louise?"

"We have a little time. I want to change clothes, anyway."

With the sound of Chopin drifting up the stairs, Louise looked through her things and thought about what she wanted to wear to the movie. She pulled out a white silk blouse with ruffles on the front and tried it on. Hmm, she thought. She got out her best pair of jeans and her new boots. Finally, she put on her Stetson and looked at herself. Her hair was getting longer and she had started curling it under. Ha, she thought, this will turn some heads downtown.

She waited until Jennie had finished a piece, then bounded downstairs with a mischievous grin. Zach smiled at her. "That's my girl! You look great."

Jennie smiled a little, too. "You look nice, Louise."

After the movie, they walked the dozen or so blocks in the warm summer air. Zach's hand was rough and hard, but Louise did not mind. It felt so good to be walking home with someone; she just wanted to savor the moment. She began to anticipate making love and finally stopped him for a brief kiss. Could she take the initiative if he did not?

The house was dark and quiet, except for the porch and stair lights. They took off their boots in the living room and climbed the stairs quietly. Reaching her room first, Louise turned toward him. For a brief moment, they looked nervously at each other, and then came together for a long kiss. As he let her go, she whispered, "Come on."

She lit a candle in her room and closed the door. Zach was taking off his shirt, so she took off her blouse and bra. Louise had modest, firm breasts, and her nipples were already hard when they touched his chest. After another long kiss, they pulled off their jeans and climbed in beside each other. His body was as hard and muscular as she had imagined. Soon he was over her and plunging into her, and their bodies began to convulse against each other. Don't rush, Zach, she thought, give me time.

He did. For the first time in her life, Louise climaxed simultaneously with a man. Afraid to cry out, she dug her fingers into his back. When it was over, he rolled off beside her and she lay for several minutes with her eyes closed. Finally, she reached for his hand and turned to kiss his neck and ear.

"Is it all right if I stay?" he whispered.

"It's all right."

She pulled the sheet up and lay against him. This was so much better than that empty room at the ranch. As she drifted off to sleep, she hoped he would be ready again before dawn. She was not disappointed. Afterward, she lay on his shoulder and listened to the birds singing, feeling enormously satisfied. Two for two, she thought, there's nothing wrong with me.

Louise was fixing breakfast when Jennie came into the kitchen and poured herself some coffee. "How was it?"

"You knew?"

"It's all over your face, Louise. You're glowing."

"Jennie," said Louise, moving close to her sister, "it was amazing! Twice!"

Jennie smiled. "I'm happy for you, Louise."

After breakfast, they took Jennie for a ride in the Anson and then flew up to Schroeder Field. Sam had been busy, and Louise said she would take the waiting customers up while he took a break. Zach hung around chatting with Sam and the other pilots who stopped in. In mid-afternoon, he took Sam up for a brief ride and then told Louise he needed to head for home. They fueled his plane and stood together next to the cabin door. Louise melted into his arms for a kiss.

"Let's do this again soon," she said.

Zach was not one to waste time or words. He held her hands. "Louise, I would like to marry you."

Louise looked at him with her mouth open. She knew this might happen, but now that it had, she was speechless.

"Zach."

"You don't have to answer right now. Take some time."

She hugged him. "Thank you, Zach. I do need some time."

"I'll come back in two weeks. You can let me know then."

She held him tighter. "I feel honored."

He slipped away and climbed into the cockpit. "So long, pardner."

Two weeks! Could she decide this in two weeks? In the excitement, Louise had forgotten that she did not have her bike. She would have to ask Sam to take her home. Did she want to confide in him?

As they poked along in Sam's old Chevrolet pickup, she looked over at him. "What do you think of Zach?"

"He seems like a good man. Why?"

"I think he's interested in me."

"Yes, he's interested in you." Sam was keeping his eyes on the road.

"I wish I knew how old he is."

"He's sixty-one."

"Really, how do you know that?"

"He told me."

"Sixty-one? I didn't think he was that old." She fell silent for the rest of the trip.

Louise had promised Zach to think it over, and she was determined to do so. She imagined herself living as a rancher's wife and wondered if she could adapt. Could she trust Tony? Could she trust herself? She was not sure anymore.

She struggled with her feelings about Zach. He wanted her, and being wanted was not something to take lightly. Was she in love with him? Maybe it was novelty—the novelty of flying a big plane, of going on interesting trips, of making love to a rugged old cowboy. Had she led him on? She should never have let it go so far. She should never have given in to her loneliness. Sixty-one! She still could not believe it.

When she could not think anymore, she sat down and addressed an envelope:

Mr. Zach Lawson
Z Bar L Ranch
Sterling, Colorado

My Dear Zach,
    Your offer touched me deeply, and I have thought of little else in the past three days.
    You have brought me fresh air and joy in the past two months, and I am very grateful to you. I just do not feel that

life on the ranch is the life I want. I could try, and maybe I would be happy, but it just does not feel right to me.

I am feeling very sad as I write this letter. I know that I may someday regret my decision, but I feel this is what I must do now.

I will never forget you, Zach.

Louise

8

Washington, DC
November 1940

On a gray, damp November day, Tom Clark sat looking through State Department cables at his desk in the Old Executive Office Building, across the street from the White House. Five thousand miles away, Germany had occupied most of the European continent and was trying to bring Great Britain to its knees with bombers and submarines. In the Far East, Japan was continuing its relentless drive into China and eyeing the colonial possessions of defeated European countries. In Washington, President Franklin D. Roosevelt was pondering ways to help the British without clearly violating the neutrality laws that isolationist senators had pushed through Congress.

Tom's phone rang and he heard the familiar voice of Harry Hopkins, closest advisor to the president. "Tom, the president wants to see you."

"I'll be right there."

Now 45 years old, only the gray around his temples belied Tom's age. He had joined the Navy in 1916 and served escort duty on convoys to Britain. Because of his degree in history and languages, he was transferred to Washington as a liaison officer to the British and French navies. Roosevelt was Assistant Secretary of the Navy at the time, and when he needed a new aide, Tom's political skills made him the natural choice.

When the Republicans took back the White House in 1920, Tom felt the country would turn inward, leaving few opportunities in the Navy. He decided to try his hand in the budding new world of Wall Street and became a stock analyst for a large trading house. He spent a lot of time visiting new companies to assess their prospects, and by investing in some of these companies, he gradually acquired a modest personal fortune. As the decade wore on, he became uneasy with the speculative fever growing around him. Too many people were going out on a limb to buy stock, and prices were getting way ahead of what companies could deliver.

When Roosevelt decided to run for governor of New York in 1928, Tom sold most of his stock and signed on to the campaign. He then worked for Roosevelt in a variety of capacities, often doing informal investigations. When the governor wanted an assessment of a situation, he would ask Tom to check it out. This continued after Roosevelt went to the White House in 1933. Officially, Tom worked for Harry Hopkins on personnel matters. Unofficially, he was available for whatever came along.

Tom crossed the street and checked through the gate to the west lawn of the White House. Although he had been to the Oval Office many times, it never failed to inspire awe, especially that great wooden desk and its occupant. As usual, Roosevelt was cheerful and courteous.

"Sit down, Tom. How's your new office?"

"Warm and dry, Mr. President," replied Tom as he sank into one of the big leather chairs facing the president's desk.

Roosevelt chuckled. "Well, we don't want you to get too comfortable. You're our best road man. There's hot tea here, would you like some."

"Thanks, I would." Tom leaned over to the small table between him and Hopkins and poured a cup.

"Tom, have you ever met Claire Chennault?" asked Roosevelt.

"No, sir, but I've heard he's in town."

"He's here with Mr. Soong, Madame Chiang's brother. He's managed to ruffle some feathers in the War Department."

Hopkins broke in. "Chennault wants to put together a volunteer group of American pilots to support the Chinese. He wants us to help him shake loose the men and planes from the Army and Navy. As you know, he's been in charge of Chiang's air force, but that's nearly gone."

"I can imagine the generals aren't thrilled," said Tom. "They already think too much of our production is going to Britain."

"General Marshall is inclined to give Chennault something," said the president, "but he's getting flak from Hap Arnold and the rest of the Air Corps boys. And then there's MacArthur, of course. He's always trying to get more support for his Philippine forces."

"We all agree that Germany is the main problem," said Hopkins. "Still, we can't overlook the Japanese threat in the Pacific. You know how many planes and ships they've been building, and we've seen what they can do in China."

"I know," said Tom, "I've been reading the cables from Chungking. They're getting pounded. I wonder how much longer Chiang can hold on."

Hopkins frowned. "I think he's getting desperate. He's willing to turn the air war over to American mercenaries. We can't exclude the possibility that he might make his own deal with the Japanese. That would let them turn their full attention to South Asia and the Pacific. They've already started moving into Indochina now that France has gone down."

"What do you want me to do?" asked Tom.

Roosevelt leaned back. "Frank Knox is having a dinner party for Chennault tomorrow night, so I'll have him invite you as a friend. I'd like to get your opinion of Chennault and his plans. I can't get too close to this myself. Half of Congress thinks I'm trying to get us into the war. By the way, I'm going down to the Caribbean for awhile. I'll be back in mid-December."

Tom got up. "I'll see what I can do, Mr. President." He nodded to Hopkins, "Harry."

As Tom headed back to his office, his mind drifted to images of Japan in 1937, before it started its latest move to control China. He had toured the country for Roosevelt then, making stops as well in Shanghai, Manila, and Singapore. What he had seen and heard left him very uneasy about the future. He had reported to the president that Japan was busy building a mobile war machine. People were working hard, and the press talked incessantly about the need for more land and resources, especially oil. Outside Japan, he had found only complacency. No one seemed to take the threat seriously, not even the Chinese. Chiang Kai-shek was preoccupied with his communist opponents, and the British with making money. General Douglas MacArthur, as military advisor to the Philippine Government, consented to a brief interview and calmly dismissed the Japanese army.

Now, three years later, the Japanese were occupying half of China and threatening to take it out of the war completely. Chiang had moved his capital upcountry to Chungking, but his airforce had nearly disappeared and the city was suffering repeated bombings. Claire Chennault, as Chiang's air commander, had tried to defend the city from his base in Kunming, but his Chinese pilots were overmatched by the Japanese in their new long-range fighter, the Mitsubishi Zero.

Tom reached for the phone and called Major Jack Pierce, a friend of his at the headquarters of the Army Air Corps.

"Hi, Jack, it's Tom."

"OK, the weather's lousy for tennis, so you must want information."

"How do you know I don't want to have lunch?"

"Lunch would mean you want lots of information."

"All right, take it easy on me. Jack, did you ever know Claire Chennault?"

There was a noticeable pause at the other end. "Yes, we were instructors together at Maxwell Field, in the tactical training school." It was clear that Jack was weighing his words carefully.

"What can you tell me about him?"

Jack paused again. "You got time for a drink this afternoon?"

"Sure. How about five o'clock at the Robin?"

Just after five, Tom walked into the venerable Willard Hotel near the White House, where every president since Franklin Pierce had stayed. The lobby of the Willard was bright and airy, dominated by pale yellow and pink tones in the marble. Stately columns supported a high, ornate ceiling, and great arched windows admitted light at the mezzanine level. Antique furniture in soft red upholstery sat on matching pink and rose Persian rugs.

Tom's eyes had to adjust as he entered the darkness of the Round Robin Lounge, with its rich paneling and great mahogany bar shaped like the federal-style oval in the ceiling plaster. Jack was in a quiet corner booth under a portrait of Henry Clay, who was said to have introduced Washingtonians to mint juleps in this watering hole of the powerful.

"I ordered your usual Manhattan up," said Jack.

"Thanks. I'm glad I was on time."

Jack was about Tom's height, a little over six feet, but more heavily built. He had played football in college and for a while in the Army.

"Is this another of your little missions?"

"I guess you could say that. I need to keep it low key." Tom knew Jack would not mention it to anyone, and Jack knew he could speak confidentially to Tom. The waitress brought their drinks, and Tom took a sip.

"So, what do you remember about Chennault?"

"He was a first-rate pilot," said Jack, "but he had to worm his way into the Air Corps. They didn't think he was pilot material. He was always kind of a black sheep, and I don't think he ever made it above captain."

"I've heard him called Colonel Chennault."

Jack smiled. "That's probably something Chiang gave him. Chennault would do that, just skip major."

"Should we take him seriously?"

"Well, the Air Corps never did, but I think they were wrong."

"Why?"

"Chennault was a pursuit man. He thought fighters could defend a target against bombers. The brass had decided we should put our money into fast, well-armed bombers. They thought fighters would be outgunned and outrun by new bombers like the B-17. Fighters should be limited to reconnaissance and supporting ground troops. Of course, the infantry brass thought the same thing."

"What did Chennault do?"

"He tried to fight the battle for a while. He was very outspoken, and he didn't always use the channels. He even testified before a congressional committee. Then they set him up as head of an acrobatic team, and he went touring the country for several years. I saw them once, flying P-12s. They were awesome."

"So they eased him out of the picture."

"Sort of. But he kept teaching tactics, and I think he was on to something. He told fighter pilots to forget the dogfights and fight as a team. And don't try to shoot it out with bombers. Dive on them and then climb and dive again. Come in behind each other, but keep some planes in reserve. He was big on formation flying."

"So you think he had a point."

"I do. And he's had some success against the Japanese with Chinese and Russian pilots."

"Have you heard any talk about him lately?"

"Not much. I heard he was in town cooking up something. He gave General Marshall some scoop on a new Japanese fighter, and it caused a stir at the Corps. Looks like it could outmaneuver anything we have, if it's for real."

"If I talk to Chennault, any advice?"

"Well, he's a pretty serious guy. Kind of suspicious, inclined to go his own way."

"Thanks, old buddy. You've been a big help."

"Don't worry, I'm keeping track."

Tom left money for the drinks on the table and said goodbye. As he left the Willard, a driver opened the door of a big black Washington taxi. Tom was suddenly aware of a familiar voice and stopped to look at a woman in a stylish black coat with long dark hair under a black beret. As the bellman picked up her luggage, she saw Tom.

"Tom, hello," she said in a surprised voice. "I just got off the train at Union Station. Do you have spies over there or something?"

Tom smiled. "Of course, these are dangerous times we live in. Hello, Anne, what are you doing in Washington?"

"I'm here for a job interview with the *Post*. I finally got out of southern France. I'll have to tell you about it."

"From the *Herald-Tribune* to the *Washington Post*, is that a step up?"

Anne looked a little embarrassed. With something less than conviction, she said, "I think the war is going to pull us in, and I want to watch how things play out down here."

"Well, if anyone can tell the story, you can."

"Thanks, I appreciate that. I've got to check in. Let's get together soon."

"OK. Here's my card."

"Executive Personnel Assistant? Hmm, that doesn't sound like you."

"We all have to make a living."

"All right, I won't ask any embarrassing questions, at least not right away. It's nice to see you, Tom."

"Same here. Good luck with the interview."

He felt a little lightheaded as he walked toward the trolley stop for the Connecticut Avenue line. Maybe it's the Manhattan, he thought. Anne Wilson had left her job at the *Washington Star-Herald* in 1937 to take a Paris assignment with the *New York Herald-Tribune*. It was her dream job, writing about the growing tension in Europe and living in a flat on the Left Bank. No other correspondents captured so well the character of the leading personalities or described so well the gulf between German ambition and Franco-British complacency.

Tom had visited Anne in 1938 and spent three idyllic days with her before she caught a train to cover the Nazi occupation of western Czechoslovakia. He had not seen her since, but he had read her dispatches from Warsaw during the German invasion of Poland in September 1939, and her harrowing accounts of the fall of France eight months later. He assumed she had made it out but had heard nothing. Now, here she was in Washington, but how long would she stay this time?

Tom drove the short distance to Secretary of the Navy Frank Knox's house in Northwest Washington. He wanted to be among the last to arrive, to attract less notice. As he entered the spacious living room, he saw the guests gathered around a stern-looking man with heavy eyebrows, a prominent chin, and a small mustache. He was answering questions from Henry Morganthau, Secretary of the Treasury, and Henry Stimson, Secretary of War.

Tom moved near but not into the group. At a pause in the conversation, Knox broke in. "Colonel, I'd like you to meet Tom Clark, a good friend of mine."

"It's a pleasure, Colonel."

"Tom," replied Chennault, looking curiously at the newcomer as he offered his hand.

"I think you know everyone else," added Knox.

Tom shook hands with the others. "Sorry to interrupt your conversation."

Knox continued, "The Colonel was just talking about the importance of keeping Rangoon and the Burma Road open to get supplies into China."

Tom nodded. "I assume the Japanese are anxious to close it."

"They're flying missions against it now out of Indochina," said Chennault. "I think it's only a matter of time before they send an army into Burma. I doubt the British can hold them off."

"Aren't your planes being assembled in Burma?" asked Tom.

Chennault looked impressed. "The fighters are. They come to Rangoon in crates."

Mrs. Knox came in and whispered to her husband, and he looked up at the group. "Gentlemen, shall we have dinner?"

As they settled into their first course, Stimson resumed the conversation. "Colonel, the Chinese have taken a beating so far. Would an American flying squadron really make a difference?"

"If I can get the personnel and planes I need, we can make a real difference. We can defend Burma and Chungking. Give me B-17s, and we can carry the war to the Japanese. We can disrupt their shipping and troop movements. We can even strike their home islands."

Morganthau seemed enthusiastic at this last suggestion. "The Japanese cities are made of flimsy materials. Incendiary bombs would set them afire."

Stimson was still skeptical. "Even if you got everything you're asking for, Colonel, you would still be seriously outnumbered."

"I've learned a lot about Japanese tactics. I'm convinced American pilots can outfly them if we have the latest planes. We would fight in teams and take advantage of our firepower. Their planes are lightly built and don't withstand hits very well. We also have a warning net of observers so we don't get caught on the ground. That's a key factor that we've worked hard on. We have a wide ring of Chinese and Burmese soldiers listening for aircraft, and each has radio contact with our bases."

Knox broke in. "Colonel, what do you think will happen if we don't get a squadron in there?"

"I think Chiang will have to throw in the towel. That means freeing up a lot of Japanese planes and troops. It also means we lose the closest air bases to Japanese supply lines, in case we end up having to fight them. The Japanese could overrun Thailand and Burma and threaten India."

Tom decided to ask a question. "Would American pilots join the Chinese Air Force?"

Chennault was ready with an answer. "No, they could work for Camco, the Central Aviation Manufacturing Company. Officially, they would be test pilots and instructors. They would be entirely under my command. Chiang is prepared to pay them well."

Morganthau chuckled. "If we loan him enough money."

When the table had been cleared for fruit and liqueur, Chennault produced a map of China and surrounding countries. He gave his listeners a thorough briefing on the military situation, the location of his airstrips, and the operations of the Japanese. Tom left with a feeling that Chennault was very competent but overly optimistic about what he could expect from his stay in Washington. However, what he said about the importance of keeping China in the war squared exactly with Tom's own opinion.

9

The next morning, Tom called Frank Knox and asked for a copy of Chennault's proposal. It was on his desk that afternoon. Chennault was asking for a lot—350 Curtiss P-40 fighters and 150 Hudson bombers to begin with. He wanted to follow that up with 700 Republic P-43s and 300 Douglas A-24 dive-bombers. He also wanted the pilots, mechanics, spare parts, and supplies to go with them. It was a very detailed list.

As Tom sat thinking about Chennault's plans, his phone rang. He recognized the unmistakable voice at the other end.

"Tom, guess what?"

"You got the job. Congratulations, Anne."

"Thanks. Want to celebrate with me?"

"How about dinner at Dupont Circle?"

"A capital idea. I've got a favorite place I haven't been to in years."

"I think I can guess. Shall I meet you in the lobby at seven?"

"I'll be there."

Tom was amazed at how easily he had succumbed to the temptation of dinner with Anne. She shows up out of the blue and he acts like he's been waiting for her. He should have at least mulled it over, he thought. He had begun to think he should settle down with someone, and Anne was definitely not ready to settle down.

Seeing her now would be just another interlude. Still, if war was coming, who knows where it could take him? Besides, how could he ignore the attraction of those dark brown eyes smiling at him?

At seven that evening, he was back in the lobby of the Willard. Anne was not one to be late, and soon she was breezing out of the elevator, looking very French and very happy. Tom recognized the burgundy silk dress from their last evening in Paris. It was *haute couture*, given to her by an admiring designer after she wrote a piece on the Parisian fashion scene. As they met, Anne put her cheek softly against Tom's and lingered for several seconds. He could sense the familiar fragrance of *Quelques Fleurs*, just a subtle amount.

"So, did they take my recommendation and make you the editor?"

When Anne smiled, her face seemed to glow. "Not yet. But they're giving me a column on the editorial page, twice a week."

"Anne, that's wonderful. That's a lot of freedom, also a lot of responsibility."

"I know. They told me the political class in this town actually reads their editorials."

He helped Anne into her coat, which fell just below her dress at mid-calf, and they headed out into a clear, crisp evening to Tom's car. Soon they were at *Le Coq Rouge*, a popular bistro near Dupont Circle. Tom had reserved a table in the back.

When the Maitre d' had left, Anne grinned. "I guess you don't want to be seen in the window with me."

"Well, I live in the shadows, you know."

"What are you doing now, exactly?"

"I do personnel work, checking out prospective federal judges and some other people before the president nominates them."

"And what else?"

"You don't give up easily, do you? Well, I do little things for the president and Harry Hopkins. I look into situations and give my recommendations."

"I thought as much."

"Seriously, Anne, I do have to be a little careful. Your job is to get stories, but my boss likes to do the surprising himself."

"Oh, Tom, you know I wouldn't take advantage of you."

Tom smiled. He was not so sure.

"*Bonsoir, Mademoiselle et Monsieur.* Would you like a cocktail before dinner?" asked the waiter.

"What would you like, Anne?"

"Something American for a change."

"Bring us a couple of old fashioneds," said Tom, "with the best bourbon you've got. The lady is celebrating."

"Congratulations, *Mademoiselle*, for whatever you are celebrating."

"*Merci. C'est une nouvelle position,*" replied Anne in perfect French.

Tom enjoyed hearing Anne addressed as *Mademoiselle*. It reminded him that she was still only twenty-nine, sixteen years younger than he was. Her accomplishments were already remarkable, and she had many more ahead of her. Being with Anne was the most pleasant thing he could think of, but it was also an elusive pleasure. Might as well make the most of it.

"I want to hear about your escape from France," said Tom.

Anne sighed. "What a shame. I was really enjoying myself there. I loved those few days we had together."

"They were wonderful days. The world always seems to intrude, doesn't it?"

"Tom, I almost didn't make it," said Anne with a sudden note of gravity. "I actually saw German columns moving down the *Champs Elysées.* I had some Jewish friends who were driving south to their parents' home in Marseilles, so I got a ride with them. Fortunately, they had hoarded some petrol—I mean gas. Otherwise, we would never have made it. There were refugees everywhere. It took four days to get to Marseilles."

"Did you have to leave a lot of your things?"

"Some. But I took the precaution in early June to ship my trunk back to New York, so I didn't have many clothes left. I thought I would get out quickly, but when I got to Marseilles, not much was leaving the port. Owners of fishing boats were taking bids to take people to Gibraltar."

"So that was late June. How long were you there?"

"I didn't get out of France until mid-October. I stayed with my Jewish friends for a few weeks, but they managed to buy their way onto an old freighter bound for Lebanon. I have no idea what happened to them. They put me in touch with a Jewish café owner who hired me as a waitress and let me stay upstairs in his flat. I kept trying to find passage out, but the price was too high."

"What about the *Trib*, couldn't they help you?"

"They tried to get me to go to London in June with the rest of their people, but I wanted to stay as long as I could. When I got to Marseilles, I couldn't get a call through to them, so I started saving money to see if I could get enough to get out. Then, in August, the police were starting to check everybody. My boss was getting worried, so I left Marseilles with a musician I had met. We rode bicycles all the way to Cannes."

"Anne, are you sure you're not making this up?"

"I swear it's the truth. Make a great movie, huh?"

"I'll say." Tom gestured to the waiter to take their orders. Unlike drinks, dinner would be very French—*saumon paté*, followed by *coquilles St. Jacques* with *haricots verts sautés*. But since French wine was getting scarce, a good Portuguese white took its place.

"OK, now you're in Cannes."

"My friend got a job playing piano in one of the big hotels and he let me stay there. He was hoping to get out of France himself, because he had been active in the Socialist Party. He heard one of de Gaulle's broadcasts and was trying to get to Britain to volunteer. So here I was on the French Riviera, too scared to leave the hotel. Then we found a convent that would take me in, no questions asked. I stayed there pretending to be a Sister for over a month."

"I'm going to refrain from humorous comments here."

"Don't get smart. Actually, I enjoyed my time there. It was very refreshing. I had very little news of the war."

"Why were you afraid of the Germans? You had an American passport."

"There were a lot of phony passports floating around. I was afraid some SS officer or local policeman would think I was Jewish and take me into custody."

"How did you finally get out?"

"My musician friend found an Italian freighter going to Sicily. The captain had a brother there with a fishing boat, who would take us to Malta."

"And you trusted him?"

"I felt I had to do something. Anyway, it worked fine. Took most of our money, but we made it to British territory. I sent a telegram to the *Trib*, and they wired me my back pay. I was able to get a flight to Gibraltar and from there to Lisbon. And here I am!"

"Amazing. What about your friend?"

"I got him on the flight to Gibraltar, and he went to British army headquarters to volunteer."

"Well, Anne, I've had a few adventures in my time, but nothing like that. I hope you kept a diary or something."

"I was afraid to keep a diary, but I began writing it down on the flight back to New York."

The *paté,* bread, and wine arrived, and the conversation turned briefly to an appreciation of good food and drink. "It's a shame to think about good French cuisine being wasted on Nazi officers," said Anne.

As they finished the *paté,* Tom leaned back and looked at Anne. "I need to get some information on the situation in China. Can you recommend anyone?"

Anne raised an eyebrow. "So, it's OK for you to use me, but not the other way around," she teased. "I do know a good British journalist who was heading for China and Burma the last I knew. He writes for the *Economist.* I've got his London phone number in a book back at the hotel. I also know an Asian scholar at George Washington University. I wouldn't be surprised if he's been to China recently."

They were both feeling the glow of the wine as they walked into the Willard lobby. "Well, let's go up and check my little black book," said Anne with amusement.

Anne's room was ample but not large. It had a mahogany four-poster bed and matching vanity table, of which Anne was making good use. Tom helped her out of her coat, and she gestured toward a door. "You can put them in that closet." It was clear she expected Tom to stay awhile, so he hung up his jacket as well.

Anne sat down with a small book and began writing on the notepad. Tom suddenly felt a strong urge to move things along. From behind, he slowly parted the dark brown tresses resting on her shoulders. He leaned down and gently kissed the back of her neck, taking in that wonderful scent that was part Anne and part French perfume. Anne stopped writing but remained bent forward to prolong the moment. Then she slowly straightened and rose from her chair.

She turned and put her hand behind his head as they began a soft, moist kiss. Tom's hand moved slowly down Anne's side and rested on the graceful curve of her waist, a spot where she radiated sensuality. She moaned softly and drew back to begin loosening his tie. "We've got some catching up to do," she whispered.

10

The next day, Tom began to follow up on the leads Anne had given him. He located the British journalist in Singapore and sent him a cable with the help of the State Department. A few days later, he had a long reply. The picture was not promising, but the author did have praise for Chennault and his efforts with the Chinese Air Force. Tom found the Asian scholar on the GWU campus, and they had a long conversation about Japanese intentions and the political factions in China.

He also made inquiries into the production commitments of the Curtiss and Republic Companies. Production was increasing rapidly, but the British seemed willing and able to take most of it. The Army Air Corps was also expanding its appetite for planes and pilots. Tom knew that General Marshall and the other chiefs were reluctant to divide the pie any further. In mid-December, he called Harry Hopkins and asked to meet with the President.

"We're having an important news conference tomorrow morning," said Hopkins. "Check with me when it's over."

The conference was already underway when Tom slipped into the Oval Office. Roosevelt seemed to be at his folksy best with the reporters sitting around him. He was telling some parable about neighbors and garden hoses and it gradually dawned on Tom that the president was getting the press ready for something big. He eased up to Hopkins, who was standing near the door. "What's up, Harry?" he asked in a low voice.

"We want to start a major program of aid to the British," said Hopkins, turning toward the wall. "We're calling it Lend-Lease."

"Would it only apply to Britain?"

"It could apply to anyone who's fighting the Axis," replied Hopkins. "Come over an hour before dinner tonight. We'll talk about China."

Tom went back to the White House at 7 p.m. Despite the late hour, Roosevelt looked bright and cheerful, obviously pleased with his new initiative. "Tom, how are things going with the mysterious Col. Chennault?"

"I like him. He's a no-nonsense guy. He's asking for the moon, but he probably expects to get a lot less."

"Has he worked his Cajun charm on you?"

"Maybe. He's charismatic all right."

"Well, we could use some charismatic leaders in the armed services," chuckled FDR.

Hopkins got to the point. "What do you think, Tom, should we get behind Chennault?"

"If we do, it's not going to sit well with the Air Corps. They like to pick up the ends of production runs when the British change their orders. The Corps is getting some good bargains that way and getting more planes for their dollars. Getting some for Chennault would mean cutting in on their little game, and he doesn't rank high on their list of favorite people."

"Sounds like it could be done, though," said Hopkins. "Would it be worth it?"

"I think so. Chennault is holding on to some bases that could be very strategic to us if we have to fight Japan. And if he can keep China fighting, the Japanese will have to commit more resources there."

"What do you think are his chances of holding on against the Japanese?" asked Roosevelt.

"Maybe 50-50. He's very knowledgeable about the Japanese military. He pays attention to detail, and I think he would use his resources very effectively. But superior numbers can overwhelm anybody. Then there's Chiang. He may be losing his grip on the situation, especially since so many people have become refugees. General Stilwell is trying to hold Chiang's army together, but it's a struggle. If Madame Chiang were not there to steady things, I wouldn't be very optimistic."

"What do you think we should do from this end?" asked Hopkins.

"Knox and Morganthau seem to be willing to carry the ball. Secretary Stimson and General Marshall are more skeptical. I think the president could pass the word that he wants the four of them to meet and work something out. We'll have to tell Morganthau that it's all right to do another loan against Chinese exports."

Hopkins was taking a few notes. "Anything else?"

"Chennault is going to need authority to recruit volunteers at bases around the country, and we may need an executive order to let the men resign from the services for this purpose."

Tom paused. "There's one thing I'm wary about. Chennault mentioned that with a bomber squadron he could carry the war to the Japanese home islands. Henry and Frank both seemed enthusiastic about that, but I'm not so sure. If American pilots get shot down over Japan, it's going to provoke a strong reaction, volunteers or not."

Roosevelt drew on his cigarette holder and seemed to be weighing Tom's last statement. "Yes, I suppose it would," he said as he exhaled. "Tom, you've done your usual fine job. Are you leaving town for the holidays?"

Tom grinned a bit sheepishly. "I'm going down to Virginia Beach for a few days."

"Enjoy it," said the president. "Who knows what we'll be doing next Christmas?"

Tom left his townhouse in Northwest Washington and headed for the large apartment building on Massachusetts Avenue where Anne had taken a flat. He did not drive very often in Washington, so his 1931 Packard 2-door Roadster was still in fine condition. He had bought the car from a businessman who went bankrupt in 1932, something he still felt a little guilty about. But he loved the car, and he always felt some pride when he went to pick up Anne.

She was wearing black pinstriped trousers, a royal blue sweater, and her beret as she opened the door. "All ready," she said as she hugged Tom and let him help her into her coat. She took his arm and kissed his cheek. "I'm so glad were doing this. Christmas at the beach! I haven't been to my folks' beach house in four years." Tom picked up her two suitcases and headed out the door.

Under a gray December sky, they made their way down U.S. 1 through Fredericksburg and Richmond, then headed out to Norfolk. Darkness was settling when they pulled up to the big, gray-shingled house, with its grand porch looking over the dunes to the Atlantic. Although the temperature was about 50 degrees, the house seemed cool and damp. As Anne unpacked their clothes, Tom split some kindling, shoveled a pail of coal out of the bin, and stoked up the furnace.

It took almost an hour before the house began to feel warm. To keep moving, they busied themselves making the bed, running the sweeper, and rinsing off dishes and pans for dinner. They had brought a metal cooler stocked with two Cornish hens, vegetables, white wine, cheese, and fruit. The house had bottled gas for cooking and hot water, and Anne was anxious to show off her

French cooking skills. It took some improvisation, but by mid-evening they sat down to an impressive candlelight dinner.

Tom raised his glass and touched Anne's. "To the chef, an amazing performance." He was thinking that Anne was truly an amazing woman.

"Thank you. It's so nice being back here."

"Did your parents build this place?"

"No, it was built in the early twenties by an executive in a ship-building company. My father bought it in 1931 when the company was losing money and cutting its payroll."

"Your father made his money in furniture, didn't he?"

"He started his company in Asheville. He never got into the stock market, so he had money available to buy several businesses during the early thirties."

"It's a great house."

"My mother loved this house. We spent the summer here before my senior year at William and Mary. My father hasn't been able to get away much in recent years, and they've hardly used it."

Like most dinners, it took less time to eat than to make. They left the dishes in the sink and took a bottle of Bailey's Irish Cream to the master bedroom. The room had a fireplace, and Tom had brought in wood before dinner. While he worked on the fire, Anne changed into a long, black, silk nightgown. Her mother was of Spanish descent, and Anne had inherited her dark brown hair and eyes, slightly olive skin, and full, sensual mouth. She had the unique gift of being sophisticated, glamorous, strong, and vulnerable at the same time.

She stacked pillows on the bed and they climbed in to watch the fire. "If we do go to war, Tom, what do you think you'll do?"

"I don't know. I'm too old to go back in the Navy. Now that Roosevelt's got another four years, I'll probably keep doing what I'm doing."

"Little things for the president?"

"Little things for the president."

"Like getting planes and pilots for Claire Chennault," said Anne sarcastically.

"Anne, I can't get planes and pilots for anyone. If the Chinese want planes, they'll have to get them themselves."

Anne knew when she was pushing things too far. She snuggled under Tom's arm and put her head on his chest. "What's he like, Tom?"

"What's who like?"

"You know, Roosevelt. What's he like behind closed doors?"

Tom sighed. Here they were in a completely romantic setting, Anne was looking incredibly sexy, and she couldn't stop being a journalist. He knew she was sincere. She just lived every part of life with the same enthusiasm. Talking about politics probably turned her on.

"He's very smooth. He always seems to know what to say. He makes everybody feel important. Sometimes I think he understands things better than any of us do. He always seems to have a vision in mind."

"My father has always liked Roosevelt, but his business friends get apoplexy at the mention of his name."

"Businessmen are very stubborn," said Tom. "They don't want to admit that Roosevelt has gotten the economy back on track."

"You think he's been good for business?"

"Roosevelt understands that you can't have prosperity unless workers have money to spend and a sense of security. The more optimistic people feel, the more they are willing to buy things. If people are buying things, businesses make money. Roosevelt has given ordinary people a sense of hope for the future."

They finished their glasses of Bailey's, and Tom put them on the nightstand. He smiled at Anne. "Speaking of hope."

Putting his arms gently around her shoulders, he kissed her lightly, and she melted into a passionate kiss. Anne's lips were full and moist, and her kisses were very sensual. Tom moved his hand slowly down the middle of her back and rested it firmly on her silk-covered waist. She whimpered, and her legs began to move. He reached down to pull her gown up slowly. Anne became more passionate as Tom allowed the tension to build in their bodies.

They enjoyed each other for a while, and then she climbed atop, pulled off her gown, and brought them to climax. He was still hard inside her as she stretched out on him. She put her hands in his hair and smiled like a kitten. "Can we stay like this all night?"

The house was chilly the next morning, so Tom got up early to fire up the furnace and make coffee. In bathrobe and slippers, he stepped out on the porch to take in the scene. The weather had cleared and there was a lovely sunrise over the ocean. He poured Anne a cup of coffee and went in wake her gently out of her contented sleep. "Can you make it out here to see the sunrise?" he asked.

The instamatic water heater was working fine, so they took a bath together in the big porcelain tub. After breakfast, they went into the village to look for gifts. They found a silversmith with a wonderful collection of jewelry, and Tom bought Anne a silver leaf to wear on her beret, with earrings to match. At a gallery, Anne saw Tom admiring a watercolor of the coastal marsh. "I know just the place for this in your house," she said.

After a leisurely lunch at a little café overlooking the beach, they stopped in the local fish market and bought some of the morning catch to make for dinner. The afternoon was sunny and mild, and they took a long walk on the beach.

"OK, Anne," said Tom after a while, "if we really do go to war, what are you going to do?"

Anne didn't answer right away, but gripped Tom's hand more tightly. She looked out at the breaking waves as a pelican crash-dived into the water. "I could stay in Washington and cover the White House," she said unconvincingly. "Would that be awkward for you?"

His silence seemed to give the answer. After a moment, he said soberly, "You know, Anne, the *Post* is going to want you back in the field. You made a big impression with your stories from Europe."

Tom felt a twinge as he said what he knew would be true. Anne was like a thoroughbred that deserved a chance to run. Tom had thought about marriage, but he wondered what frustrations would follow. Maybe the delight of her company for a while was all he should wish for. They walked for a time without speaking. Finally, Anne reached up and kissed him on the cheek.

"Who knows if we're going to war, anyway?"

11

Sioux City
May 1941

May was Louise's favorite month. March would have occasional flying days, and there would always be some in April, but by May, the days were longer, the field was dry, and the weather was usually good. Everyone struggled to get through winter on the plains, but no one more than Louise.

One thing in her life had changed. For Christmas, Jennie and Rose had given her a new bicycle, and not a moment too soon. As she rode toward Merrill on a Wednesday in late May, Louise laughed at herself. Thirty years old, she thought, and giddy about having a new bike. What a life!

She turned into Schroeder Field and noticed that the Stinson was not there. Sam must have a customer. Finding no one in the terminal, she went down to the hangar and began putting tools and supplies back where they belonged. Before long, she heard an engine and went out to see the Stinson touching down. Leaning against the wall, she saw that Sam was the only one getting out.

"What did you do, lose your passenger?"

"Louise, I've been to Omaha. Come on over to the office."

She followed him in, and, for once, he did not immediately put his feet up. "What were you doing in Omaha?" she asked as she settled into the other chair.

"Meeting with some guys at the airport. They're running the CPT program for Creighton University, and they want to start an extension at Sioux City."

"What's the CPT program?"

Sam handed her a sheet of paper. "Civilian Pilot Training. The government started it a while back, just in case we got drawn into the war. It works with colleges and trains pilots. That's the course outline."

"They want you to do it in Sioux City?"

"They've had four inquiries from up in this area. If we can find six more, we can run a class."

"We?"

"Louise, you know damn well I couldn't do this without you."

"Of course you could, but if you want to think you need me, it's fine with me. Did you tell these guys about me?"

"I did, and they were thrilled. Listen to this: one place in every class has to go to a woman. So you've got to find us one."

Louise had not seen Sam with a gleam in his eye for a long time. That alone would be reason for her to pitch in, as if she needed a reason. The whole idea sounded too good to be true.

"How much will the course cost?"

"Nothing to the students. The government pays. Creighton will pay us a thousand dollars for each class of ten. They'll provide two Cubs and gas."

"How long does a class run?"

"Three months. If we could recruit four classes a year, that's two grand for each of us."

"Wait up, young man, we haven't got our first class yet."

They both laughed. Sam put his feet up, and Louise began to pace around the little office. "OK," she said, "how are we going to do this?"

Louise's life was suddenly hectic. She had to keep up with her job, carry out a marketing effort, make arrangements with Harry at the airport, go over the course with the men in Omaha, find a place for the ground school, get student logbooks and materials assembled, and still take some of the weekend rides at Schroeder Field. She loved it.

Miraculously, a final publicity effort on the Fourth of July put them over the top, and they ended up with six people on a waiting list. Two weeks later, they stood before nine young men and one young woman in a room at the business college and began teaching the basics of flying. It was not long before they had a routine— Louise lectured and Sam told anecdotes. The students responded with enthusiasm, and in mid-August, they began their first lessons in Piper Cubs at the airport. Sam and Louise had to suspend Saturday rides at Schroeder Field.

Graduation from the course required that the students do several maneuvers, including recovering from a stall and spin. Well ahead of time, Louise began going up with Sam and practicing them in both the Stinson and a Piper. It was a harrowing experience to do a spin with a student, trying not to take over unless it was truly necessary. Louise found that she had a reservoir of nerve of which she had not been aware.

Two of their first graduates were accepted for flight training in the Army and one in the Navy. Louise felt she was doing something important, and she began to follow international news more closely. In mid-October, they started their second class, realizing that winter weather would drag it out longer than the first.

In the meantime, something else had happened to Louise. On a Sunday morning in September, Harold Wilkins came up to her after church services.

"Miss Mitchell, how about a ride in my new car?"

Louise was surprised, but she smiled. "Sure, why not?"

Harold was assistant manager at the First National Bank down-town. He was not bad looking, although his hair was receding and he was getting a little soft around the waistline. He had married a classmate shortly after graduating from high school, but she grew tired of marriage to someone who was trying to get a business degree and working full-time. It was still the 1920s and she wanted to enjoy it, so Harold had graciously given her a divorce after three years.

After a short drive along the Missouri River, he dropped Louise back at home.

"Thank you, Harold, that was very enjoyable."

"My pleasure, Louise, I hope we can do it again."

The following Sunday, Louise again met Harold outside the church. "Would you like a drive today, Louise?"

"Harold, would you mind giving me a ride to Merrill?"

"Not at all. Going to do some flying?"

"I've got practicing to do. I hate to miss a day like this."

They drove to Louise's house and she changed into her flying clothes. She made sandwiches while Harold took the front wheel off her bicycle and put it in his trunk. In less than an hour, they were at the field enjoying a little picnic with Sam. They did this a few more times when the weather was good, although she could not get Harold up in an airplane.

While the new class was in ground school, Sam and Louise resumed Saturday rides for a month. One Saturday afternoon in early November, Harold drove up to Schroeder Field and watched Louise bring in her last tour of the day.

"Harold, this is a surprise."

"May I take you to dinner, Louise?"

She was able to stall for a moment while she hung up the keys. "Well, sure, that would be nice."

He drove her home and she put on a wool sweater and skirt. They went to a nice place, and she had an enjoyable evening. Louise was coming to feel that Harold was a very decent person. He worked long hours at the bank and fully expected to be manager before long. He was active in Kiwanis and the Masonic Lodge, and coached a youth baseball team. He was, in short, a solid citizen.

Louise did not, however, feel much chemistry with Harold and so did not mind that he was not the type to make sexual advances. For the time being, he seemed content to see her at church and have an occasional date. That was good, because she did not have much time to spend with him. Someday, she might have to consider the situation more seriously, but for now, it was pleasant and comfortable. If Harold enjoyed her company, why turn him away?

Winter was coming, and it would be difficult to find flying time for the little Cubs. This year, the approach of winter seemed a lot more tolerable to Louise. She was busy, she was making some good money, and she had a friend. Most of all, she was doing something with Sam, something worthwhile. The heartaches of the previous autumn were gone.

12

Washington
November 1941

It was a week into November, and the last of the autumn leaves were falling as Tom walked toward the White House. He was thinking about the contrast of the worsening international situation with his own happy year of seeing Anne two or three times a week. Hitler had launched an invasion of the Soviet Union in June, and his troops were knocking at the doors of Moscow. American relations with Japan were deteriorating, and the U.S. ambassador in Tokyo was warning of impending war.

Roosevelt was staring out the window as Tom entered the Oval Office with Harry Hopkins. "Good morning, Mr. President," said Hopkins.

FDR was suddenly jovial. "Well, here's Tom and Harry, where's Dick?"

Tom grinned. "I'm afraid he's under the weather, Mr. President."

As they sat down, Hopkins began, "Tom and I have been talking about Japanese intentions, and we both think they're getting ready to make some moves."

"So do I," said FDR.

"I'm concerned about our readiness to defend the Philippines," said Tom.

Roosevelt drew on his cigarette holder and exhaled. "You know, General Marshall was just here, and he doesn't think the situation is very urgent. He's been getting very optimistic reports from MacArthur about Philippine defense plans. At the same time, we keep getting these pleas from MacArthur for more of everything."

"Generals always want more of everything," said Hopkins.

"I know, but I wish I had a better idea of what the situation is out there."

"I think I just heard my cue," said Tom.

"Would you like to seek an audience with the General?" Roosevelt enjoyed referring to MacArthur privately as the General, a habit he picked up when MacArthur was Army chief of staff in the early 1930s. The General would probably have approved, had he known.

"My last audience was more of a lecture," said Tom, "actually more of a performance. It was very entertaining, but I came away not knowing what to think. By the way, you keep calling him the General. President Quezon made him a field marshal."

Roosevelt laughed. "I know. He's the only American field marshal I know of."

Tom left the meeting thinking that this was not going to be one of his easier missions. Back in the gothic structure on Seventeenth Street, he put through a call to Fort Sam Houston in San Antonio, Texas. He left a message for Gen. Dwight Eisenhower, who for several years had been MacArthur's chief of staff in the Philippines. Eisenhower called back a few hours later.

"Yes, General, thanks for getting back to me so soon. I'm going out to the Philippines on a little fact-finding mission for the president. I'd like to stop and see you on the way."

"Another trip to Manila, eh?" replied Eisenhower. "I remember when you stopped there in '37. All right, but I haven't been there for nearly two years."

"I just want to get a little background, General. I'll be there tomorrow afternoon."

Tom called his travel contact in the Air Corps and asked if anything was leaving the next day for Kelly Field in San Antonio. As luck would have it, several officers who had been in Washington for staff meetings were heading back to Kelly in a C-47, and Tom could hitch a ride. That evening, he packed his seabag and went to spend the night with Anne. She drove him to Andrews Field the next morning and brought his car back.

By mid-afternoon, Tom was descending to the concrete at Kelly Field. He was able to ride with two of his fellow passengers over to nearby Fort Sam Houston and found Eisenhower at the administration building. "Let's get out of here and take a walk," said the general.

As they strolled in the Texas sunshine, Tom laid out his mission. "We've been getting a lot of confusing impressions about the state of Philippine defenses. MacArthur sends urgent appeals for more men and equipment, but he also talks publicly as if he can turn back any invasion. He even has General Marshall thinking that things are in good shape."

"Mr. Clark, you will never find anyone more difficult to understand than Douglas MacArthur. Part of it is that he enjoys listening to himself talk. He loves rhetorical flourishes. He thinks out loud, and that's why he seems to be a bundle of contradictions."

"Yes, I got a little taste of it on my last visit."

"Some of the bravado and ceremony he indulges in is warranted, to stir up local pride. The Filipinos are very ambivalent about their ties to the United States. They want our protection, but they are also afraid of being in the crossfire if we go to war with Japan. When I was there, we had a hard time getting money from their government to support an army. After the Japanese went into China, President Quezon began talking about neutrality and early independence. Of course, that made it more difficult to get Congress to help from this end."

"Where did things stand when you left, General?"

"The so-called Filipino Army barely existed, maybe 4,000 troops at most. What weapons they had were antiquated, mostly Enfield rifles. The American garrison wasn't much more than an outpost. The airfields were primitive, which didn't matter because there weren't many planes anyway."

"We've been reinforcing them this fall," said Tom, "and shipping equipment."

"So I've heard. The question is whether there will be enough time."

"General Marshall says that MacArthur doesn't expect a Japanese attack before April."

"Well, I wouldn't know. If they have that much time, they may be all right."

"Did you think the Philippines can be defended?" asked Tom.

"Any place can be defended if you've got the right combination of men and weapons. In Luzon, you would want to prevent the landings. Since there are several landing points, you would need good intelligence and plenty of air power, preferably both land-based and carrier-based. If the troops get ashore, you've got to prevent their supplies and reinforcements from getting ashore."

"So you agree with MacArthur's plan?"

"I agree with the strategy of stopping the landings, providing he's got the forces to do it. We certainly didn't have them when I was there, not even close. MacArthur recognized the role of air power, but I didn't think he put enough emphasis on it. He had this thing about torpedo boats. It had some merit, but I think you would need air power to stop the Japanese."

"What if the Japanese struck early, and we weren't ready to stop the landings?"

"Well, you could hold out for a while on the Bataan Peninsula and on the southern island of Mindanao. But I think what I would do is pull back to Australia and build up the forces from there."

"What about using the Pacific Fleet?"

"I'm not a Navy commander, Mr. Clark. You would have to ask them."

That evening, Tom took a taxi to visit the Alamo. He sat on a bench and watched as the sun's final rays gave the old fortress a ghastly flesh-colored appearance. It made him wonder if Jim Bowie, Davy Crockett, and the other valiant defenders were haunting the place. They had held out against overwhelming odds for many days, expecting reinforcements that never came. He wondered if another Alamo was waiting somewhere in America's future.

The next morning, Tom was able to get a ride out of Kelly to the air base in Long Beach. He liked to hitch rides on military aircraft whenever he could, not just because it saved money, but because he heard a lot of interesting talk on these rides. His luck ran out at Long Beach, and he had to get a commercial flight from Los Angeles to Honolulu. There he stopped to chat with Admiral Kimmel, commander of the Pacific Fleet at Pearl Harbor. Kimmel was adamant that his responsibilities did not extend to defending the Philippines. He had to protect Guam, Wake, and Midway Islands, not to mention the Aleutians and the Hawaiian Islands themselves.

Tom had to wait a day for a B-17 that was being delivered to the Philippines, so he visited some of the military installations on Oahu. The ambience bothered him. The military personnel seemed so comfortable, so wrapped up in their tennis tournaments, boxing matches, and football games. Sports seemed to be their primary interest. He looked down on the beautiful harbor protected by its narrow channel to the sea. So many ships were in port. It looked like a giant bathtub waiting for a child to come in and play with the boats.

Tom had a sense of foreboding the next day when he boarded the big bomber at Hickam Field. The Pacific seemed so vast. Among other things, he had learned that deliveries of equipment to Manila were taking as long as six weeks from the factories. He hoped MacArthur was right about the Japanese timetable.

The flight to Manila was long and uncomfortable, with a refueling and rest stop at Wake Island. Following the sun and setting their watches back, they landed at Clark Field just before sunset the next day. Tom was tired, and rather than trying to get army transportation, he decided to take his chances with one of the local taxis. A long ride took him to the Manila Hotel, where MacArthur lived in the penthouse suite. He noticed several Americans gathered among the palms in the open-air lounge, but he was not up to socializing just then.

The next morning, he called the penthouse and spoke to MacArthur's chief of staff, who told him in a chilly tone that the General could see him upstairs at 11 a.m. Tom went up at the appointed time, wondering what kind of reception he would get. To his surprise, he was greeted by Jean MacArthur, the General's wife, who said her husband was waiting for him on the balcony. "May I bring you some tea?" she inquired graciously.

Tom thanked her and joined MacArthur on the balcony overlooking Manila Bay. He had not wanted to look like a politician, so he had worn his lightest-weight khaki shirt and trousers. He was grateful to see the General in khaki as well, albeit wearing his gold-braided cap. Trim and straight, MacArthur looked younger than his sixty-one years. He greeted Tom warmly and gestured to the landmarks in the panorama below. To the left, U.S. Navy ships were anchored at Cavite, and across the bay was Bataan Peninsula. The island of Corregidor was visible in the distance, standing like a sentry near the narrow mouth of the bay.

"So, you've come to see how I'm doing," said MacArthur.

"You might say that, General."

"Well, things are a lot better since I took command of the garrison in July. I'm starting to get some planes in here and get the airfields improved. My troop strength is growing, and it's helping me recruit Filipino soldiers. President Quezon is behind me one hundred percent. But I have a lot of work to do. Getting anyone's attention in Washington is like pulling teeth. No offense, Mr. Clark, but General Marshall is the one who should be out here, and he ought to bring Arnold and Stark."

"I agree I'm a poor substitute, General," volunteered Tom.

"No matter, I want you to get a good look around. I'm going to give you a letter to take back to the president, so he will be sure to know what we need."

"General, I understand you think the Japanese will not attack the Philippines before spring."

MacArthur had begun to pace. "That's right. By Christmas, the weather here will make landings impossible. If the Japanese move this year, it will be in Indochina and Thailand. Then they may take on the British in Burma or Malaya, and that would tie up most of their forces. They haven't fought a western power yet. It won't be like fighting the Chinese. They would not risk getting bogged down here at the same time. If I get what I need for my defense plan, the Japanese may not strike here at all."

"If the Japanese know we're building up our air force here, do you think they might try a preemptive strike?"

"That would be very risky. Even with the P-40s I've got here now, I would take a terrible toll on their attacking force. I'm sure you've heard what Chennault and his volunteers are doing to them in China."

Tom persisted, "Would you know they're coming?"

"I have two radar stations, and I have people on the coast keeping watch. You know, I have been ordered not to take actions that might start hostilities. I cannot send reconnaissance planes over the Japanese bases."

This struck Tom as a rigid interpretation of orders, but he let it pass for the time being. "Look, Mr. Clark," continued MacArthur, "I have an excellent plan to stop a Japanese invasion and I have the support of the Filipino people. All I need is for Washington to deliver on its promises."

"I hear you, General."

"We are sitting at a crossroads in Asian history. The days of European domination are coming to an end. The people of Asia want to determine their own future, and they look to the country of Washington and Jefferson and Lincoln to set the example."

MacArthur stopped pacing and pointed his corncob pipe at Tom. "We do not rule other peoples, Mr. Clark, we lead them. That is our destiny. If we do not make a stand against the Japanese out here, we are forsaking our destiny."

Tom found himself mesmerized by MacArthur's voice. Suddenly, the General glanced at his watch and said, "I want to catch the 11:30 news broadcast, then we'll have some lunch. Afterwards we can go over to headquarters and look over the plans. I want you to meet General Brereton, my new air commander. He's doing a bang-up job."

Tom thought MacArthur was being very decent, and he regretted some of the jokes they had made at the General's expense. They sat on the balcony under an umbrella and enjoyed a shrimp salad with white Australian wine. Then they got into the General's open car with his chief of staff and set off for his headquarters. In a room of maps, MacArthur paced from one to another and gave Tom an overview of the military geography of the Philippines. It was clear that the General had thought a good deal about the strategy of defending the islands. Still, Tom was uneasy.

"General, as you know, the War Department has favored a different plan for the defense of the Philippines. They believe that in case of attack, we should immediately withdraw to Bataan and hold it until forces are ready for a counter-offensive."

MacArthur stiffened. "I do not intend to simply concede Luzon and Manila to the Japanese. I would be breaking faith with the Filipino people who have supported me so loyally. The people of this Commonwealth have entrusted me with their protection and I do not propose to let them down. I will meet the invaders at the water's edge, where conditions favor the defender. You do not win wars by retreating at the first smell of gunpowder, Mr. Clark."

"Suppose the Japanese attack comes much earlier, before we're ready." Tom felt a rush of adrenaline, knowing that MacArthur was not accustomed to being challenged.

The General glared for a moment, then smiled and headed for the door. "Don't worry, Mr. Clark, I will not be taken by surprise."

They walked to an office in the back, where a serious-looking, solidly built man was going over plans with an aide. "Tom, I'd like you to meet General Brereton, my new air commander. Lewis, could you take this young man under your wing for a little while? Show him what we're doing."

Brereton shook hands, but he did not seem pleased with the assignment. "Well, sit down, Mr. Clark," he said impatiently. "I've heard you're from the White House. What would you like to know?"

"How is the buildup going, General?"

"The buildup, that's an interesting word for it." Brereton paused and looked at a map on his wall. Suddenly, he seemed more interested in Tom's visit. "Let's take a little ride. I need to go over to Nichols Field to look at some things. Major Howard, can you get us a jeep?"

The general's aide saluted and hurried out. Brereton handed Tom an aviator's cap and they walked out into the tropical sunshine. The air was sweet with the smell of oleander and bougainvillea. They sped past whitewashed buildings and men dressed in white suits as they headed for the small airfield south of the city. On arrival, Tom saw a grass landing strip, a few small buildings, and several P-40s. They drove out to one end where a bulldozer was working to clear additional land. "This is one of our projects," said Brereton. "Right now, nothing bigger than a P-40 can land here. We've got two fields in the entire Philippines where B-17s can land. You landed at one of them. I'm sure you were impressed."

"It wasn't exactly what I was expecting, General."

"Well, Clark is the only field that's got any anti-aircraft guns. It's got a few. No radar station, though."

"A lot of planes are on their way here, General. Do you have room for them?"

"We put them wherever we can. What's worse is that we can't take care of them. We haven't got a maintenance depot and we haven't got any spare parts."

"You know, General Brereton, I was expecting to see a beehive of activity here. I know it's a hot, humid climate, but things seem pretty relaxed to me."

"No kidding. You certainly wouldn't think war was imminent, would you?"

"Do you think war is imminent?"

"I have no idea. I would like to be flying reconnaissance missions and taking photographs, but I've been told that would be provocative. I'll tell you something, Mr. Clark, there are a lot of

Japanese nationals living in the Philippines. I'll bet you the Japanese have plenty of information on us."

"Have you made your case to General MacArthur?"

"I've tried. I get very little time with him. His chief of staff is always in the way. And now they've got me running around the region meeting with allied air commanders—coordinating. I've got to fly to Jakarta tomorrow morning."

"I'm sorry to be taking up your time like this."

"Listen, Mr. Clark, make sure the president knows the situation out here. I don't have any special intelligence sources, but I can tell you one thing. If the Japanese intend to take the Dutch East Indies and Malaya, they can't afford to leave the Philippines in our hands. We would threaten all of their supply lines from here."

Brereton dropped Tom off at the Cavite naval base, where he met for a while with Admiral Hart. Tom had the impression that Hart was not much involved in MacArthur's planning, that the Admiral was not even comfortable being in the Philippines. He talked a lot about the logic of operating from Australia. Mentally worn out, Tom accepted a ride back to Manila, where Hart's aide dropped him off at the hotel. He sprawled on his bed and was soon asleep.

13

About 8 p.m., Tom awoke in his room at the Manila Hotel and realized he was hungry. He freshened up and went down to the lobby, where he ran into a correspondent he knew.

"Hi, Jim, what are you doing out here?"

"Looking for something to write about, what else? Maybe I can write about you. What are you doing out here?"

Tom smiled. "Have you had dinner? I'm famished."

Jim Andersen was a handsome, blond-haired journalist who worked for United Press International and freelanced for magazines like *Time* and *Life*. He had a nose for news and an uncanny knack for being in the right place at the right time. He and Tom found a table along the side of the screened, open-air restaurant that surrounded the big circular bar. Huge ceiling fans turned overhead, providing a little relief from the warm evening air.

"I thought you would be in London, Jim, or maybe Moscow."

"Too bleak. There are some sacrifices I won't make for a story. Actually, I was in Moscow last month. Just between you and me, I think the Germans are in for a tough winter. The Russians have bent all right, but I don't think they're ready to break."

"We're starting to get some equipment to them," said Tom.

"It's badly needed, and I think it will be a good investment. The German lines are really strung out. I still don't understand why Hitler did this."

"I know. He was very careful until he launched this offensive. He must have thought the Soviet Union would disintegrate under pressure."

Jim nodded. "The Russians are funny people. They can be very cynical one minute and jovial the next. They're used to hardship. I don't think they'll fold their tents that easily."

"How did you get out?" asked Tom.

"I took a train across Siberia to Vladivostok. It was quite a trip. What a vast country! The Soviets have been building a lot of industry around the Ural Mountains."

"Did you go to Japan?"

"I tried. Couldn't get a visa. It's the first time I haven't been able to get in somewhere. I managed to get on a British plane to Hong Kong with some RAF officers. Otherwise, I might still be in Russia."

"Are you just stopping over here?"

"Maybe. I've got a lot of notes to write stories from, and I like it here. The women are wonderful."

"Ah, the ethics of journalism."

"A more pertinent question is what a presidential aide is doing out here."

"Just routine briefings, representing the president. If it were really important, they would have sent somebody else."

"The RAF officers I met said the Japanese are building up their air strength in Indochina and Formosa. They were worried about an attack on Hong Kong, and they thought the Japanese might try to take Rangoon and close off supplies to China."

Tom was listening attentively. "That would mean war between Japan and Britain. That's a big step."

"These guys were pretty sure something was afoot. What would we do if Japan attacked British possessions?"

"I don't know. It would put us in a difficult position. We're trying to help the British all we can, and I guess we would try to get equipment to them out here. But we're trying to concentrate on stopping Hitler."

"I wonder if the Japanese might decide that now's the time to roll the dice and take on everybody out here, including us," mused Jim.

"That's hard to believe. It would sure make our decisions for us, wouldn't it?"

"Are we ready for something like that?" Jim was pressing for something newsworthy, and Tom paused to ponder the question.

Just then, a soft voice broke into the conversation. "You gentlemen look like you've finished your dinner, would you like to join us for a drink?" Tom looked up to see a beautiful, young Filipino woman in a white silk dress decorated with a floral design. He noticed that another young woman was watching them from the bar. Before he could answer, Jim accepted the invitation.

Tom felt uneasy as they put money on the table for dinner and took their glasses of wine to the bar. Jim sat next to the girl who had come to their table, leaving Tom to sit next to the other. "Hello, I'm Maria," she said with a shy smile.

"I'm Tom." He shook her hand lightly. He was thinking that she was lovely, with sympathetic eyes, and maybe twenty-one. He assumed they were call girls, certainly classy ones, but he suspected they might also be on the lookout for American husbands. How had he gotten himself into this situation? A year ago, he might have welcomed it, but now he was interested in holding on to Anne.

"I haven't seen you here before," said Maria, with just the touch of a Spanish accent.

"I came in yesterday," said Tom.

"Are you a businessman?" she asked.

He thought she sounded rather innocent to be a call girl, and he caught himself feeling attracted to her. "No, I work for the government."

"Oh, what kind of work?"

It suddenly occurred to Tom that they could be working for the Japanese. "Oh, nothing very interesting. I do security checks at our military bases. Make sure they're guarding against sabotage. Train the local police to look for spies. Stuff like that."

"I'm sure it's interesting work," she said with a smile. She did not seem very interested, and Tom thought he was probably being paranoid.

"Are you staying at the hotel?"

"Yes," he answered tentatively.

"We could go to your room if you like."

So the meter was running on the small talk, thought Tom. He nodded and left money for her drink on the bar. Jim and his companion followed them out, and they all got into the elevator together. The girls whispered to each other, and Tom did his best to avoid looking at any of them. He and Maria got off first, at the third floor, and as he left the elevator, he felt Jim pat him on the back.

He led her to his room and unlocked the door. Inside, she looked at him expectantly in the dim light, and he thought what a joy it would be to lie next to her. He reached for his wallet and took out five dollars, a princely sum in Manila. "Maria," he said, "I think you're a beautiful woman, and I know I would love to go to bed with you. But there's someone waiting for me back home, someone I care about very much."

He handed her the money. "Would you sit on the balcony with me for a while?"

She hesitated, looking at him curiously. "OK," she said.

Tom made it back to Washington in time for Thanksgiving. Anne's parents came into town by train on Wednesday. Anne had bought everything to make dinner at Tom's place, so she and her mother set about the business of baking turkey, squash, sweet potatoes, and the rest of the traditional meal. Tom noticed that Anne's parents were very proud of her, but also relieved that she seemed to have settled in Washington. There were a few subtle hints that they also approved of him.

On Friday, he met early with Roosevelt and Hopkins.

"Well, how did it go with the Field Marshal?" asked FDR, grinning.

"He was very kind to me," said Tom. "He gave me the run of the place."

"You seem to have a way of getting along with people."

"Well, it helps to be representing the president. And I've learned a few things from you over the years."

Roosevelt chuckled, taking his cigarette holder from his teeth. "I hope you've been selective about what you've learned."

Tom went on to express his concern about Japanese intentions and the vulnerability of the Philippines. They all agreed that stopping Hitler in Russia was still the main objective, but they would try to expedite the shipments to Manila. Tom walked back to his office hoping that he was wrong and MacArthur was right.

14

The first Sunday morning in December was unusually warm and bright, and Tom awoke to beams of sunlight in Anne's bedroom. He got up to open the curtains and stretched himself. As Anne stirred and squinted, Tom hovered over her. "Looks like a beautiful day, Miss Wilson, how about lunch at Harper's Ferry?"

Anne pulled him into a hug. "I'd love to, Mr. Clark."

Tom drove home to change clothes. He pulled on some brown slacks and a tan Shetland sweater and headed back to Anne's place. She came out of her building dressed smartly in navy slacks and blazer over a light blue cashmere sweater. Watching her, Tom again marveled that this remarkable young woman was part of his life.

The Washington Monument was gleaming as they crossed the Potomac and headed west on the Lee Highway. They stopped for a stroll around the Manassas battlefield, where Lee's troops had routed Union forces in the first battle of Bull Run. Then it was on past beautiful horse farms in the Virginia piedmont to Front Royal on the Shenandoah River. From there, they drove north through Charles Town to Harper's Ferry, where the Shenandoah finds a gap in the mountains and joins the Potomac. After walking around the historic old town, they stopped in the Cliffside Hotel for a leisurely lunch.

"The world seems far away," said Anne. "It's hard to believe there's still a war going on."

"I know. Out here, it's hard to imagine that the Russians are desperately trying to keep the Germans out of Moscow and Leningrad. The hardships must be terrible."

"I thought we'd be in it by now. It seems like your boss has done everything he can to provoke Hitler."

"Well, we've done everything we can to help the British and Russians. I think he's very discouraged that so many people can't see the danger. The isolationists are still a force in the Senate."

"Why didn't he ask Congress for a declaration of war when that U-boat sunk our destroyer. They probably would have given it to him."

"I'm not so sure. He didn't want to risk losing a vote like that. Even if it carried by a few votes, it would have been hard to take the country into war with a slender margin."

Anne wasn't convinced. "I think Roosevelt missed his chance. Hitler isn't going to do him a favor and declare war on us, not while he's got his hands full in Russia. Once he finishes off Stalin, he'll have the most powerful empire on earth. Then what are we going to do?"

"The president doesn't want to be the one to declare war because then the Japanese would have to honor their treaty with Hitler, and we'd be fighting in Europe and the Pacific at the same time. But to tell you the truth, Anne, I'm inclined to agree with you. I think we're going to have to fight Germany and Japan both, and the only question is when."

"If Roosevelt doesn't take the bull by the horns pretty soon, we're going to wake up and find that most of the world is under German or Japanese occupation, without us ever firing a shot."

Tom sighed and gazed out the window at the cliffs across the Potomac. "Well, let's not spoil this beautiful day worrying about it. Maybe we should talk about us for a while. Would you like more coffee?"

Anne smiled warmly. "You're right, maybe we should talk about us."

"I think your parents had the impression you were settling in Washington."

"My parents are afraid I'm going to be an old maid."

"They're also very proud of your work."

"Yes, they are. My sister has given them two grandchildren, whom of course they dote on."

"I didn't think you would be in Washington this long."

Anne smiled. "Did you think I was just passing through?"

"We're beating around the bush here, aren't we?"

"We are beating around the proverbial bush, Mr. Clark."

"You know, Anne, it's possible that we are not going to war after all."

"I've been thinking about that myself." She paused. "Where is our waiter, anyway?"

Suddenly, conversation in the room stopped as guests turned to look at the owner, who was tapping a glass.

"Ladies and gentlemen," he said with a grave expression on his face, "please excuse the interruption. We have been listening to the radio in the kitchen. The Japanese have bombed our navy at Pearl Harbor, in the Hawaiian Islands."

The sun was low in the sky when Tom and Anne arrived back in Washington. Anne wanted to have a look at the Japanese embassy, so Tom turned the car up Sixteenth Street. Nearing the embassy, they saw a police barricade in the street and a noisy crowd beyond it. They decided not to stay, and Tom headed toward Dupont Circle, where he stopped in front of the *Post* building.

He held Anne close for a long time, then gathered himself
enough to say, "The world is intruding again."

Anne looked at him sadly. "Is it? I don't know."

They left each other with a lingering handshake, and Tom hurried down Connecticut Avenue to the White House. Security had
already been beefed up, and he had to pass three checkpoints to
get to the Oval Office. Roosevelt was meeting with Secretaries
Knox and Stimson, General Marshall, Sumner Welles of the State
Department, and, of course, Harry Hopkins. The president was
listening grimly to Marshall's latest report of the losses at Pearl
Harbor: five battleships sunk and 14 ships heavily damaged, at
least 2,000 casualties, most of the American planes destroyed on
the ground. The only bright spot was that the fleet's aircraft carriers were all at sea.

"I don't understand," said Roosevelt, "how could we lose so
many planes?"

"General Arnold had warned General Short about possible sabotage," replied Marshall. "General Short had lined up his planes
in the center of the fields where they could be better guarded."

Tom winced. Thinking about the poorly defended airfields he
had recently seen in the Philippines, he decided to say something,
"General Marshall, may I ask a question?"

Marshall looked his way without answering, and Tom continued,
"Was the same warning about sabotage sent to the Philippines?"

"Yes."

"Is it possible that our planes at Clark Field could be lined up
the same way?"

Marshall seemed a little annoyed. "The attack on Pearl was a
surprise, but MacArthur knows the danger in the Philippines.
He'll be ready."

Tom decided not to back down. "With all due respect, General
Marshall, when I visited there last month, I had the feeling that

General MacArthur underestimated the threat from the Japanese air force."

Roosevelt knew when to step in. "General Marshall, it wouldn't hurt to check with General MacArthur would it? We should make sure he knows what happened to the planes in Hawaii."

"Agreed, Mr. President. I'll get word to him as soon as possible."

Tom remained quiet for the rest of the meeting. Afterward he helped Hopkins with suggestions for Roosevelt's speech to Congress the next day. At midnight, he arrived home exhausted and fell asleep in his clothes.

Awakening at 7 a.m., he turned on his radio just as the announcer was saying, "To repeat this bulletin, United Press International is reporting that Japanese planes have attacked Clark Field and other airfields in the Philippines. It appears that American losses have been heavy."

Tom found out later that Air Corps Chief of Staff Hap Arnold did in fact call General Brereton in Manila and warn him to disperse his planes. Brereton put his P-40s and B-17s in the air in anticipation of a morning air raid, but it did not come. He wanted to launch a preemptive strike against Japanese bases on Formosa, but could not get a meeting with MacArthur to get authorization. In the confusion, the American planes returned to base and were lined up on the field when the Japanese struck at noon, destroying over half of the American aircraft in the Philippines. Two days later, they attacked the naval base at Cavite, leaving nothing but a few PT boats and submarines.

15

Tom and Anne barely saw each other in the week after Pearl Harbor. By Saturday, they were finally ready for a relaxing evening, and Tom picked Anne up for dinner at Potowmack Landing in historic Alexandria. He thought she looked exceptionally radiant in a blue velvet dress with matching shoes. As they drove, they exchanged stories about their week's activities.

"I've been over to Arlington to see the new Pentagon," said Anne. "They have nice briefing rooms now."

"Did you get some good information?"

"It was mostly bad news. They were pretty evasive when it came time for questions. Looks like it's going to be more difficult to talk to people around here now."

"Maybe even me."

Anne took his arm and smiled. "Now Tom, you're not going to clam up on me, are you?"

"No comment."

They both laughed. They also both knew that their relationship was a little awkward for him. He wanted to answer her questions if he could, because she meant a lot to him. He also knew that she was careful about how she used their conversations.

They had reserved a table by the window, but the curtains were closed in observation of the blackouts. It was a small reminder that life had changed. Seafood was still good, however, and they ordered the catch of the day. Wine was another matter. Little remained from Europe, so they tried a Riesling from western New York.

"It's not bad," said Anne, as she sipped her wine. "Was Roosevelt surprised that Germany declared war on us Thursday?"

"Yes, he was."

"Was he relieved?" Anne's journalistic skills were never far below the surface.

"Well, it's not the situation he hoped for. He wanted to join the fight against Germany and deal with Japan later. But at least the decks are clear now, and we can go to work."

"How are we going to divide things? Is the Pacific going to get any attention?"

"Stopping the Germans in Russia is still a top priority. I'm not sure at this point how it's going to play out. We've still got a lot of work to do to train and equip our forces. Congress made it very difficult to prepare for this, and now we have to make some hard choices."

"But we've got forces in the Pacific already, and they're in real danger, it seems to me. We can't just leave them out on a limb, can we?"

"I'm doing everything I can to get help to China and the Philippines. But I have to admit that I'm glad I'm not the one making the tough calls. I don't envy Roosevelt."

They talked about the changes in their lives in the past week. The international bureau of the *Post* had quickly become the focus of activity, as local news took a back seat. There was a continuous atmosphere of crisis. Nothing enticed the public's interest more than the rumors, some of which were true, of attacks on West Coast cities or sightings of German submarines off the East Coast.

As they finished dinner, Tom was talking about the myriad of projects he had been trying to keep track of in the past few days. He trailed off as he noticed that Anne was peering into her glass of wine and seemed lost in thought. After a few moments of silence, she looked up and said quietly, "You know, my editor wants me to go to Hawaii."

Tom was expecting something like this, and he stifled a sigh. "When does he want you to leave?"

"Right away. If I don't want to do it, he'll send someone else. I won't lose my job."

"You mean you haven't agreed yet?"

"Well, the Pacific is getting all the attention right now, but what happens when Europe heats up? I might be stuck out there."

Tom was surprised to hear Anne talking this way. She had always been ready to follow the news and had always found a way to go where the action was. "Anne, you're highly regarded at the *Post*. If you wanted to get back to Europe, they would get you there."

She seemed a little agitated. "So you think I should go."

Tom suddenly realized that Anne was struggling with her feelings as much as he was. He hesitated, feeling very uncertain of what to say.

"I'm not sure what I think," he began slowly. "This past year has been the happiest of my life, but I always assumed it would end. You're a terrific journalist. I can't expect you to stay in one place."

Anne did not answer right away, and Tom wondered if he had said the wrong thing. Then, without looking up, she said wistfully, "It has been a wonderful year, hasn't it?"

They sat silently for a few minutes. Finally, Tom felt he should take the initiative. "We don't have to give up on each other. The war won't last forever."

Anne reached out and took his hand. "You are so noble, it's exasperating."

At Anne's place that night, they made love with a passion that was extraordinary even for them. All day Sunday, Tom wondered if Anne would follow her journalistic instincts or decide to stay in Washington. He went to his office but found it difficult to concentrate on the barrage of information swirling around him. Late in the afternoon, he answered his phone and heard only, "Hi," followed by a pause.

"What's up?" he managed.

"I'm leaving Tuesday."

Tom steadied himself. "That's not much time. Can I help?"

"Could I borrow your car tomorrow?"

"Of course. I'll bring it over tonight and you can take me to work in the morning."

On Tuesday morning, Tom drove Anne to the new National Airport, where she checked in for the TWA flight to Los Angeles. As they waited for boarding, he tried to make light of the situation. "You lucky dog, Hawaii in December. And I'll be stuck here in this stuff."

"I'm not going out there to sit on the beach, you know. I'll have to learn all about naval warfare. You should come along and advise me."

"I wish I could. Listen, don't take unnecessary chances. There could be more air raids out there."

"Do you think the Japanese might try to take Hawaii?"

"I doubt it, but then I was surprised by Pearl Harbor, so who knows?"

The PA announcer called Anne's flight, and they looked at each other nervously. She reached her hand behind Tom's neck and pulled him into a kiss. "Wait for me," she said with tears starting to fill her eyes. Tom handed Anne her bag, and she walked toward the line of people heading out the door. At the last second, she turned back, put her hand to her lips, and disappeared.

Two weeks after the first air raids, Japanese troops landed at several locations in the Philippines and met with little resistance. They steadily drove the defenders back until MacArthur realized that retreat to Bataan and Corregidor was the only way to save his army. His move surprised the Japanese and was executed skillfully, except that much food and equipment had to be left behind. On half-ration, American and Filipino troops began a heroic defense that was soon a leading story in newspapers back home.

Just after Christmas, Tom had a letter from Anne, dated almost a week earlier. She was staying at the Moana Hotel in Honolulu, talking to everyone she could about the events of December 7th. One of her first stories was about a tall, young woman pilot named Cornelia Fort, who had been giving a lesson that morning when she suddenly found herself in the midst of Japanese planes heading for Pearl Harbor. Anne was also making new contacts in the Army and Navy and probably sniffing out things she was not supposed to know. Having dealt with French censors, she knew how to get some interesting information past the watchful eyes of the press officers.

The letter made Tom feel better about his decision to encourage Anne, and he went about his work with renewed enthusiasm. On the Sunday after New Year's Day, he opened his copy of the *Post* as he sat with coffee and a bagel. Suddenly, his eyes fixed on a column on the left side of page one. It carried the headline, "U.S. Troops Dig In on Bataan Peninsula." The byline was riveting: "Special to the *Post* from Corregidor, by Anne Wilson."

16

Sioux City
December 1941

Saturday had been a clear day, allowing Sam and Louise to accomplish a good deal with their students at the Sioux City airport. Sunday began with glorious winter sunshine, and Harold gave Louise a ride to Schroeder Field after church. They sat in the little terminal having lunch, wondering if the weather would bring out some customers for a ride over the snow-covered fields. Mrs. Schroeder arrived and turned on the radio.

"Harold," asked Louise, "you give me rides, are you ever going to let me take you for a ride?"

"I've been thinking about it. I've just about got my courage up."

"You'd be in good hands, Harold," said Sam. "This is as good a pilot as you'll find in these parts."

"I know she is. Maybe after our lunch settles."

"All right!" said Louise. "We're getting to you."

"I said 'maybe'."

They all laughed. In the lull that followed, Louise thought about what Sam had said. He was always saying nice things about her as a pilot and a friend, but never as a woman. She wondered why.

"Well," said Sam, "if Harold doesn't go up, we may not have any business today."

The music ended on the radio and the 1:30 news broadcast came on. Suddenly, Mrs. Schroeder spoke up, "Listen!" She turned up the radio.

"The attack has been confirmed in a statement from the White House. The first reports are that damage to our Pacific Fleet has been heavy and many lives have been lost. It is assumed that the Japanese planes were launched from aircraft carriers. Repeating this bulletin: Japanese planes have attacked the U.S. fleet at Pearl Harbor in the Hawaiian Islands. Stay tuned to this station for further reports."

They sat in silence looking at each other. Finally, Louise broke the ice, "Japan has attacked us? We're going to war with Japan?"

"I guess so," said Sam.

"What about Germany?" asked Louise.

"Beats me. Maybe they're going to attack us, too."

"What are we going to do, Sam? Do you think they'll still want our program?"

"I would think so. I'd say we ought to move it along as fast as we can. Get the students out on Sundays."

"What are you going to do, Harold?"

"I don't know. I'm sure the Kiwanis will meet right away to see what we can do."

The news convinced them that no one would be coming out for a ride. Louise decided to head back to Sioux City with Harold and follow the reports with her sisters.

In the coming weeks, she and Sam squeezed as much student flight time as they could out of the winter weather. Their students talked a good deal about the war, realizing that getting into flight training could save them from being drafted into the infantry. Three more of the original graduates were accepted into the Army Air Corps. The young woman from the first class came to see

Louise about what she could do. For the moment, all Louise could suggest was to take more lessons with Sam.

Louise had little time for a social life, so she was pleased when Harold invited her to New Year's Eve at the Masonic Lodge. She had been saving the money from the classes and decided to go shopping. She surprised herself by picking out a green satin dress with a low back and a V-shaped neckline that became a strap around her neck.

At the party, there was a great deal of talk about the war, but hardly anyone except Louise was actually doing anything. To the probable annoyance of their wives, a number of men gathered around to listen to her talk about flying. This was a new experience, and she had to admit she enjoyed it. In her heels, she was taller than some of the men.

She realized after while that Harold was feeling neglected, so she excused herself and went to where he was sitting with a colleague from the bank. "Harold, let's dance."

"It'll have to be a slow one, Louise. I don't do the swing."

"OK, the next slow one," she said as she sat down.

Soon they were on the floor, and Harold proved to be fairly light on his feet. Louise was in an expansive mood, and she felt rather comfortable in Harold's arms. It was the most romantic thing they had done so far, and when the band struck up Auld Lang Syne, she gave him a nice kiss. Then she found herself being kissed by several other men. She almost felt like she was being discovered. These were married men, however, and the evening was soon over.

"I had a lovely time, Harold," said Louise as he dropped her at home.

"You were the life of the party, Louise."

"Oh, Harold, I hope I didn't embarrass you."

"No, no, I was proud of you. There were some envious men there tonight."

"Harold, it's sweet of you to say that." She leaned over and gave him a brief kiss.

"Good night, Louise."

"Good night, Harold."

Despite their best efforts, Sam and Louise were not able to finish the class until the end of February. By then, they had another class ready to go and a waiting list. Four of their graduates went directly into the Army Air Corps, two went to Navy flight training, and one to the Coast Guard. Louise was becoming a minor celebrity in aviation circles. In March, the local newspaper ran an article about the program with a nice picture of her and Sam.

For the time being, she was content with her life in Sioux City. Working with students was stimulating, and she enjoyed the deference they gave her. A few of them wrote to her after going into the service, saying that their CPT training had given them a real edge. She and Jennie had to contend with rationing, but their needs were not great and their life was still comfortable. Harold got involved in war-bond drives. He was appreciative of Louise's company and patient about her busy schedule. Although she was slightly uneasy about it, their relationship mirrored the rest of her life—comfortable.

Louise followed the news of the war closely. She felt she was part of the national effort, and it was a good feeling. Despite the succession of bad news that winter, she would sometimes daydream about the exotic locations where the fighting was taking place. Occasionally, the Sioux City paper carried an article from the Philippines by a woman correspondent. Louise wondered what this woman was like and how she had gotten into the precarious situation on Corregidor.

17

In the first months after the attack on Pearl Harbor, the Japanese defeated the British in Malaya and Singapore, won the Battle of the Java Sea to leave the Dutch East Indies defenseless, and seized the American islands of Wake and Guam. By February 1942, the advance of the Rising Sun was stalled in only two places, Bataan and Burma. In their drive to take the Burmese port of Rangoon, the Japanese were meeting stiff resistance from Claire Chennault's American Volunteer Group, newly dubbed the Flying Tigers by the press.

Tom was worried about Anne, knowing that Corregidor was subject to frequent air raids. He also knew that if she could find a way to cross to Bataan and report directly on the fighting there, she would. American and Filipino troops were giving ground slowly, and their struggle was being followed intently by the public back home. In the White House and War Department, a debate ensued over what to do about the stranded troops. The Navy was unwilling to commit its crippled Pacific Fleet to breaking the Japanese blockade of the Philippines. A convoy en route there at the time of Pearl Harbor had diverted to Australia, and very little of the materiel it carried ever reached Corregidor. Virtually the only supplies making it to the defenders came by submarine.

Besides the logistical problems, the question of relieving Bataan was bound up with the issue of dividing resources between Europe and the Far East. Roosevelt and the War Department were committed to helping Britain and Russia defeat Germany before turning their attention to Japan. Stopping the Japanese in the Philippines, or even evacuating the defenders, might require a sizable commitment of air and naval power that was badly needed elsewhere. Still, leaving the American and Filipino soldiers to their fate was a difficult threshold to cross, and key players in Washington wavered in their resolve.

Tom found himself in an awkward position, concerned as he was about Anne's safety. At a meeting in mid-January, he suggested a major commitment of submarines to break the Japanese blockade. The Navy, however, was preoccupied with potential threats from Japanese carrier task forces and vehemently opposed any diversion of their forces. Roosevelt did order three additional submarines to run the blockade with supplies and evacuate wounded personnel.

As February progressed, the debate began to focus on the issue of whether to bring MacArthur himself out. The General was resisting any suggestion that he should leave his troops, but Roosevelt and Marshall had concluded that for both military and political reasons, MacArthur should be saved and put in charge of allied forces in Australia.

Tom was thinking about Anne in late February when the familiar call came from Harry Hopkins. Soon he was huddled again with the president and his chief aide. Roosevelt was looking weary, as he often had during this bleak winter, but he brightened a little when Tom entered.

"Tom, I've got something for you. Frank Knox mentioned to me that one of our submarines took some reporters out of the

Philippines. He didn't know which ones, but they went to Melbourne."

"Thank God," breathed Tom. "I hope Anne went with them."

"I hope so, too," said the president. "Tom, you've met MacArthur twice. What do you think it will take to get him to leave?"

"Well, he's a soldier from the old school, so I don't think he would disobey a direct order. But I think it would be easier on him if he knew he was going to lead the counter-offensive against the Japanese."

"That may not come for a while. Defending Australia may be his only mission for some time."

"If we tell him that now, he may just go out and get himself killed. He's a very proud man, and he's given to histrionics. I think you've got to give him something to hang on to."

Hopkins joined in. "What happens when he gets to Australia and finds out there isn't much to work with? Even the Australian troops are mostly in North Africa with Montgomery."

Roosevelt answered the question. "I expect he'll start a campaign to get the troops, planes, and ships to mount an offensive. He'll probably make a nuisance of himself, but if we let him die on Corregidor, he's going to haunt us. The Republicans will make a martyr of him."

"I'll say this for MacArthur," said Tom, "we have so many timid commanders, at least he thinks offense. He's willing to take some chances."

"That reminds me," said Roosevelt, "your old friend Col. Chennault is on the agenda again. What's this all about?"

"Well, Mr. President, you remember that right after Pearl Harbor we floated the idea of taking the American Volunteer Group into the Army? General Marshall and General Arnold agreed to make them squadrons of the 10th Air Force, which is setting up in India. I thought Chennault had agreed, but now it seems he's resisting."

"Wouldn't it be easier to get reinforcements and supplies to him if he were back in the Army?" asked Hopkins.

"It certainly would. We've managed to get some things through to him, but it's like pulling teeth. Everybody seems to think that if it's ticketed for China, it's fair game. The new P-40s made it to the Gold Coast in Africa, but it looks like Chennault will have to send his own people to pick them up."

"So why is he balking at converting his group?"

"I'm not sure. Maybe he thinks he got bargaining power right now and is holding on to his cards."

"I wouldn't want to lose Chennault," said Roosevelt. "He's done yeoman service for us, pretty much on a shoestring. And his Flying Tigers have gotten good press, something we haven't had much of."

"Why don't I pay the Colonel a visit and check out the situation?"

"Tom, I don't like asking you to do that. It's a dangerous trip."

"Well, we are in a war, Mr. President. It's dangerous for a lot of people."

Hopkins encouraged the idea. "We could use some first-hand information from China. We can pass the word to the Air Corps to get you there, and Chennault will know you're coming this time."

"Then it's settled, I go to China."

Back at his office, Tom called Anne's editor, who said he had heard nothing from her for several days. Tom asked for a call as soon as the *Post* got word of her whereabouts. Two days later, the phone rang several times at Tom's house, but he was already on an American Airlines flight to Miami.

18

In Miami, Tom got on the first of several DC-3s he would see in the next few weeks. The Army called them C-47s, and they were fast becoming the workhorses of the Air Transport Command. The next stop was Trinidad, where he had to wait a day for a plane to Natal, on the coast of Brazil. There was little hint of war in Trinidad. He walked the beach for hours under a blue sky, wondering where Anne was, wondering what the troops in the Philippines were enduring, wondering what he himself was heading into.

He shared the flight to Natal with some pilots and ground crews who were headed for duty with the 10th Air Force in India. A few thought they might be headed for China. A flying boat took them across the Atlantic to Liberia, but then it was back in a C-47 to British bases in Khartoum and Aden. The group was just about exhausted when they landed in Calcutta, on the eastern coast of India.

In Calcutta, Tom had to wait for a flight into China. The following day, a DC-3 of the Chinese National Airline Company arrived, bringing several of Chennault's pilots who were making their way to Africa to pick up new P-40Es. Tom boarded the return flight and headed across the Bay of Bengal.

Since he had left Washington, the situation in Burma had worsened. Both the British Royal Air Force and the Flying Tigers had abandoned Rangoon after holding off the Japanese for nearly three months. Now the lifeline of supplies through the port and up the Burma Road was gone. The Japanese air force was turning its attention to the rest of Burma, and flights across the country were becoming increasingly hazardous.

Soon they were flying over the mountain ridges and river valleys that traverse Burma from north to south, and Tom was glad for the fleece-lined leather flying jacket that a thoughtful supply sergeant had given him in Calcutta. As the pilot settled into a northeasterly course, Tom noticed they were losing altitude.

"Do you know what's up?" he asked a fellow passenger.

"I heard we're stopping in Lashio to pick up some mechanics. Probably some of my buddies."

As they bumped down on the runway, Tom noticed that hardly any planes were parked at the field. They taxied toward a low building, and two men ran out carrying seabags on their shoulders. The pilot opened his window, and one of the men yelled, "Have you got enough gas to get to Kunming?"

"Sure," answered the pilot.

"Then get this thing in the air. We've got a raid coming in any minute."

The copilot opened the side door and the men scrambled in. Quickly the plane swung around and wheeled into place for takeoff. The pilot gave it everything he had, and the DC-3 shuddered as it rolled down the gravel runway. When it just cleared the trees at the end, Tom murmured, "Thank you, Mr. Douglas." Circling away toward the northeast, Tom could see flashes of light and puffs of smoke rising from the airfield.

Before long they had cleared the last mountains and were heading into a beautiful high valley, with rice paddies and irrigation canals that appeared from the sky as an intricate flowing tapestry. A huge lake stretched out ahead, and the pilot followed it to a more routine landing at Wu Chia Ba airfield in Kunming. As Tom climbed down from the plane, a tall woman approached him. She was wearing khaki shorts, a white blouse, and a sidearm.

"Mr. Clark? I'm Olga Greenlaw. Welcome to China."

So this was Olga, wife of Chennault's executive officer and already something of a legend. In early middle age, she was certainly attractive. "It's a pleasure to meet you, Mrs. Greenlaw."

"Olga, please. I've got a jeep waiting."

The sun was beginning to set behind the mountains as Tom slung his old seabag over his shoulder and followed Olga to a jeep driven by a Chinese soldier. He climbed into the back seat, and off they went through a maze of people, carts, bicycles, and animals to see Claire Chennault.

Chennault and some of his pilots were housed in a hostel at the north end of the city. Olga showed Tom a room he could use and left him with the promise, "I'll call you in a little while for dinner."

Tom thought the quarters were reasonably well appointed, certainly better than barracks. He washed up, shaved, and put on a fresh khaki shirt. Soon Olga reappeared, now in a floral-decorated, yellow silk dress. "Ready to meet the Old Man?"

Chennault remained seated as they entered the dining room. He looked much older than Tom remembered, and more frail. "Welcome, Tom," he said as he extended his hand. "I'm sorry, I've had bronchitis off and on all winter. This is my exec, Harvey Greenlaw. How was your trip?"

"Long and tiring," replied Tom, "and a little too exciting at Lashio. Are you expecting any raids here?"

"We haven't been hit for a couple of months. We fought off a raid in late December. Beat them up pretty good, and they haven't been back. But our guys had plenty of action over Rangoon."

"You and your men did a great job. Believe me, it helped morale back home."

"Which hasn't brought me any more planes," teased Chennault in a hoarse voice.

"I'm sorry about the new P-40s, Colonel. The Army promised they would deliver them all the way."

"Well, maybe it's part of their squeeze play. They probably never thought we would go to Africa and get them ourselves."

A Chinese waiter appeared. "Won ton soup," he said quietly. The group turned its attention to a delicious meal accompanied by small talk. As the waiter cleared the table, Chennault lit a cigarette and asked a pointed question.

"Tom, are you speaking for the president while you're here?"

Tom was expecting this. "Up to a point, Colonel. I know the president does not want to lose your services or those of your men. But there isn't any question that it would be easier to build up your forces if you were back in the Army."

"I don't know if the Army wants me. The setup they're talking about seems intended to get rid of me."

"Attaching you to the 10th Air Force under General Brereton?"

"I don't mind Brereton. It's Stilwell and his crowd up in Chungking that worry me. Vinegar Joe has got his own air officer, and I don't think much of him. Are you going up to see Stilwell?"

General Joseph Stilwell had just been named chief of the U.S military mission in China, and Chiang Kai-shek had made him commander of the Chinese expeditionary forces in Burma. Tom knew the feisty general only by reputation.

"Yes, I guess I am. Do you think General Stilwell will try to take over air operations here?"

"I can work with Vinegar Joe all right, if it's just between him and me. But I don't want anyone else in between."

"Colonel, the president is determined that you will command American air operations in China. He is prepared to do whatever it takes to assure that. That includes bomber squadrons that are sent here."

"Once again, I'm being asked to take a lot on faith."

"I know we promised a bomber group earlier, Colonel. We were still working on it when Pearl Harbor happened."

Chennault looked at Olga. "What do you think, Olga? Do you think I should be a general in the U.S. Army?"

Olga was clearly enjoying the conversation. "Well, I think you would make a splendid general. What would they make me, a captain?"

Tom laughed with everyone else, then he became serious. He knew he was offering Chennault his best chance. "Colonel, I can't say much to General Stilwell if you're undecided."

Chennault took a long draw on his cigarette and watched the smoke rise slowly toward the ceiling fan. No wonder he can't get over bronchitis, thought Tom.

"I don't know how many of the pilots we could keep here, they're pretty worn out. You might be able to keep some by giving them regular commissions, but offering reserve lieutenant isn't going to cut it."

"I can't make any promises about that," said Tom. "I'll do what I can. The president does not like to meddle too much in military business."

Chennault was ready to show his hand. He spoke slowly, "If we keep the AVG intact until the contracts are up in July, and we assure them they'll get the kill bonuses they were promised, most of them will stay for now. We might get some squadron leaders to stay longer."

"I think we can do that," said Tom.

"Well, if you can deliver Stilwell, I'll join your army."

"That's good enough for me. Will Chiang go along?"

Chennault smiled. "Chiang needs planes. I'll assure Madame Chiang that this is the best way." Chennault was playing one of his best cards, his loyal friendship with the Chiangs, and the gesture was not lost on Tom.

Olga knew her cue. "Gentlemen, do we have to talk business all evening? I'd like to hear what's going on back in the states."

The next morning, Tom joined his hosts for a quick breakfast, after which they piled into two jeeps and headed for the airfield. At the command post, Chennault went to a large map on the wall and gave Tom a briefing on the military situation. It was not promising. The Japanese would probably take the remaining airfields in Burma and then the only supply route into China would be over the Himalayas from northern India.

"If you stay very long, you may have to fly over the hump yourself," said Chennault."

"Are the red thumbtacks your observation posts?" asked Tom.

"Yes, we would be in serious jeopardy without them. The RAF had some radar in Burma, but it didn't give them much warning. Ready for a look around?"

The morning fog had given way to a beautiful sunny day, but Chennault bundled himself up and climbed into the back of a jeep with Olga in the driver's seat. "It's easier for me to talk from back here," he said. "You see those two beat-up Tomahawks over there? Cracked-up planes, that's been our main supply of spare parts. We've been criticized for lack of military discipline, but we've got some the best mechanics you'll find anywhere. We don't let anything go to waste."

Tom pointed out toward the runway and looked back at Chennault. "Colonel, why do you have those planes parked in a row over there? They look like sitting ducks."

"Show him, Olga." Olga wheeled the jeep toward a half-dozen P-40s with the trademark shark's teeth painted on the front. When they got up close, Tom realized that they were plywood dummies, with plenty of bullet holes in them.

"Some Chinese carpenters make them for us. From the air they look like the real thing."

"Well, they fooled me," said Tom. "Colonel, do you mind if I look through some of the mission reports this afternoon?"

"Not at all. Just remember, these are some colorful guys. You'll meet some of them at dinner tonight."

Tom spent several hours at a corner desk in the command post. He had wondered about the sensational press accounts of Flying Tiger victories over the Japanese air force. Despite their presumed losses, the Japanese seemed to have an endless supply of planes to put in the air. As Tom read through pilots' accounts of several battles, he began to suspect that two or three pilots were often claiming credit for the same Japanese plane. It was not something he wanted to confront anybody about, especially since these pilots were expecting bonuses for enemy planes destroyed. He thought the claims were sincere, but it illustrated the difficulty of assessing damage in the heat of battle. He filed it away for future reference.

19

Dinner with the AVG pilots was a lot of fun. Tom listened to their stories and suspected that they got better with each telling. When they found out he was close to President Roosevelt, he took a lot of good-natured kidding about bonuses and Army commissions. Next morning, he packed his bag and jumped into a jeep with a Chinese driver. At the airfield, he got on a CNAC plane and headed north to Chungking, Chiang Kai-shek's provisional capital. As he stepped down on the runway there, he was met by an Army captain in a fresh uniform. "This way, sir. General Stilwell is expecting you."

They drove to a one-story building that looked like it might have been a warehouse, and Tom was led into an area closed off by plywood partitions. Half a dozen officers were seated around a table, and several large maps were on the wall.

"Mr. Clark, welcome to China. I'm General Stilwell. Let me introduce you to my staff."

There were a few pleasantries. Stilwell asked three of his staff to give briefings, then he made some remarks of his own. He talked about his plans for using Chinese troops in Burma to reinforce the beleaguered British. As the meeting broke up, Tom went to Stilwell and said quietly, "General, may I speak to you privately?"

Stilwell turned to the waiting officers. "Thank you, gentlemen, that will be all for now."

When they were alone, Tom began, "General, I learned a lot here today. I appreciate the trouble you and your staff went to on short notice."

"You're welcome. What have you got to tell me, Mr. Clark?"

"The president wants Colonel Chennault to command all air operations in China."

Stilwell hesitated, but Tom said nothing more. He looked calmly at the general, who finally asked, "Is he willing to come back in?"

"Yes."

"When?"

"As soon as everyone agrees. But the AVG keeps flying until the contracts are up in July. Then we create three new squadrons. We try to keep some of his best people as squadron leaders."

Stilwell paused again, weighing his response. "We'd have to make him a brigadier."

"As soon as possible. You'll have the full support of the president. And it would help if you would recommend regular commissions for any AVG pilots who would stay."

"Do you know how the Washington brass would take that?"

"I know, but we're in a war now, General. This is not the peacetime army any more."

"Is anybody else on board with this? What about Arnold and Brereton?"

"Right now this is between Colonel Chennault, the Chiangs, you, and the White House. If you can live with it, we want the four of you to have a meeting. The Chiangs will then send a formal proposal to the president."

Tom knew that he was appealing to Stilwell's sense of self-importance, and it worked. The general looked at him shrewdly.

"You're asking me to stick my neck out. You're sure this is what the president wants?"

"I'm certain of it."

"Then why doesn't he just order it? He's the commander-in-chief."

"The president doesn't like to order things if he can get an agreement instead. But he won't leave you out on a limb."

"All right, young man. I'll do the best I can."

"Thank you, General."

Tom headed for the restroom and breathed a sigh of relief. He felt he had just overcome a major stumbling block, and with less difficulty than he expected. He wondered if Chennault would be surprised. Soon he was back at the airport checking on ways to get to Calcutta. He would have liked to see the charming Madame Chiang again, whom he had met in Shanghai in 1937, but he felt it was best to let Chennault handle things this time.

As luck would have it, a B-17 had flown into Chungking two days earlier, bringing some personnel for Stilwell's command and also making an appearance to boost Chinese morale. The Flying Fortress was America's most powerful bomber at the time, with a payload of 6,000 pounds and four turrets with 50-caliber machine guns. Tom climbed into the big plane and pulled down one of bucket seats that surrounded the bomb load area. He was the only passenger out of Chungking, but the flight would stop in Kunming to pick up seven AVG pilots heading for Africa to bring back more of the new Kittyhawks.

At Kunming, Tom got out and walked over to Chennault's command post. He found the colonel immersed in maps with two of his pilots. Seeing Tom hesitate at the door, Chennault asked his men to wait outside a few minutes.

"Back already. How did it go with Vinegar Joe?"

"You're on, Colonel. He's willing to support your terms."

"Well, that's something. So what happens now?"

"You and he need to meet with the Chiangs. Then have Chiang send a formal proposal to the president. He should say that he has consulted with you and General Stilwell and believes the two of you will support his proposal."

Chennault nodded and smiled. "Not bad, Tom, a nice little end-run. Did you ever play football?"

"Just tennis and baseball, Colonel, but let's not call it a squeeze play. I've got to get back on that B-17. I may not get another chance to ride one. Thanks again for your hospitality."

"Anytime, as long as you bring something with you," laughed Chennault.

The big bomber lumbered into the air and headed southwest toward Burma. This time, Tom had some rowdy good company, and there was more talk about the future of the AVG. Tom asked whether any of them would stay in China after their contracts were up, but he let them believe that he was only on a fact-finding mission. Suddenly, the copilot emerged from the cockpit and yelled, "Bandits at nine o'clock!"

Only one gunner had made the trip, and he climbed quickly into the overhead turret. Tom and his fellow passengers sprawled on the cold floor as the pilot throttled up to 300 mph. The top turret began firing its two 50-caliber guns, an almost deafening sound. A few Japanese bullets whistled through the fuselage and ricocheted inside.

"Is anybody hit?" yelled the copilot.

"I think we're OK," yelled back one of the AVG men.

"We're at top speed. I think they've broken off."

The gunner was climbing down. "I think I hit one. Looked like he was trailing smoke."

"Well, they hit us for sure," said the copilot, "is everybody all right?"

Another Flying Tiger sat up. "They were probably on their way to a mission and decided to make a pass. We were a target of opportunity."

"It's a good thing they didn't know we were all in here," said another, "or they wouldn't have let us go."

Tom picked himself up off the floor and knelt for a moment on one knee. "And I thought I was lucky to get on a B-17," he said in a strained attempt at humor.

Fortunately, the rest of the trip was uneventful, and they landed in Calcutta late that afternoon. Two weeks after leaving home, Tom was back at his townhouse in Northwest Washington. At his office the next morning, he had a message from Anne, who was now living at a boarding house in Melbourne. She was expecting to stay for a while to see if there would be news potential. There was also a message from Hopkins that MacArthur had made it out of Corregidor on a PT boat with his family and staff. He was somewhere in northern Australia.

Tom began a memorandum to the president with his recommendations for White House policy toward China. Knowing that FDR did not like long documents, he began by clearly spelling out the understandings he had reached with Chennault and Stilwell, and the assurances he had given on the president's behalf. He then characterized the situation in Burma and China, and made a pitch for increasing the American presence there.

That evening, Tom wrote a long letter to Anne. "I miss you," he began. "I was terribly worried about you on Corregidor. Isn't it possible to cover the war without getting into the most dangerous situations? I know, of course, that you will always go after the best stories, but I wish you would be just a little more careful." He went on to tell her about his trip to China, leaving out the parts where he had come under fire.

A week later, he read a front-page dispatch from Anne in the *Post*. She had caught up with MacArthur in Adelaide, where he had given a statement to the press. She quoted him as saying, "The President of the United States ordered me to break through the Japanese lines for the purpose, as I understand it, of organizing the American offensive against Japan, a primary object of which is the relief of the Philippines. I came through and I shall return."

20

As spring passed into the warm, humid Washington summer, Tom received occasional letters from Anne. They were full of useful observations, indicating that MacArthur's press officer was not trying to censor the mail as he did the news dispatches. Anne's stories in the *Post* were as close to real news as anything coming out of Australia. Somehow, she found things to say that got through the censorship and still conveyed a sense of what was happening. She resisted the habit of other correspondents to fawn over the General, and Tom suspected that his staff viewed her with a wary eye.

In April, Claire Chennault had become a brigadier general in the U.S. Army Air Forces and commander of air operations in China. On July 4, the American Volunteer Group, as Chennault said, "passed into history." It was replaced by three squadrons of the 10th Air Force.

The Japanese were moving to cut off the flow of supplies to Australia, apparently in preparation for an invasion. The U.S. Navy had disrupted the Japanese timetable in the Battle of the Coral Sea, turning back a convoy headed for Port Moresby on the southeast coast of New Guinea. Now the enemy was building airfields in the Solomon Islands and planning another move against Moresby. From there, they could mount an offensive against

Australia itself. In late July, MacArthur moved his headquarters from Melbourne to Brisbane, 1,200 miles to the northeast. This meant that Anne was now closer to the action.

With Australia's best divisions still in North Africa, MacArthur was dependent on militia units and the slowly building American air, naval, and ground forces. He wanted command of all Pacific forces, but the Navy held out for a theater of its own. In Washington, debate ensued over the strategy to follow against the Japanese. Both MacArthur and Admiral King, Chief of Naval Operations, put forward plans to take the major Japanese base at Rabaul, but there were not nearly enough resources available for such an effort. The prevailing view in the capital, pushed hard by the British, was that defending Australia was the goal for 1942.

In August, American pilots and a returning Australian brigade repulsed a Japanese landing at Milne Bay on the eastern tip of New Guinea. Frustrated in their seaborne efforts, the Japanese were now making an incredible attempt to take Port Moresby by hiking through the jungles and over the mountains from the north coast. Just before Labor Day, Tom received a letter from Anne, mailed some ten days earlier. She talked about life in Brisbane, then concluded:

Today, we were herded together for an impromptu briefing, background only. It was quite a show. The General came in, saluted, and started pacing. He went on for two hours and all we did was take notes. Then he saluted again and was gone. The upshot is that he's going to take on the Japanese in New Guinea. They're trying to come over the mountains to take Moresby, and he thinks that's the place to stop an invasion of Australia. The Aussie reporters are nervous as hell. Some of them think Moresby could be another Dunkirk, except it's across the Coral Sea instead of the English Channel.

Please don't fret about me, Tom. You know I've got nine lives and I've only used four of them. Anyway, I haven't seen a Japanese plane since I left Corregidor. The biggest danger here is the Aussie truck drivers.

I think about you often. Can't you wangle a visit out here? Doesn't your boss need some first-hand information?

Missing you,
Anne

The truth was, FDR did want some first-hand information. So did General Arnold, commander of the Army Air Forces. Tom learned about it the second week in September, in a call from Harry Hopkins.

"Tom, Hap Arnold is taking off tomorrow on a Pacific tour. We want you to go as our liaison. Can you make it?"

"Are you kidding, Harry? I could make it this morning if I had to."

Early next morning, Tom was at Andrews AAFB, dressed in khaki shirt and brown pants, carrying his seabag and flight jacket. He boarded a B-17 that had been modified for travel by General Arnold and his staff. Tom was looking forward to some chats with the general. There would be time for chats, as the Flying Fortress made its way the 10,000 miles from Washington to Dallas to Long Beach to Honolulu to Samoa, and finally to Brisbane.

Hap Arnold had the most genuine aviation credentials of any officer in the Army. He had learned to fly from Wilbur and Orville Wright and had become an apostle of air power. Desperately trying to prepare for war in 1939, he had persuaded Congress to authorize the Civilian Pilot Training Programs at colleges around the country. He had also pushed manufacturers to design new fighters and bombers in anticipation of big contracts, knowing that development and testing took plenty of lead-time. In 1942, these initiatives were paying off. Tom wanted especially to talk about Boeing's progress with the new, long-range B-29 bomber.

It was early afternoon when the Australian coast appeared at Brisbane. His head swimming with aviation history, Tom followed the officers down the stairs to be greeted by General Kenney, MacArthur's new air commander. Soon they were off to MacArthur's headquarters to receive one of his legendary dissertations. It was full of assertions, plans, aspirations, and frustrations. Arnold thought the General seemed shaken by his recent experiences, but Tom thought it was vintage MacArthur.

For security reasons, Tom had not been able to let Anne know of the visit. When the meeting broke up for dinner, he excused himself, found a taxi, and gave the address of Anne's hotel. After a short ride, he was standing in front of a small, four-story build-ing with turn-of-the-century character. He went to the desk and asked if they could buzz Anne's room. When she had not appeared after a few minutes, Tom wrote a note for her mailbox.

"Where do your guests usually go for dinner?" he asked the clerk.

"You could check the cafés down the street. There's three in the next few blocks."

With his jacket slung over his shoulder, Tom went out into the early evening sunshine. Beside the first café was a courtyard din-ing area, and he stopped to survey the small crowd. His eyes came to rest on a dark-haired beauty sitting across from a blond-haired man. As he approached the table, she looked up and did a double take. "Tom!" She jumped up to meet him in a hug. "You're here. Why didn't you let me know?"

"Security. I'm traveling with General Arnold."

"I'm so glad. I'd like you to meet Jim Andersen. We came out of Corregidor together."

"Hi, Jim," said Tom, with a hint of irritation in his voice. "I'm surprised you're still in the Far East."

"There's as much news here as anywhere," said Jim with a smile.

"So you two know each other?" Anne sounded a bit uneasy.

"We go back a ways," said Tom. "I saw Jim in Manila before Pearl Harbor."

"We were just having a drink before dinner," said Jim. "Why don't you take my place. I'm sure you two have a lot to talk about."

"You're a dear, Jim," said Anne quickly. "I'll see you tomorrow."

When they were seated again, Tom offered an apology. "Sorry to drop in on you out of the blue. I should have called before coming over."

"Don't be silly, I love surprises. You look terrific."

"So do you. I like your outfit." Anne was wearing dark brown pants and an olive green sweater, with a press patch on the shoulder.

"Do I look official?" she said with a grin.

"You look like the great journalist that you are. How do you like it here?"

"Brisbane is nice, but it's been a frustrating place to work. All the news is carefully controlled. I get some good information from the Aussie personnel, but I can't get it past MacArthur's press officer. I wish I could get to Guadalcanal."

Tom sighed. "You want to drive me crazy again, don't you?"

"I'm sorry. I know you worry, but it's my job to report the news."

"I know. I would just like to think that you'll be around after the war."

"After the war. It's hard to imagine that right now, isn't it?"

"We're starting to win a few battles. Production is really going strong now. We're going to have a lot of stuff in the field before long."

"Out here?"

"Here, too. Russia has been taking a lot, but they've borne the brunt of the fighting against the Germans. That's where the die are cast right now."

"This is still a shoestring operation out here. Are you going to talk to Gen. Kenney?"

"I hope so. He and Hap Arnold are together tonight. Today we had our MacArthur lecture."

"What do you think of the General?"

"Complex man. Inspiring one minute, pompous the next. I think he lives in a world of his own, half real, half imagined."

"Well said. Some of the correspondents worship him. Some of us find him amusing. His staff has some unsavory characters on it, and I think they feed his delusions. He has a lot of power around here, but he doesn't seem to get much help from Washington. Or the Navy, for that matter."

"He's very popular with the public back home. Nobody seems to realize that he was responsible for the debacle in the Philippines. The Republicans use him every chance they can to harass Roosevelt. His requisitions don't even seem to acknowledge that we're at war with Hitler."

Anne was looking down. "The Philippines. I knew a lot of those men, and the nurses. Sometimes I still cry about it. I just hope some of them survived."

After a pause, Tom had to satisfy his curiosity. "By the way, did you go to Bataan?"

"I was there twice. One day with MacArthur on his trip, then Jim and I got back for three days."

"Wait a minute. Are you saying MacArthur only went to Bataan once?"

"As far as I know, he only spent one day there. I'm pretty sure of it."

"Well, people back home have a totally different impression."

Their food arrived and the conversation turned to Australian cuisine. Anne had selected a local wine, and Tom agreed it was excellent. After dinner, they walked for a while in the light of a nearly full moon. "I appreciate your letters, Tom. I know you must be very busy back there."

"I'm busy, but I like writing to you. It gives me a chance to sit back and think, and remember."

Anne pulled him against her. "You mean a lot to me, Tom."

He looked into her eyes, searching for meaning, then bent and gave her a soft kiss. She held him for a longer kiss, and then put her head against his chest. "How long can you stay?"

"Tomorrow for sure, then I don't know."

"You're leaving with Arnold?"

"He's going to meet with Nimitz at New Caledonia. I should be there."

"So we have two nights. Let's go back to the hotel now."

If Tom had any doubts about Anne's feelings, she gave no hint of anything that night. They made love with all the old passion, and she fell asleep in his arms. Tom lay there with all the conflicts turning in his mind. How could he expect to hold on to this woman, who was living and working in a world of men halfway around the world? Anything could happen in the coming years. She was sure to find her way to the fighting, and Japanese bombs were not likely to discriminate between GIs and beautiful correspondents. What was she doing with Jim Andersen? Was it just professional friendship? Would he ever tell her about that night in Manila?

Tom realized that he was silently making a fool of himself. He was privileged to be loved by the most wonderful woman he had ever met, even if it was love on the run. A night like this could make up for all those nights alone. If Anne would become his wife after the war, the wait would be worth it. He dozed off into a well-earned sleep.

As the first rays of light crept into Anne's room, she stirred and began to kiss his neck. She reached down to see if he was hard, and slipped her leg across him. Soon she had him inside her and was moving forward and back in a slowly increasing rhythm. She raised up and looked at the ceiling, moaning as he touched her hard nipples. She gasped as Tom burst inside her. Gradually, her body relaxed and she settled on top of him. "Welcome to Australia," she whispered.

Tom took a quick bath and caught a cab to MacArthur's headquarters. He went to General Kenney's office and asked a corporal if General Arnold had arrived yet.

"Are you Mr. Clark?"

"Yes."

"General Arnold left you a message to meet them at the air base. They're going to Moresby."

"Can anybody give me a ride?"

"Sure, follow me, sir."

Arnold's B-17 was warming up as the jeep dropped Tom off. "You're just in time, Mr. Clark," said a captain standing near the steps, "let's go."

Inside, Arnold invited Tom to sit and listen as Kenney described his buildup of air power at Port Moresby and the missions he was sending out of there. "It's absolutely critical to hold these fields," said Kenney. "We're bringing in everything by air, even trucks. We cut them in two and weld them back together. We can hit supply ships from there if we can find them in time. We can hit Rabaul itself, but it would be a lot better to have bases on the north coast. The weather over the mountains can be treacherous."

In a few hours, they were starting a descent toward the dark green coast of New Guinea. The British colonial town of Port Moresby came into sight, along with several airfields carved out of the jungle. As they stepped out into the steaming air, Tom was aware of a stench, like rotting plants. Everything seemed to be damp, despite the hot sun shining at the moment. They piled into three jeeps and began a tour of the area. In the harbor, a damaged old ship lay anchored. As they watched, two B-25 light bombers made low-level passes at it, dropping practice bombs at the last minute. Both attempts missed short of the target. A third B-25 came in 50 feet off the water and dropped its bomb just short of the target before pulling up over the ship. The bomb glanced off the water into the side of the vessel. General Kenney and his staff let out a loud cheer.

"What in hell are you doing, George?" asked Arnold.

"Trying something new, General. We haven't been hitting anything from high altitude, and those damn torpedoes we've got are less than worthless. We're trying to work out low altitude and skip bombing. If the B-17s can draw the enemy's fighters up to high altitude, our light bombers and P-40s can come in just over the waves."

"You're going to use B-17s as decoys? Do you know how hard I've been fighting for long-range bombers?"

"Don't get me wrong, General. We use B-17s all the time against Rabaul and the Jap airfields on New Guinea. But we've got to find a better way to attack ships. The Navy's getting its best results with dive bombers."

"Well, George, I put you out here to get results. I'm not going to tell you how to do it. Keep me posted on how this works."

"You can depend on it, General."

It was starting to rain, and they pulled on the slickers they had been given.

"I'd like to visit some of the wounded," said Arnold.

"I'm sorry," said Kenney, "the hospital's quarantined. We've got more men down from sickness than bullet wounds."

"Then how about the troops."

"We'll give it a try," said Kenney.

The jeeps started on a road toward the jungle, which became less of a road as it wound into the seven-foot grass and on into the dense canopy. Sunlight began to break through again, and steam rose from little swamps. Tom could see orchid trees and colorful birds, but he wondered how men could live in such a place, let alone fight in it. He was thankful for the knee-high rubber boots they had, because several times they had to get out to push the jeeps through a foot of water. They edged off the muddy road twice to let ambulance jeeps pass in the opposite direction.

"You mean the Japanese crossed the mountains on a road like this?" asked Tom, as they finished pushing one of the jeeps out of the mud.

"Road? Trail is more like it," said Kenney. "If there's a road up there, they cut it."

About six miles into the jungle, they came upon a company of Australian troops resting on its way to the front. "How far to the fighting, Captain?" Arnold asked the commander.

"Maybe 20 kilometers, General. The Nips are making a big push to take Imita Ridge. We aim to stop 'em."

"What happens if we don't stop them?"

"They'd take the high ground around Moresby and level it with mortars. They've carried a lot of heavy mortars over those hills."

"Have you been fighting here long, Captain?"

"This is my second time up the trail, General. We got back from North Africa a month ago, and I did some recon ahead of my company. The rest of our brigade has been up there for three weeks."

"I guess this is a different kind of war for you."

"It's hell, sir. We were hot in the desert, but this is hell. The only good thing is it's worse hell for those poor bastards that hiked over the mountains."

"May I say hello to your men before you move out?"

"Certainly, sir."

Arnold and Kenney moved among the troops shaking hands, while Tom and the others chatted with those nearby. These were veteran troops, and they knew the tricks of survival. To a man, however, none had imagined the conditions they now found themselves in. Tom wondered how human beings, presumably the only intelligent creatures on earth, could fall into such a situation. He wondered, too, if he could convince Anne to stay in Brisbane.

As they waited for their jeeps to get turned around, Tom ventured a comment. "These seem like good troops, I wonder why General MacArthur has a low opinion of them?"

Kenney eyed him cautiously. "These are the first regular Aussie troops we've had. Up to now we've had to depend on their militia. Kind of like the National Guard units in the states."

"Does General MacArthur know the conditions here?"

"He's been given good reports," said Kenney.

The jeeps were ready and they piled in. Tom was not riding with Kenney and Arnold, and he knew he had already touched a sensitive nerve. He resolved to keep his thoughts to himself for the rest of the visit.

21

It was dark when they landed back in Brisbane, and Tom knew that Anne would be wondering what happened to him. He called her hotel from the base and waited for her to come down to the phone.

"Where have you been? I've been worried sick," she said with obvious irritation.

"I'm sorry, I just got back from Moresby."

"Moresby? You went there without telling me? You couldn't get me on the trip?"

"Anne, it took me by surprise. I barely got on the plane myself. There were no reporters."

"Well, can you at least tell me about it?"

"Sure. May I come over, then?"

"Of course, you lout, get over here."

Anne had started a bottle of wine when Tom arrived, and they sat on the bed talking about what Tom had seen. "What do you think of the New Guinea strategy?" asked Anne.

"I'm not an expert, by any means, but it seems basically sound to me. If you can bottle up the Japanese on a jungle trail, where they have trouble supplying their troops, it's better than trying to fight them on a broad front in Australia. What worries me is MacArthur's belief that you always pursue a retreating enemy.

Once we turn them back, we could end up exhausting our own people if we follow them over those mountains."

"What's the alternative, just let them go?"

"We missed a chance to put an airfield on the north coast, but I think I would still try to do it, further east. Then bomb their garrisons constantly until we can make an amphibious assault."

"That could be pretty bloody."

"Maybe, but not compared to going over the mountains and fighting through the jungle. Anyway, we know MacArthur is going to do it his own way."

"Well, General Clark, we'll see if you're right."

"I guess I'm glad I don't have to make those decisions." He put his glass on the floor and took Anne into his arms. "I'm better qualified to make these decisions."

"You're very well qualified," she whispered, as they began a long kiss.

At MacArthur's headquarters the next day, Tom avoided the generals and sought out the mission reports from Kenney's flyers. He found a private corner and spent a few hours reading through them. After lunch, the traveling party climbed aboard the B-17 and headed for New Caledonia. Tom sat quietly and thought about Anne, wondering if this had been their last goodbye.

That evening, he listened as Arnold tried to hash out differences with Admiral Chester Nimitz, commander-in-chief of the Pacific Fleet. The Army and Navy never liked entrusting their forces to an operation commanded by the other service. Arnold was suspicious of the Navy's willingness to support MacArthur's operations, and Nimitz was dubious about MacArthur's understanding of naval power. The Navy wanted Army reinforcements for the Marines on Guadalcanal, but Arnold questioned the Navy's resolve in supporting them. Tom was especially appalled to learn that naval commanders had withdrawn their ships from Guadalcanal before putting ashore all the supplies and equipment intended for the Marines there.

While they slept that night, a climactic battle ensued on Imita Ridge, as Australian forces threw back a furious Japanese attack. Several days later, the decimated Japanese army began retreating over the mountains. MacArthur ordered Australian and U.S. troops to pursue them, setting in motion a bitter campaign to dislodge the Japanese on the northeast coast of New Guinea, a campaign that took four months and cost 8,500 casualties.

Back in Washington the last week in September, Tom wrote his report for the president and gave it to Hopkins. Two days later, he walked to the White House in the bright autumn sunshine. This time, Secretaries Knox and Stimson were in the Oval Office. Tom joined them for tea, thinking the group seemed unusually serious.

"I've read your report, Tom," said Roosevelt. You're not as diplomatic as usual."

"I tried to be, Mr. President. There were some things I felt needed to be said."

"Frank thinks you're a little hard on the Navy, and you an old Navy hand."

"I don't want to pick on the Navy, Mr. Secretary. I'm just concerned that we aren't recognizing the novelty of the Pacific Theater. I think we're in a huge chess game out there, and it's going to involve a lot of coordinated operations. We can't afford to have the services fighting with each other. If we put troops ashore somewhere, we've got to support them."

"We don't have a lot of ships to play with out there," said Knox. "We've got to be careful."

"Careful is one thing, but what happened at Gaudalcanal went beyond careful."

Roosevelt intervened. "Tom, are you suggesting we reopen the issue of a unified command in the Pacific?"

Tom took a moment to sip his tea and compose himself. "I thought about that a lot on the trip back, Mr. President. In principle, yes, we should have a unified command. I'm concerned that we're not going to make the best use of scarce resources in the Pacific. But I understand the political problem we've got. We can't relieve MacArthur of his command, and I can't honestly ask the Navy to accept him as supreme commander. We seem to be stuck with two theaters."

"Well," said Roosevelt, "there's nothing to prevent me from doing some jawboning. Nothing to prevent Frank and Henry from doing some either, right, gentlemen? I want a coordinated plan and serious efforts to get along. I'm going to put that word out myself."

It was Hopkins' turn. "Tom, you recommend that we speed up deliveries to the Pacific. We've just committed ourselves to a major offensive in North Africa. We can't be everywhere at once."

"I understand, Harry. I just think there are opportunities in the South Pacific that we may lose if we give the Japanese a lot of time. I think they're overextended right now, and if we pick our battles carefully, we can disrupt their supply lines."

Tom looked at Knox. "That reminds me, Mr. Secretary, when is Admiral Halsey going to be back in command?"

"Any day now," said Knox. "Nimitz is putting him in command of the South Pacific."

"I wish I could see the first meeting between Bull Halsey and the General," said Roosevelt. Everyone laughed before he continued. "Tom, I thought your comments about landing craft were very interesting."

"We're going to need a lot more shallow-draft boats in the Pacific, because of the reefs. It may be the most critical shortage we have."

"I want you to be my point man on this. I want to get that pipeline moving. Let me know whenever you need my help."

"Yes, sir."

"Well, gentlemen," said FDR, "I think we've had an excellent meeting. Tom, thank you for your candor."

Tom left the White House thinking how difficult it was to get everybody pulling in the same direction, even to fight a war. He went about the task of expediting the movement of landing craft to the Pacific. In mid-October, as he glanced at the front page of the *Post*, his eyes froze on the headline.

JAPANESE SHIPS POUND MARINES ON GAUDALCANAL
Second Night of Heavy Bombardment at Henderson Field
Special to the Post from Anne Wilson

22

Sioux City
October 1942

Jennie was sitting in one of the large wicker chairs, watching Louise come down the street beneath the canopy of great oaks. Home from a day of teaching secretarial skills at the National Business Training School, Jennie was having tea and reading her mail on the porch. Today she had a most interesting letter.

Louise sank into the other chair. "Anything for me?" She noticed that Jennie was smiling like a cat that had swallowed a canary.

"No, but I've got some news that will interest you. I have a letter from an old friend in the Navy Department. She's working for the Army Air Forces now, in the Air Transport Command. She says her boss, Nancy Love, has started a squadron of women pilots to ferry airplanes from the factories to Army bases. She says they're still looking for experienced pilots."

Louise sat up straight. "You're kidding. What kind of experience do they want?"

"A minimum of 500 hours, that's the only thing Mary says. But she says the first group of women is very impressive, and very rich."

Louise was calculating in her head. Rising from her chair, she said excitedly, "I can do that, Jennie, I know I can. Help me write to your friend."

Jennie gathered up her tea and mail and followed her sister to the big oak dining table. She got out a pad of paper and began to take notes as Louise paged through her logbook. Louise had easily more than 500 hours, but she would really look impressive if she had not put so many into Sam's book. They made notes of several of the visiting planes that Louise had flown, including, of course, the twin-engine Anson. That ought to pique their interest, she thought.

They composed a letter to Mary, and Jennie typed it on her shiny black Royal. As Louise pondered it a few more times, Jennie began to make dinner. Louise was still bouncing as she came in from the garden with vegetables for salad. Then she had an unsettling thought. "I hope they're paying a decent wage for this. I want to keep up my part of the house expenses."

"I can manage all right," replied Jennie. "Besides, I think Rose would like to move back here now. She's tired of living alone."

"Really? Gosh, I hope she wouldn't think I was moving out to let her move in."

"No, there's plenty of room here for all of us. Rose would understand."

After her initial euphoria, Louise was unusually quiet as they ate dinner, seemingly lost in thought. As Jennie finished eating, she asked quietly, "Louise, what are you going to do about Harold?"

Louise sighed, as if reality had just intruded on her dreams. "I don't know. He would never understand my going off like this."

"Well, you didn't seem very enthusiastic about his proposal."

"I hope I didn't let it show. I know he really mustered up his courage."

"Have you actually been thinking about accepting it?"

"Harold would probably be a good husband. He's considerate and unselfish, and he has a secure position."

"He also idolizes you."

Louise found it hard to imagine that Harold would be a good lover, but he might surprise her. It had occurred to her that maybe she should take the initiative and find out. After a few minutes, she poured herself and Jennie some more wine. "What do you think I should do, Jennie?"

"Well, there's no harm in sending the letter. You don't have to commit yourself yet. Take some time to think it over."

Louise *was* thinking. She was turning her glass and watching the facets of the stem catch the light. "I've turned down two other men. This could be three strikes and I'm out."

"What about Sam?"

"Sam." Louise took a drink and thought about her mentor. "Sam is the nicest man I know. I used to have a crush on him. He could have had me for the asking."

"Maybe he'll ask you now."

Louise gazed into her glass with a distant smile. "He'll never ask. Sam thinks I'm his niece. He wants me to be a pioneer. I can hear him now, 'This is it, Louise, this is your chance. Don't look back.'"

"What about the program?"

"He thinks it won't last much longer. This is probably our last class. He could finish it up."

"Well, Louise, you're just going to have to look into your heart and decide."

Over the next week, Louise pondered her response if she were invited to join the women's flying squadron. She told Sam about it, and his reaction was just what she expected. "Do it, Louise. You can fly all the latest planes and see the country. And you'll be helping win the war."

If only it were that simple. Louise thought about Jennie and Rose, middle-aged and mainly each other for company. She thought about Harold. She could make him very happy if she accepted his proposal, but she doubted he would wait for her to come back. On the other hand, she might meet someone else during her travels, maybe another pilot.

Finally, it came down to flying. Louise loved to fly more than anything in the world, and this was the chance of a lifetime. In Sioux City, with her modest income, the best she could hope for was to own part of a Piper Cub some day. This was a chance to fly military aircraft, powerful aircraft. A man in her situation would not hesitate, she thought, why should I?

A week after Louise mailed the letter, Western Union delivered a telegram. She ran to Jennie and read it aloud:

PLEASE REPORT ASAP TO AIR TRANSPORT COM-MAND SECOND FERRY GROUP NEW CASTLE ARMY AIR FORCE BASE WILMINGTON DELAWARE STOP TRAVEL AT OWN EXPENSE STOP MUST PASS FLIGHT CHECK ON ARRIVAL STOP
NANCY LOVE WAFS GROUP LEADER

Jennie took her hands. "Congratulations, Louise."

"Thank you." Louise looked at the telegram again, and her excitement waned a little. "Jennie, this could be expensive."

"It's all right. We can make the investment."

"What if I don't pass the flight check?"

"You'll pass."

"But I don't know what their standards will be. It's not a sure thing."

"Louise, you've been training pilots for them already. Are you trying to talk yourself out of it?"

Louise grinned and hugged Jennie. "I don't deserve a sister like you."

Louise spent the next two days getting together everything she thought she would need to spend the winter in Delaware, which she assumed would be chilly and damp. Rose took her to Johnson's Luggage Shop and bought her a new metal trunk, one Louise could handle alone if necessary. She had to go to the First National Bank to withdraw $200 from her savings account, so she took the occasion to tell Harold. He stared at her blankly.

"I won't be gone forever, Harold. I'll be back when the war's over."

Despite her assurances, he was crestfallen. "I can't believe you're doing this, Louise." He turned away, but she had seen the tears starting to fill his eyes. She did not want to waver.

"I'm sorry. I have to go now."

23

On Saturday, October 12, 1942, there was hardly a cloud in the autumn sky as Louise boarded a train to Chicago. She murmured a quiet prayer that her trunk would survive the change of trains and make it to Washington with her. Sioux City was not on the main line, so the old steam engine pulled just three coaches and a mail car. It made slow progress through the gently rolling hills and cornfields of Iowa, seeming to stop longer than necessary in places like Waterloo and Dubuque. Her seat companion was an older woman who was uninterested in conversation, but Louise did enjoy her first crossing of the Mississippi, where she saw the bluffs of Dubuque in the late afternoon sun.

They arrived in Chicago's cavernous station at nine that evening, but it was still a bustling place. Louise had never seen such a collection of humanity. Carrying her suitcase and overcoat, she found a huge trainboard and scanned the timetables to locate her next train. Unable to get a reservation on a Pennsylvania RR train to Philadelphia, she had decided to follow Jennie's 1917 path. She had reserved a Pullman berth on a Chesapeake and Ohio train to Washington that left Chicago at 11:05 P.M. She finally found the entry, showing departure a half-hour late.

Louise had eaten the food she brought with her, so she started looking for a place to get a snack. There was a cafeteria, but the line at the service counter was surprisingly long. Then she noticed a pushcart with smoke rising from a grill. Feeling adventurous, she spent 25 cents on a Polish sausage on rye bread with sauerkraut. She had to eat standing up, but at least she avoided getting anything on her wool suit. Another seven cents got a bottle of root beer, and Louise began wandering until she saw a man get up from the end of a bench. Seizing the chance, she sat down and watched the show around her.

About eleven, a scruffily dressed man approached Louise and asked politely if he could have her empty bottle. She happily obliged and, after finding a ladies' room, began looking for the platform assigned to her train. It was already backing in, and she found Pullman Car No. 108, with a sign saying "Washington" on the side. The bunks were in place when she entered her compartment, and Louise decided to take the upper one. She got out a cotton nightgown, hung her suit in the tiny closet, and climbed into bed. She was fast asleep when her traveling companion entered and took the lower berth.

Dead to the world, Louise was oblivious to stops in Gary, Lafayette, and Indianapolis. She awoke to the call of the porter announcing the train's approach to Cincinnati. Poking her head out of the curtain, she saw an attractive woman, about her own age, all dressed and refreshed.

"Hello there," said her companion, "how'd you sleep?"

"Like a log, thanks. I hope you didn't mind that I took the upper berth."

"No, it worked out fine. My name's Janet Simmons."

"Louise Mitchell. Are you going to Washington?"

"White Sulphur Springs, West Virginia. I'm going to be the head chef at the Greenbriar."

"Really! Is that a big place?"

"You bet it is. It's a beautiful resort owned by the railroad. By the way, we're going to be in Cincinnati for a little while. Want to get some breakfast?"

"Sure, let me get washed up."

Louise threw on her robe and went to the end of the car, where the porter gave her a towel and bar of soap. She combed out her hair the best she could, put on some makeup, and headed back to get dressed. As they climbed down from the car, the porter reminded them, "Fifty minutes, ladies."

They went upstairs into a beautiful concourse lined with mosaics representing the industries of Cincinnati. It opened into a huge art-deco rotunda in the shape of a half-dome. The place was full of uniformed men milling about with their seabags. Around the upper walls of the rotunda was a continuous mosaic depicting the history of the city. Louise gazed from one end to the other and said excitedly, "Janet, this is the most beautiful building I've ever seen."

"Yes, I'm from Chicago, and I'm impressed."

The made their way across the great marble floor and noticed a sign saying, "Rookwood Tea Room."

"Let's have a look," said Janet.

They went into a parlor lined with light green tile. It was bright and cheerful, full of marble-top tables. The serving counter was ornamented by decorative tiles of floral design. A menu board offered a variety of pastries, juices, coffees, and, of course, tea. They claimed a table and went up to make their choices. Once seated, Janet asked, "So, Louise, what's taking you to Washington?"

"I'm going to try out for a women's flying squadron, ferrying planes for the Army."

Janet sat back in her chair. "You're kidding! I thought only men could be pilots."

"And I thought only men could be chefs."

"Well," said Janet, laughing, "here's to World War II." She paused. "I guess I shouldn't laugh about that. But I have to say, I would never have gotten this chance without the war."

"And I would probably be getting ready to marry the local banker," said Louise. "What are you leaving behind?"

"A decent job as assistant chef at the Drake Hotel and a sax player who couldn't make up his mind."

"Was it a hard decision?"

"I thought about it for a while. But then I said, 'Why am I getting this opportunity, to turn it down?' I felt like fate was knocking on my door."

Louise smiled in recognition. "I felt the same way. It seemed like all those years of giving people rides in a little plane were suddenly going to pay off. I didn't feel I could pass it up."

"What will you do in this squadron."

"Pick up planes at factories and fly them to bases. That's about all I know."

"Well, it sounds exciting to me. Now I'm envious."

"I think being head chef in a big resort would be quite a challenge. I'd love to come and see you there some day."

"Standing invitation," said Janet, raising her cup. "Will you give me a plane ride?"

Louise raised her cup in return. "It's a deal. We'd better head back to the train."

As the streamlined engine headed across the Ohio River and eastward on the Kentucky side, Louise and Janet became fast friends. The hills were a mass of yellow and green. Smoky, unfamiliar towns came and went—Ashland, Huntington, Charleston. In the heart of the mountains near the Virginia border, they stopped at White Sulphur Springs. "There it is!" said Janet, pointing to a gleaming white, Greek revival building on a low hill. "My new home!"

Louise followed her off the car and gave her a long, tearful hug. "I'm so glad you were my bunkmate. Good luck."

"Don't forget to write. I can't wait to hear about your trips."

The conductor was calling, so Louise climbed aboard and waved from her compartment. She felt much better about what she was doing.

24

About eight Sunday evening, the C & O train pulled into Union Station in the nation's capital. Louise went to an information desk and inquired about nearby hotels. The agent said there was a decent hotel on North Capitol Street, within walking distance. She asked about her trunk, and was told she could buy a ticket on a morning train and check her trunk to Wilmington. So far, so good, thought Louise.

Monday morning she was on a Pennsylvania RR train, feeling very refreshed. From the Wilmington station, she called the New Castle base and spoke to Jennie's friend Mary, who sounded friendly. "I'll see if I can get you a ride. Call me back in 15 minutes."

Louise went off to find her trunk and then called Mary back. She was told that a jeep would pick her up in about half an hour. A jeep, thought Louise, I think I'm going to like this. The driver had two stripes on his sleeve. At about two that afternoon, he dropped Louise off at a low, gray building on the base. He helped her take her trunk to a reception office inside, where Mary greeted her cheerfully. "So you're Jennie's little sister. Give me your logbook, I'll tell Mrs. Love you're here."

Louise sat and watched as men in uniform came and went. After about twenty minutes, a slender, poised young woman in a gray-green jacket and trousers appeared. "Miss Mitchell," she said with a faint smile, "I'm Nancy Love. Welcome to New Castle."

Louise was nearly speechless. She was expecting a middle-aged woman, but Nancy Love appeared to be younger than thirty, strikingly beautiful, with liquid eyes, fine features, and platinum hair.

Before Louise could say much, Nancy continued, "Lieutenant Thomas will check you out and then we'll talk. I'm concerned about your lack of cross-country experience."

It seemed to Louise that warmth was not one of Nancy's qualities. She sat again and waited until a handsome young man in flying gear came in. "Miss Mitchell, I'm Lt. Thomas. There's a flight suit at the hangar you can use."

Louise's heart was beating fast as she climbed into the jeep and Lt. Thomas sped away toward the field. Not only would she have to prove her flying skills, she would have to do it in a plane with an attractive man. Lt. Thomas, however, was all business. They got into a Stearman biplane, and he told her to taxi to the end of the runway and do her preflight checks. Soon Louise was focused on the airplane, and she began to feel confident. She had flown a couple of these and knew what she was doing. They took off and circled a few times, then her examiner began to call out a series of maneuvers, all of which Louise had taught to students. He gave no hint of his opinion, just instructions. They touched down twice on the runway and took off again, and each time Louise felt that she made her approach perfectly.

Back on the ground, Lt. Thomas said in a matter-of-fact way, "Turn in the flight suit and we'll get back to the office." Louise wondered if she had failed. As she sat again in the reception area, Mary asked if she wanted some coffee.

"Thanks, Mary, but I'm already on edge."

She waited at least half an hour before Mary finally said to follow her back to Nancy's office. Nancy was looking at a file as Louise entered. She glanced up and gestured to a chair. Louise was preparing herself for the worst when Nancy leaned back and smiled in her enigmatic way.

"Lt. Thomas said you handled the Stearman perfectly. You don't have much experience in bigger planes or cross-country flying, but we can give you a 30-day trial. The pay is $250 a month, minus the barracks and mess fee. If you make it, you'll have to buy at least two uniforms, a dress one like this, and a shirt and slacks combination for casual. You'll need shoes for both. The Army supplies your flight gear, but if you lose any of it, you'll have to reimburse us."

"I understand," said Louise. She was wondering if she could manage on her meager resources, but she had not come all this way to be easily discouraged.

"Mary will get you a ride to the barracks, and someone there will show you the vacant rooms. Be back here tomorrow at 0900 for orientation."

Louise lugged her trunk up the steps at the end of the long barracks building, which sat off by itself at one side of the base. In the hallway, she saw an open door and stopped in front of it. "Hello?"

A young woman with wavy brown hair jumped up from a chaise lounge. "Hi there, I'm Kate Burns from Pittsburgh."

"I'm Louise Mitchell from Sioux City. I just got checked out."

"You're the third today. C'mon, I'll help you find a room." She showed Louise three that were available. "If I were you, I'd take this one on the left, away from the wind."

"Thanks, I will," said Louise. By this time, several other women had gathered nearby and begun to introduce themselves. Most seemed to be in their late twenties or early thirties, and rather sophisticated. Louise had a good feeling about Kate, and about a tall, awkward-looking, young woman named Cornelia. As soon as she could, she retrieved her trunk from the end of the hall and began hanging things on a rod in one corner. The room had a bunk, chair, table, and a small dresser. Her head swimming, Louise wondered how long this would be her home.

The next day, she and the other new arrivals were fitted with flight suits at the quartermaster's shop. "Fitted" was a misnomer, because army flight suits were not cut for women. They were issued fleece-lined leather jackets, helmets, goggles, gloves, canvas travel bags, and parachutes, and told to take good care of all of them. Then they went on to learn the intricacies of government travel regulations. They would get a per diem when they were on missions, but it would be paid only after they submitted proper vouchers. One more out-of-pocket expense, thought Louise.

During her first week, Louise flew only once more. A different instructor took her up for three hops between the base and Wilmington's small municipal airport. On her second landing at the base, she was waved off by a ground crewman who was watching her approach. Louise had no idea why she was told to pull up, but decided later that it was part of the training.

Nancy's comment about cross-country experience was burned in her memory, so she concentrated hard on the chart-reading exercises and navigation lessons, such as how to adjust for wind that could blow a small plane off course. In the third week, she and the other recent arrivals were led on a flight to eastern Pennsylvania, involving stops at two small airports. Louise loved the experience of flying with the group, but she still worried that she would wash out. In mid-November, she received a message to report to Nancy's office.

Louise dreaded the meeting, but to her surprise, Nancy greeted her rather pleasantly. "The Piper factory in Lock Haven has some Cubs for us. Betty's going to take three of you new girls up to get them. Be ready at 0800 tomorrow."

Louise barely slept that night and was dressed and packed at the crack of dawn. They rode in an army truck to the train station, where they caught a local to Philadelphia. From there, it was a slow trip to Williamsport in central Pennsylvania, where a large black car from the Piper factory met them at the station. It was nearly 4 p.m. when they arrived at the factory and Betty decided that there was too little daylight left to head back to New Castle. They went off to a small hotel in Lock Haven, where Louise was glad that they decided to double up in two rooms.

The next morning, they waited two hours at the factory for the weather to clear. Betty spent the time reviewing the checkpoints along their route. She was a diminutive woman, one of the oldest in the group, and Louise thought she looked nothing like a pilot. But it was clear that Betty knew her stuff, and Louise felt very confident following her lead. When they were finally in the air, Louise kept close track of their progress on her chart and was delighted at how well she recognized things. After following Betty in for perfect landings at New Castle, they delivered their planes to the operations officer. Louise felt she had done well, but again there was no positive feedback.

The next day, she was again asked to report to Nancy Love. Again, Louise was nervous.

"Miss Mitchell," Nancy began in a businesslike tone, "are you still interested in flying with us?"

"I certainly am," replied Louise, with a determination that surprised even her.

Nancy smiled. "Then we must take you to the tailor shop. Welcome to the WAFS."

25

By Thanksgiving, life was becoming hectic in the WAFS barracks at New Castle. Louise had made another trip to Lock Haven, delivering a piper to a training contractor in Georgia. The flight leader was a tall, impressive woman who knew the tricks of navigation well, and Louise felt she was learning fast.

Piper Cubs had a short range and cruised at 75 mph, so taking one from Pennsylvania to Georgia involved a series of stops at small airports and at least two overnight stays. On this trip, bad weather forced a full day layover in Greenville, South Carolina. In this mountain city, Louise had her first exposure to bluegrass music. A tall thin man in a large cowboy hat played fiddle and led a trio that included a banjo and guitar. She was surprised at how much she liked the music, but trips like this could strain her budget. She had already made two more withdrawals from her savings account.

Louise liked most of her fellow pilots, but she was especially fond of Kate, whom she had met first. Kate was lively, somewhat irreverent, and determined to enjoy this wartime opportunity. In her company, Louise felt increasingly confident in her new environment. Together, they were an attractive pair. The WAFS dress uniform was a wool, gray-green pantsuit with light gray shirt and overseas cap. Daytime wear was khaki slacks and white shirt with black oxfords. Louise and Kate loved to roll up their sleeves, pin their wings on their shirts, and let their wavy brown hair hang down on their shoulders.

As the WAFS pilots flew more missions, the initial tension between them and the men on base began to ease. Louise had been too preoccupied with learning her job to pay much notice to the men in uniform who were everywhere around her. She liked her instructors, but these relationships were kept on a very professional level, something Louise appreciated. She wanted, above all, to prove her worth as a pilot.

On the Saturday evening after Thanksgiving, Louise and Kate were both on base and decided to go to the dance at the officers' club. They bundled their overcoats over their dress uniforms and headed across the base into a chilly wind. The club had a nice room with a small stage and a good supply of tables around an open area. A haze of cigarette smoke hung over the crowd, something Louise could have done without. A small combo of enlisted men was playing the tunes of the big band era. Glancing around, Louise noticed Nancy Love at a table surrounded by officers. She was laughing and talking, and the men seemed to be hanging on every word. Nancy was an impressive woman, thought Louise, no doubt about it.

"Is there room for us?" Kate was asking at a table with two WAFS and four young men. Everyone moved closer together, and Kate scrounged some unused chairs from neighboring tables. An enlisted man took their drink orders, and Louise took Kate's suggestion to try a B-17. She found herself sitting next to a young lieutenant with short brown hair, boyish good looks, and wings on his jacket. She guessed he was about twenty-two.

"Hello, Lieutenant, I'm Louise Mitchell," she said with new-found assurance.

"Pleased to meet you, ma'am," he replied in a pleasant, singsong accent, "my name's Terry Fawcett."

"Where are you from, Lieutenant?"

"Lexington, Kentucky, ma'am. How about you?"

"Sioux City, Iowa. It seems so far away now. I can't believe I left there less than two months ago."

"I know what you mean, ma'am."

"How long have you been at New Castle?"

"Two months. It's my transition training, to P-40s. I'll probably ship out soon."

"Well, I'm only flying Cubs. I'd love to climb into a P-40."

"Maybe you will, ma'am, if they send all the rest of us overseas."

His tone was sincere, and Louise smiled appreciatively. She was surprised and pleased that this young man thought of her as a potential P-40 pilot. "Where did you train, Lieutenant?"

"I had primary training in Macon, Georgia."

"Ha!" laughed Louise. "I delivered a Cub there."

"Then I went to basic and advanced school in Texas, at Randolph Field."

"I've heard Randolph is the best training base. Have you been back?"

"Once, to drop off an AT-6. It was kind of fun going back on business. How long have you been flying, ma'am?"

"I did my first solo in a Challenger, in 1930. I was 19 years old." Louise had answered spontaneously and with pride, but suddenly she realized how much distance she had put between herself and this young man.

"And you've been flying ever since?" He had turned toward her and looked genuinely impressed.

"Yes, at a small field in Iowa. I gave rides and lessons. Before I came here, I was instructing in the CPT program in Sioux City."

"Ma'am, that's something to be proud of."

"Thank you, Lieutenant." Louise was feeling both satisfaction and regret at this turn in the conversation. She quickly reminded herself that he was nearly ten years younger than she was, and he was certainly treating her with appropriate respect. She wondered if he would soon excuse himself. She sipped her B-17, which was good but strong.

After a pause, the lieutenant looked up from his drink. "Miss Mitchell, would you like to dance?"

Louise smiled. "Well, this is a dance, isn't it?"

He rose and pulled her chair back for her. She followed his lead of taking off her jacket and hanging it on the chair. Louise had not danced to swing music, but she felt she could pick up the moves if her partner knew them. He did. In a few minutes, she and this young man from Kentucky looked like natural dance partners, and people were starting to watch them. The lieutenant was both strong and gentle, and his touch sent a warm feeling through Louise's body. Not to be outdone, Kate led another young pilot to the floor and captured some of the attention. After three numbers, the women traded partners and danced a few more. When they arrived back at their table, their companions gave them a round of applause.

For the next hour, everyone listened as the men at the table told stories about the new pursuit planes. Two had heard about accidents involving Bell's P-39 Airacobra, a fast plane designed with the engine behind the pilot. They agreed that they would not volunteer for P-39 duty.

At a pause in the conversation, Lieutenant Fawcett turned to Louise and said apologetically, "Ma'am, I'm afraid I have to leave on a mission tomorrow morning. I'm taking a P-40 from Buffalo to Panama. I need to get to bed now."

"I should say, Lieutenant. Good luck, and thank you very much for the dancing."

"It was my pleasure, ma'am. Happy flying."

Louise and Kate stayed at the table for a while longer, then excused themselves. As they headed back to the barracks, Kate couldn't resist asking, "So, what did you think of him?"

"Which one?"

"You know which one, Lieutenant Fawcett."

"Kate, he's ten years younger than me. All he called me was 'ma'am'."

"Yeah? Well, he was looking at you when you didn't notice."

"He was?" Louise stopped and took Kate's arm. "Kate, he's very nice, and he's a great dancer, but that's all. I'm not looking to mess anything up by getting involved with a young pilot. By the way, do you think Nancy was upset with us?"

They started walking again. "Nancy already thinks I'm a little too wild. She told me to watch myself, that we had to maintain a professional image. Then look at her flirt, husband and all. But I guess for her it's just politics."

"Do you think we were too wild tonight?"

"Nah. We weren't loud or silly. We just danced, and pretty well, I thought. Where'd you learn to dance like that?"

"I was just following him. I used to dance a lot when I was young, but not for a long time. It was really fun, wasn't it?"

They climbed the stairs to their rooms. "I'm going to get into my flannel PJs," said Kate. "C'mon down for a while."

Louise changed into her nightgown and robe and headed back to Kate's room.

"Would you like something to take the chill off?" Kate had a bottle of bourbon and two small glasses. She was right, Louise felt warmer immediately.

"I feel like I'm living a dream, Kate. Do you feel that way?"

"I think we all do. Even Nancy and Betty, and they've flown a lot. I just hope we get to fly something besides Cubs and primary trainers."

"Do you think we will?"

"Yeah, I do. But we have to prove ourselves first. That's why Nancy's so careful, she knows we're not accepted yet. The truth is, we've got better pilots in our group than a lot of the men here."

"Wouldn't you love to get behind about 400 horsepower? Really get up in the air?"

"Why not 500?" laughed Kate. "Let's make it a New Year's resolution."

They touched glasses and laughed some more.

"So, Louise, how come you haven't married, if I'm not too nosy?"

Louise took another sip and stretched out on the bunk. "No, you're not too nosy. I'm not really sure why. I got involved in flying and that seemed to bother a lot of guys. There weren't many good prospects in Sioux City. I had one guy for a while, but he wasn't a very good lover and I got tired of it. I had another guy who was just too old."

"How old?"

"Too old."

"That old, huh?" They both laughed.

"The past year I dated a banker, a very nice man, but kind of dull. He never tried to get me into bed, and I wasn't very inspired either. He was broken-hearted when I left. I felt guilty about it."

"What are you going to do if you meet someone here?"

"Kate, all I want to do right now is fly. When the war's over, I'll worry about men again."

"So you didn't feel anything at all tonight?"

"Can I turn the tables here? What are you going to do if you meet someone?"

"You have to answer my question first," laughed Kate. "My curiosity is too great."

"You are a devil. OK, I hope he liked me. I hope I didn't blush when he asked me to dance."

"Ha! I knew it. I bet you were wondering if he was as good in bed as he was on the dance floor."

"Kate, stop it. I just met this poor young man." Louise sat up and finished her bourbon. "Now, smart aleck, are you looking for a man here?"

"Maybe, but only for after the war. I don't want to stop flying until I have to."

"So you're going to put several in the bank and withdraw one later." They laughed again and Kate poured a little more in their glasses.

"I like that idea. That's what I'm going to do, put them in the bank."

26

Louise was feeling a bit hung over, but she made it to breakfast Sunday morning. In the afternoon, she wrote a long letter to Jennie, as she had done every Sunday. She told her sister about the dance, but left out her feelings about the young lieutenant. That evening, she answered a knock at her door and opened it to see Nancy. Oh no, she thought, I knew I shouldn't have danced last night.

"Miss Mitchell," began Nancy coolly, "do you think you're ready to handle a PT-19?"

"Uh, I'm sure I am, Mrs. Love." Louise tried to gather herself. "I've been up twice and I've studied the tech manuals backward and forward."

"Be at the hangar at 0900 tomorrow to check out in one. If you do well, you leave for Hagerstown after lunch. Get to the Quartermaster first thing tomorrow and get winter gear. And be sure they give you some long johns."

"Yes, ma'am." Louise could barely conceal her excitement.

Nancy started to leave, then turned back. "Miss Mitchell, I thought you handled yourself well last night, but don't get attached to any of these young flyers. Keep your mind on your work."

"Yes, ma'am." Louise closed the door and let out a long breath. "Thank heavens," she said aloud.

She sat down and added a postscript to her letter, then bounded down to Kate's room. "Guess what," she bubbled, "I get to check out in a PT-19 tomorrow, and maybe a mission."

"Great," said Kate, giving her a hug, "we'll be on a mission together."

"No kidding? I hope I don't screw up the check out."

"You won't, you're plenty good enough."

"Nancy said I would need long underwear. Do you think so?"

"Absolutely. I didn't bother with it on my first PT mission, and I was cold in that open cockpit. Make sure you've got a warm scarf. Oh, and if you're nice to the ops crew, they'll give you a clipboard that straps to your thigh. Then you might be able to keep your charts from blowing away."

"I'd better study the techs again. No bourbon tonight, my friend."

Louise was at the officers' mess by 7 a.m. and the quartermaster's shop by eight. She was issued fleece-lined leather pants to go with her jacket, wool-lined boots, wool underwear, and a warmer flying helmet. She lugged the new gear and her parachute to the operations hangar and changed into the flight suit. Feeling so heavy that she could hardly walk, she imagined that she must have looked like a penguin. She was looking around the hangar when she heard a familiar voice behind her.

"Ready, Miss Mitchell?" Lt. Thomas was also in winter flying gear, but looking as if his had been tailored for him. Louise felt a little better knowing she had the same instructor who had checked her out on her first day. She followed him out of the hangar to where two ground crewmen were pulling a sleek blue and yellow PT-19 into position. Lt. Thomas climbed into the rear cockpit.

"As soon as you're settled in, start the engine and we'll check out the headphones."

Louise eased herself into the bucket seat and was again glad that she was 5 feet 7. She wondered how smaller women managed in these planes. She reviewed the controls and started the engine. "Boy," she murmured. "175 horses sound a lot better than 65!" She put on her headphones. "Mitchell here."

"Taxi out to warm up and we'll do the preflight."

Soon Louise was feeling a rush as they pulled smoothly away from the ground and climbed to 8,000 feet. As before, Lt. Thomas calmly called out maneuvers, and again Louise did them easily. She loved the plane and knew that she could fly bigger ones. After half an hour, Thomas told her to get into a landing pattern. She made her approach and turns, easing the plane onto the runway just the way the manual described it.

Climbing down from the wing outside the hangar, Louise took off her helmet and waited. For the first time, Lt. Thomas looked at her with a slight smile. "Mrs. Love wants you ready to leave from the mess hall at 1300 hours."

Exhilarated, Louise changed clothes again and charmed an operations corporal into giving her a clipboard. She was struggling toward the barracks when he pulled up in a jeep. "May I give you a ride, ma'am?"

"You *are* an angel, Corporal."

Back in her room, Louise carefully packed her uniform and enough things to get her through a few days if the weather got bad. She slung her parachute over her back, picked up another bag with her boots, helmet, and leather pants, and headed for the officers' mess. After lunch, she and five other WAFS piled into a truck for a quick trip to a waiting C-47, in which they made the short hop to Fairchild's factory in Hagerstown, Maryland. Louise was surprised to find that Nancy was going as flight leader. She had heard that deliveries were piling up and guessed that was why she herself had been pushed ahead.

In Hagerstown, they found six PT-19s waiting for delivery to a training field in Montgomery, Alabama. After going over the charts with Nancy, they donned the rest of their gear and climbed into the cockpits. Louise was sweating underneath everything, but she trusted Kate's advice. They made their preflight checks before heading to the runway so they could take off close behind each other. Nancy took off first and circled until the rest could get into a loose diamond formation. As they headed south along the Shenandoah Valley, Louise gazed at the blue sky and the wooded country below. She could not help feeling proud that she was part of a team doing something important, and she wished her mother were still alive to hear about it.

As darkness approached, Nancy headed for their first stop at Roanoke, Virginia. Following her in, the WAFS pilots made perfect landings and taxied in for refueling and overnight parking. Nancy sent a telegram back to New Castle, while Kate called to get them hotel rooms. Louise was grateful that she could share a room with Kate, making her six-dollar per diem stretch a little further. After dinner, she and Kate hung up their uniforms and stretched out on their beds, exhausted but too keyed up to sleep.

"Do you think you'll keep flying after the war?" asked Louise.

"I hope so. I can't imagine giving up flying."

"What about marriage, and children?"

Kate was usually quick with an answer, but this time she thought for a moment. "If I can marry another pilot, he would understand."

"Somebody's got to be home if you have kids."

"Maybe we'd have enough money to get a nanny. Not everybody has to fly for the airlines. Betty flew for Grumman as a test pilot."

"What about all the men coming back? Won't they take all the jobs?" asked Louise.

"Aviation is going to be big. I'm sure there'll be room for us."

"I wish I could be as optimistic about everything as you are. I feel like I'll wake up some day back in Sioux City and go to the church and marry Harold the banker. Or maybe I'll go back and he won't want me."

"Louise, will you stop putting yourself down. You're going to attract plenty of attention before this is over. There's no reason why we can't all marry pilots. I should think they'd be thrilled to have us."

"I'm seven years older than you, Kate."

"There are pilots your age, too. Listen, you're on your first PT mission, just enjoy it. This war's a long way from over." Kate's voice was showing some uncharacteristic irritation, and Louise realized she had to stop feeling sorry for herself.

"You're right, I don't know why I get into these moods. Good night, Kate."

"Good night."

Their phone rang at 5 a.m., and by 6:30, they had eaten and were on their way to the field. It would be a full day of flying to reach Montgomery, with two stops along the way. Louise loved the challenge of following their progress on her charts, which she barely managed to keep on the clipboard. The six of them were a comical sight as they piled out in the mild Alabama air, tired, hungry, and anxious to find the restroom. But Nancy was smiling as she gave them the receipts for their planes. "Well done, let's find a hotel."

Back at New Castle after three days on the road, Louise wondered if Lt. Terry Fawcett was back from Panama yet. She could not help glancing around the officers' mess, but there was no sign of him. A day later, she was headed back to Hagerstown with three WAFS colleagues for another delivery. This trip took her to Oklahoma, and she was gone four days. She still did not see the young lieutenant. Finally, she mustered up the courage to ask one of the young men who had been at the table with them.

"Fawcett? Yeah, he was here for a few days, but he got his orders. He's on his way to North Africa."

"Oh," said Louise, trying to hide her disappointment. "I wanted to wish him good luck."

27

Anne's first dispatch from Guadalcanal had confirmed Tom's worst fear about her determination to get to the heart of the action. After that, he scanned the *Post* every day for one of her cabled reports. At least twice a week, he had evidence that she was still all right. Her stories were captivating. She was helping in the hospital, and the wounded soldiers gave her plenty of information about the desperate fighting on the perimeter of Henderson Field. In the columns of the *Post*, these young men came alive for readers, as did the doctors and nurses. With apparently little censorship, Anne's journalistic gifts were flourishing.

Tom followed the drama with mixed feelings. He was enormously concerned for Anne's safety, yet proud of what she was doing. In spite of himself, he returned to his doubts about a future with her. As much as he loved and admired her, he felt she was using up her nine lives in a hurry. If she survived the war, she would still be in the prime of her career and still inclined to live on the edge. Tom was feeling more and more that he wanted a companion in his life.

There was little time for such thoughts, however, as Christmas 1942 approached. He was busy with various tasks assigned him by Roosevelt. In Russia, German forces were stalled at Stalingrad, in what was shaping up as a critical struggle that might turn the tide on the eastern front. Allied forces had taken the initiative in New Guinea, the Solomon Islands, and North Africa, but the Japanese and Germans were giving ground grudgingly and exacting a heavy price. The end was far from being in sight.

In January, as fighting on Guadalcanal entered its final phase, Tom accompanied Roosevelt to Casablanca for a conference with Winston Churchill and the Combined Chiefs of Staff. He again found himself arguing the case for increased support of the South Pacific Theater, and this time Marshall and King were pushing the same view. The British, however, argued stubbornly for a strictly defensive stance against Japan. They also resisted any commitment to an invasion across the English Channel, instead keeping the focus on Mediterranean operations.

Tom's friend Jack Pierce was there as an aide to General Arnold, and as the conference closed, they sat in the rooftop restaurant of the whitewashed hotel. The Mediterranean sun beat down on a colorful marketplace nearby. "We're drifting, Jack," said Tom, gazing at the blue sky and sea. "We still don't have a strategy for winning this war."

"What about the bombing campaign? Don't you think we can destroy the German war industry?"

"Maybe. But I'm becoming skeptical about high-altitude bombing. I wonder if we're really doing the damage we think we are."

"Don't let my boss hear you say that. He's put his reputation on the line for strategic bombing. He can hardly wait to get the B-29s out there."

"I have a lot of respect for your boss, and I really enjoyed traveling with him. I think high-altitude bombing has its place, but I don't think it's going to win the war."

"What is going to win it?"

"In the Pacific, coordinated attacks and disruption of supply lines. Isolating the Japanese forces and cutting them off. Eventually blockading the home islands."

"What about the Germans?"

"I don't like to see us spending time and resources in the Mediterranean. Sooner or later we're going to have to cross the channel and take on the Germans in France, and I'd rather do it sooner, before they finish their coastal fortifications. I hate to say this, but I think Stalin has a point when he says we're leaving him to do the major fighting."

"Well, I think Marshall and Eisenhower would agree with you, but Churchill is adamant. I wonder if he's ever going to agree to cross the Channel."

"Not unless Roosevelt insists on it," said Tom.

In early February, Tom noticed a break in Anne's stories from Guadalcanal. Calling the *Post*, he was told that she had flown to Admiral Halsey's headquarters in New Caledonia, which was a great relief. He sent off a letter, hoping it would find her.

A month later, he joined Roosevelt and Hopkins as the sun set on a lovely spring day. "I've had a letter from Anne," said Tom. "She says that Halsey and MacArthur seem to be getting along fine. She thinks the General has met his match."

"I think she's right," said FDR. "Maybe that's one less feud to worry about. Now, I understand you boys want to talk about China. We haven't done that for a while."

"Tom thinks we need to intervene on Chennault's behalf again," said Hopkins.

"What does he want now, the first B-29s?"

"I hope somebody's going to want them," said Tom. "No, the problem is that Chennault's old nemesis is now the commander of the 10th Air Force, and they're not getting along. I promised

Chennault that he would control air operations in China, and I think we should back him now."

"What do you suggest?" asked Roosevelt.

"We're up to eight squadrons in China, six fighter and two bomber. I think we could make them a separate air force, with Chennault in command."

"Does Hap Arnold agree with this?"

"I'm afraid General Arnold still sees Chennault as a maverick. We would have to direct him to do it."

Roosevelt leaned back and looked at the ceiling. "My generals, what would I do without them? So you think this is necessary?"

"I think Chennault can run a very effective campaign if he has control. He's performing a valuable service."

"OK, draft a memo to Arnold."

"One more thing. I know General Stilwell is frustrated already, but I think Chennault should get first priority on supplies going over the Hump."

"You really want to rub it in, don't you."

"With all due respect to General Stilwell, I just don't think he can accomplish much with the Chinese army. I've come to the conclusion that Chiang is just plain incompetent, and he doesn't control much of the army anyway. Chennault can at least harass the Japanese and contribute to our Pacific war effort, and it's important to hold his airfields for raids on the home islands."

"Well, I've been thinking the same thing," said FDR, "but I do want to keep Stilwell in the game. If the British get serious about retaking Burma, I want Stilwell to be ready to help."

There was a knock on the door, and the president's secretary entered with a cablegram. As he read it, his face brightened into a smile. "It's MacArthur's report on the Bismarck Sea," said Roosevelt excitedly. Several days earlier, American planes had repeatedly attacked a Japanese convoy trying to reinforce troops in New Guinea.

"Twenty-two ships, over 100 planes, 15,000 troops, what a tremendous victory!"

Tom was uneasy about the figures, especially knowing MacArthur's flair for public relations. "It certainly is good news, Mr. President."

"I must send congratulations to MacArthur and the commanders involved," continued Roosevelt.

"You can do it in person," said Tom. "General Kenney has just arrived to meet with the Joint Chiefs. It would be a good opportunity to get first-hand information on the war out there."

"Terrific. Let's get him over here. Make sure we have a photographer, Harry."

"Mr. President," said Tom, "there's something I think we ought to keep in mind."

"What's that?"

"I've been reluctant to say this, but based on my experience, I suspect the enemy losses are being greatly exaggerated."

"On purpose?"

"Not necessarily, although I think there's a natural desire to accept the highest estimates. It's more a matter of the confusion that goes on in battle. Pilots may claim credit for the same enemy plane, or assume more damage to a ship than has actually happened. I saw signs of it in the reports I read in Kunming, and again in Brisbane."

"What are you suggesting, Tom?" asked Hopkins."

"Well, I don't think we should make an issue over MacArthur's report. It's good for morale, military and civilian, to have a victory like that."

"It's good for my morale," chuckled FDR.

"Make no mistake," added Tom, "this is an important victory. The Japanese will find it hard to reinforce their New Guinea troops after this."

"So why worry about the numbers?" asked Hopkins impatiently.

"I think we should keep it in mind when we're evaluating progress in the different theaters, so we don't make overly optimistic assumptions. And I think we should somehow let the commanders know that we're a little skeptical."

"Well, Tom, I'll give this some thought," said Roosevelt, with a tone that meant the meeting was over.

The next morning, General Kenney brought a large map and was very articulate in pleading his case for more planes, personnel, and engineering units to build airfields. In the primitive South Pacific, building forward airfields was a key to moving forces and cutting off enemy troops. FDR listened intently as Kenney explained his flexible use of air power to achieve objectives.

After nearly an hour, Roosevelt took over. "General Kenney, this has been one of the most helpful presentations I've had since Pearl Harbor. I am most appreciative that you have given us this time."

"Thank you, Mr. President." The gruff general was positively beaming.

Roosevelt continued enthusiastically, "Your victory in the Bismarck Sea was astonishing. I should think the Japanese would have little to defend Rabaul after such losses."

Kenney became somewhat animated. "Oh no, Mr. President. The Japs still have plenty of strength at Rabaul, and we've still got a tough fight on our hands in New Guinea."

"Well, General, I'm delighted with what you've accomplished with so few resources. You know, we're still very concerned about Germany, but I'm going to tell General Marshall to do everything he can for you."

"Thank you, Mr. President." Kenney rose and saluted, and Roosevelt returned it with a broad smile.

Tom was amused at the way Roosevelt had handled the situation. There's still nobody like him, he thought as he walked back to his office. As it turned out, General Kenney left Washington with less than what he wanted, but a little more than the Joint Chiefs had intended to give him.

That afternoon, Tom answered the phone and heard Anne's voice, surprisingly clear. "Where are you?" he asked.

"I'm in LA, on my way to Washington."

"Are you all right?"

"I'm getting over malaria. I look a little wasted."

"When did you get it? Why didn't you tell me?"

"It started at the end of January. I just didn't want you worrying."

"Well, get home here and let me play nurse for a change."

"I'll be there tomorrow afternoon, about 5:30 on TWA. Can you pick me up?"

"Wild horses couldn't stop me."

At National Airport the next day, Tom watched patiently as passengers stepped down from the Los Angeles flight and headed for the terminal. When it seemed the plane was empty, a flight attendant stepped out and turned back to help someone. Anne appeared, looking thin and unsteady, and followed the attendant slowly down the stairs. Tom met her inside the door and took her in his arms.

"I must be a sight," she said.

"You're a sight I'm very glad to see. How are you feeling?"

"Tired, but I'm getting better all the time."

"Were you in the hospital on the Canal?"

"I got some medication there, but I didn't want to take up a bed, so I went back to New Caledonia. Admiral Halsey was so cute. He came to see me and said he had read some of my stories."

Tom smiled. "I've never heard Halsey called cute. Anyway, everybody I know has been reading your stories. You're a celebrity in town."

"I don't feel like a celebrity right now."

They looked over the luggage spread on the floor, and Anne pointed to hers. Tom got her settled on a bench near the front door of the terminal and went to get his car. A little later they were at his townhouse, and Anne stretched out on the couch. Tom laid a wool army blanket over her.

"This should make you feel right at home. How about some sherry?"

Anne reached out and Tom knelt down to kiss her. "This is kind of fun," she said.

A week later, Anne was feeling strong enough to spend several hours a day at the *Post*. One evening in late March, she talked a colleague out of some ration stamps and stopped at the local grocery to pick up things for a candlelight dinner.

"*Boeuf bourguinon*," said Tom. "You are really something."

As they finished and sat nursing their wine, Anne looked across the table. "I had a long talk with my editor today."

"What about?" asked Tom, as if he did not already know.

"What I should do now. He wants me to go to North Africa."

"Are you well enough to leave Washington?"

"I'm much better, thanks to you."

"You know, there are a lot of interesting stories here at home."

"Do you think I should stay here?"

Tom sighed. "I would love to have you here. Why do you have to be so damned good? You've got millions of women rooting for you."

"Funny, that's what my editor said. I never really thought of it that way. I just love my job."

Tom's eyes rested for a moment on the Matisse he had bought in Paris in 1938. "Anne, we both know you've got to go back. You'd be restless here; you'd be a pain in the neck."

"I would not," she said indignantly. "You make me sound like a fanatic. I'm not Wonder Woman with a typewriter."

Tom laughed. "A lot of people think you are."

"Tom Clark, you may end up sleeping on the couch tonight."

He rose and kissed the back of her neck. "I'd rather have sex with Wonder Woman."

A week later, Anne was on her way to Tunisia.

28

By March 1943, planes and pilots were heading overseas in large numbers to Britain, Russia, North Africa, and the South Pacific. The Ferry Division was struggling to meet delivery orders, and the small band of WAFS pilots had scarcely any days off. Some had now been transferred to bases in Dallas, Long Beach, and Romulus, Michigan. Nancy had gone to Long Beach, leaving Betty in charge at New Castle, where Louise and Kate were still busy flying PT-19s and an occasional BT-13.

The restrictions on the WAFS were gradually falling away under the pressure of wartime demands. Word had gotten back that Nancy had become one of the few American pilots to check out in a P-51 Mustang, and Betty was getting ready to check out in a P-47 Thunderbolt. The P-47s were assembled at Republic Aviation's factory on Long Island, and the company had two instructors at New Castle to train ferry pilots. Needless to say, Kate had befriended one of them.

One day she grabbed Louise's arm after breakfast. "C'mon, my friend Bob from Republic is showing the training film and he said we could join in."

They watched the film with four male pilots, and afterwards Bob gave them all tech manuals and had them sit in the cockpit of a P-47. Sitting high in the air but unable to see past the huge engine in front of her, Louise laughed and exclaimed, "Now, this is an airplane!"

Over the next few weeks, Louise and Kate carried the Thunderbolt manuals with them on missions and spent every spare moment studying. Back together on a Sunday night, they took turns asking each other what to do in a multitude of situations. Finally, Kate broke out the bourbon. "We're ready," she proclaimed, "we're going to do this."

"How?" asked Louise. "We haven't been cleared to go near the things."

"There's got to be a way. I'll sleep with the base commander if I have to."

Louise laughed along with her friend, suspecting that Kate was only half kidding. "You know, I think Bob wants us to fly them. I think Republic really needs us."

"I *know* they do," said Kate authoritatively.

The next morning, Kate was off on a mission and Louise went to the ready room to be on call. As she was trying to get some time in the Link simulator, their friendly Republic instructor came up to her. Bob was a little older than Louise and good-looking, with the casual air of a civilian about him. "Miss Mitchell, you've flown BT-13s, haven't you?"

"Sure, a couple of times," said Louise.

"Have you flown that Texan over there?" He pointed to an AT-6 in the hangar, an advanced trainer with a 600 horsepower Pratt and Whitney engine.

"No, but I'd sure like to," she said as enthusiastically as she could. Louise suspected what he was up to. The Texan was a step up from the 450 HP BT-13, though still a long way from a Thunderbolt.

"Wait here, I'll see if they'll let me check you out."

Louise waited breathlessly. She knew that this scene would have been unthinkable a few months ago, but things were changing fast, and everybody felt overwhelmed by the demands they were getting. Bob was back in 15 minutes, with authority from somebody.

"Let's go."

They climbed into the big trainer and Louise took a few minutes to look over the instrument panel, then started the engine. As the 600 horses warmed up, she began the preflight checks while her instructor radioed the tower, requesting permission to taxi. Weaving slightly in order to see ahead, Louise neared the runway and called the tower, "WAFS Mitchell in the Texan, permission to take off."

"Cleared for takeoff, Miss Mitchell."

Louise brought the Texan onto the runway, revved the engine, and released the brakes. She pushed the throttle all the way forward and felt the G force against her body as the AT-6 took off and climbed quickly to 8,000 feet, where they began the familiar series of maneuvers. The plane was more responsive than anything she had ever flown, and Bob told her to pull the turns as tightly as she could. She came back in for a smooth landing, but he told her to take it up again.

"Now let's do that landing a little faster."

Louise brought it in at 105 mph, pulling hard on the stick as they touched down. "Take it up again," yelled Bob. Louise wondered if she was doing something wrong. As they circled toward the landing pattern, she heard in her headphones, "Try it at 120."

Louise had been flying planes that could barely do 120 mph, let alone land at it. She took a deep breath and headed down. So this is what dive-bombing is like, she thought. The runway was coming up fast, but she was determined not to pull up too soon. At the last minute, she braced herself and pulled hard. The Texan's engine sounded like it might stall, but the wheels bounced a little and rolled down the runway at 123 mph. As she brought the plane to a stop, Louise couldn't resist, "Was that fast enough?"

"A few more of these and you'll be ready for a Thunderbolt, Mitchell."

Louise couldn't wait to tell Kate, but she was off on another PT mission the next day. By the time she got back, Kate had checked out in the Texan as well. Over the next few weeks, they took every chance they could get to practice takeoffs and landings in it. Kate brought one in at 132 mph, and they decided that they had better stop trying to beat each other before they killed themselves and ruined a good airplane.

Their diminutive squadron leader Betty had already checked out in a P-47, using wooden blocks attached to the rudder pedals. Betty must have known what Louise and Kate were up to, but she studiously ignored them. In mid-April, the two were in the ready room together when Bob approached them. "How about a little taxi practice?"

He did not have to ask twice. The ground crew brought a Thunderbolt out of the hangar and charged the battery. Kate piled into the cockpit, while Bob and Louise stood on the wing and went over the layout. As they climbed down, Kate started the big engine. She warmed it up, called the tower, and began to weave down the taxiway like a drunken driver. Near the runway, she made a big turn and headed back to the hangar.

It was Louise's turn, and she climbed in excitedly. As she started the engine, reality began to set in—she had 2,300 horses in front of her and no instructor's seat behind her. Each of the four blades on the propeller was longer than she was. On each wing, she could see four 50-caliber machine guns, and on the stick was the button for firing them. "Louise Mitchell," she said to herself, "are you sure you want to do this?"

She released the brakes, and six tons of airplane began to weave toward the runway. She handled it fine down and back and began to feel comfortable, but she was glad she was still on the ground. As she wheeled it around and stopped at the hangar, Bob bounced up on the wing. "How does it feel?" he shouted above the noise of the idling engine.

"Great!" shouted Louise, with as much composure as she could muster.

"Take it back to the runway and rev it up. If you want to try it, call the tower."

Louise was dumbfounded. Surely, he was not serious. But Bob had already climbed back down, what was she going to do now? If she did not take this chance, when would there be another one? She could see Kate glaring at her with hands on her hips, and she knew her friend was fuming. "Well, if I'm going to leave this world, at least it will be in a blaze of glory."

Again, Louise weaved the powerful plane toward the runway, with the instruction film racing through her mind. She did the pre-flight checks, pulled into position, and revved the engine. Then she took a deep breath and called the tower. "WAFS Mitchell in the Thunderbolt, ready for takeoff."

"Cleared for takeoff, Miss Mitchell. Good luck."

Louise released the brakes and gave it full throttle. She thought her eardrums would break, if the G force did not crush her first. The tail wheel was up and she could see the end of the runway rushing at her. She pulled steadily back on the stick and could barely keep from passing out as the P-47 roared into the sky. At 10,000 feet, she leveled off and glanced at the airspeed indicator—315 mph. "My God," she blurted out, "I'm flying a Thunderbolt!"

"What was that, Miss Mitchell?" came the voice in her head-phones. She had her hand on the mike button.

Louise began to do some 30-degree turns, first right, then left, trying to keep a heading. She thought she should turn back before she got out too far, so she soon banked the plane around toward the base and looked down to find a landmark. In the distance, she saw a river flowing into a large bay. Must be the Delaware, she thought, but as she got closer she realized it was the Susquehanna flowing into Chesapeake Bay. She had been 100 miles out from New Castle, almost to Hagerstown.

Within minutes, Louise had to radio the tower for permission to land. She knew she had to plan her turns a lot further ahead than what she was used to, but as she headed into the first one, she realized she was not going to make the pattern. "Permission to try again," she called.

"Take your time, Miss Mitchell, the sky's all yours."

Louise did not want to miss another one. She gave herself more room and pulled it as tightly as she possibly could. The P-47 came around and she could see the runway ahead of her. She put down the landing gear, uttering a prayer as the red warning light went off. With every ounce of concentration she could muster, she held the nose steady and cut the airspeed. With a jolt, the front wheels hit the pavement and Louise struggled to hold the plane straight. Soon she was down on three wheels and slowing to a stop just short of the taxiway. As she turned, she heard the controller, "Welcome back, Miss Mitchell."

"Permission to breathe again," replied Louise.

Back at the hangar, Louise felt giddy as she climbed out of the cockpit. Kate climbed quickly past her without a word and jumped in. The concrete seemed to be rolling as Louise walked slowly up to Bob.

"Congratulations, Miss Mitchell, you're a pursuit pilot."

"Thanks." Louise was still trying to steady herself as she took off her helmet. "Bob," she said sheepishly, "I know this is a military base, but would you give me a hug?" Laughing, Bob put his arms around her and held her for several seconds.

A half-hour later, Kate brought the Thunderbolt in for a smoother landing and cruised up to the hanger. Bouncing down, she strode up to Bob and Louise. "How was that, Professor?" she asked with an air of cockiness.

"Looked good to me," answered Bob. "C'mon, I'll sign your logbooks."

Taking their leave of Bob, Louise glanced at Kate. "Going to lunch?"

"Not today. Got to get a haircut."

Kate was off without another word. Louise figured she was sore and needed some time to cool down. That evening, she ventured down to Kate's room and knocked timidly. "May I come in?"

Kate shrugged her shoulders and started to pace.

"Nice haircut," offered Louise.

"Cut the crap, Louise, what have you and Bob been up to, anyway?"

Louise was startled. She sank into the wooden chair. "Kate, there's nothing like that. I don't think Bob meant anything by sending me up first. It just happened that way."

Kate was looking out the window. "Well, congratulations, Miss Mitchell, you're the second woman to fly a P-47."

"Third," said Louise, "I found out today that Nancy beat us both."

"Really?" This seemed to make Kate feel a little better. She wandered across the room and turned to look at Louise. "So nothing's going on with Bob?"

"I swear it, Kate, nothing."

Kate stood there looking at her friend and her face gradually lightened into a grin. "That was a helluva ride, wasn't it?"

29

At the beginning of May, New Castle's WAFS received an influx of eight new pilots from Jacqueline Cochran's training base in Texas. Cochran was Nancy Love's archrival for leadership of the women pilots serving the Army. Brash and ambitious, she had won General Arnold's approval to establish the training program five days after the Air Transport Command had approved Nancy's formation of the WAFS. The original WAFS numbered only 25, but Cochran's program was soon training pilots by the hundreds. In 1943, the Ferry Division needed them badly, although there was plenty of skepticism about their qualifications.

Louise and Kate were glad to see the newcomers, because it meant they could get away from some of the PT missions and do some real flying. They were taking every opportunity to log time in the Thunderbolt, and in early May, they climbed into a C-47 with Betty and headed for Republic's factory at Farmingdale, Long Island. For three days, they took off from the factory, circled the Statue of Liberty, and landed their P-47s on a strip at the Newark docks, where they would be loaded on ships bound for England or North Africa. Piling into a staff car, they would ride back to Republic and climb into another Thunderbolt.

After the first few, it was rather boring work, but it had an unforeseen value for the Army. The WAFS soon became so sensitive that they could detect variances in performance that might require adjustments or repairs. When this happened, they would call for permission to take the planes up higher for a little shakedown cruise, and some they returned to the factory. Louise took a plane back on the third day, but her next one performed beautifully on the short hop to Newark. As she parked it near the dock and turned off the engine, she had an inspiration. She always carried a small box of stationery in case she was stranded for a while. She took out a sheet and began to write:

To the brave pilot who gets this plane:
I hope it takes as good care of you as it did of me.
God be with you.
Louise Mitchell
2nd Ferrying Group
New Castle AAFB, Delaware

She put the note in an envelope and stuck it in the chart pouch where the pilot would find it. From then on, Louise put a similar note in each combat plane she delivered.

As they finished dinner on the third evening, Betty told the waitress that they needed three straws. "Here's the deal," she began, "Republic has two Thunderbolts to go to their Evansville plant for modifications. Fairchild has four PT-19s for Sweetwater, Jackie Cochran's new base in Texas. One of us has to take three of the new girls to Hagerstown and deliver the PTs."

Betty used her pocketknife to cut one of the straws and then mixed them up inside her fist. Kate reached over and drew a long one. "Thunderbolt for me!" she said gleefully.

Louise reached and drew the short one. "Oh well, at least the girls will enjoy making a delivery to the new trainees."

"Here's a little reward, Louise. You can put the girls on a plane home and go to Dallas to pick up an AT-6. We need another one at New Castle."

The next morning, Louise was on one of Republic's company planes bound for New Castle, where it would pick up two other WAFS for the Newark shuttle service. These two had checked out in P-47s with the full approval of ATC headquarters. Louise spent the rest of the day getting her uniform cleaned, her vouchers filed, and everything else ready for a trip that would probably take a week. Early the following day, she and three of the recent graduates were in a C-47 bound for Hagerstown.

Two long days of flying brought them within range of Avenger Field in Sweetwater, Texas. When they delivered their planes at noon the next day, she and her companions were treated like celebrities. Louise was accustomed to blank stares when she landed at obscure airfields, so the reception at Sweetwater was gratifying. Leaving her friends to party a little in the Texas dust, she persuaded an instructor to give her a lift to Dallas in a BT-13. The next morning, she headed home in a gleaming new AT-6.

Tom Clark was making his way back to Washington from a visit to CINCPAC in Hawaii. He had made it as far as Little Rock on military transports, but now he was stranded, having missed the only commercial flight to Washington that day. He could get a connection through Atlanta the next day at 8 a.m., but it would be a fifteen-hour trip from Little Rock to Washington. As he pondered his options at the operations center, one of the traffic controllers came up to him and said casually, "There's a ferry pilot refueling over there, headed for Delaware. Maybe you can hitch a ride in the back seat."

"Thanks, I'll check it out."

It was warm and Tom had his leather flight jacket slung over his shoulder. He walked out to where a fuel truck was servicing an AT-6. "Hey there, where's the pilot?"

"In the canteen, getting some lunch."

Tom went into the canteen and glanced around. The only pilot he saw was a burly young man with red hair. He went up to him and asked, "Is that your AT-6 out there?"

"Ain't mine, sorry."

Tom noticed a flying helmet on the end of a table and a parachute on one of the chairs. He wandered over and waited. In a few minutes he noticed someone in a flight suit coming toward him, carrying a tray of food. "Hi there," said a cheerful woman's voice, "you looking for me?"

"I guess so," said Tom, unable to hide his surprise. "Is that your AT-6 out there?"

"It is for the next two days. What's the matter, did I park in your spot?"

Tom grinned. "No, I was looking for a ride. I heard you're going to Delaware and I need to get back to Washington."

"Well, sir, that would be very illegal." Louise was enjoying this little encounter. She put her tray on the table and sat down. "Are you somebody important that I'm supposed to know?"

"Not really, but I do have a priority one. White House travel orders."

"Whoa, that's higher than mine. You could confiscate my seat."

"I'm afraid that wouldn't get either one of us home. Do you mind if I sit down?"

"Be my guest. Have you eaten yet?"

"Not since breakfast."

"Why don't you get something quick and let me think about this."

Tom left his jacket and went off to get a sandwich. When he returned, he put his tray down across from Louise and offered his hand. "I'm Tom Clark. I work for President Roosevelt."

"I'm Louise Mitchell. I work for everybody."

She liked the firm but gentle handshake. He was tall and tan, with brown hair graying at the sides and a boyish smile that gave her a good feeling. "So what are you doing in this fix?"

"Well, I'm on my way back from CINCPAC. I got this far on transports, but now I've missed everything out of here, civilian and military. I'm supposed to have dinner with the president tomorrow evening and give him a report. He's leaving town the next morning."

"Well, my goodness, you are cutting it close, aren't you?"

"Not very good planning, was it?"

"Look, I don't know if we can work this out. To begin with, I don't fly that thing after dark. I'll be overnighting in Nashville, so I won't be near Washington until late tomorrow afternoon. For another thing, if anybody knew I gave you a ride, I'd be in hot water. And on top of all that, I've got my bag in back seat."

Tom was becoming fascinated with this pert young woman. "I've only got a small bag and a briefcase. I've flown with ferry pilots before."

"You've flown with *male* ferry pilots before. There are all kind of rules on us."

"Suppose I order you to take me," said Tom with a grin. "My boss is the commander-in-chief."

Louise grinned back. "Wow, you're pulling out all the stops! Seriously, Mr. Clark, I'd like to help you out, but I don't think I can."

"OK, I understand. I've enjoyed meeting you, Miss Mitchell."

Louise got up to leave and pulled on her parachute. "Good luck, Mr. Clark," she said with a sympathetic smile.

She went out the door and stopped at the fuel counter to sign for the gas. As she headed toward her plane, she murmured aloud, "Damn it, I wonder if he's still there." She hurried back into the canteen and caught Tom's eyes as he was finishing his lemonade. He stood up as she approached. "Do you think you can get a parachute?" she asked.

Tom showed his credentials to the man at the operations desk and assured him the White House would reimburse them. The man shrugged his shoulders and went into a large closet. He came out carrying a weathered parachute and handed it to Tom. "Don't worry about it," he grunted.

Tom got the rest of his gear and headed out to the plane. Louise had her bag on the wing and was gazing into the back seat. As Tom climbed up, she said, "You'll have to get in and I'll put things around you. It's not going to be first class. You'll want that jacket on, by the way."

Louise helped him strap the parachute on his back and he eased into the seat. She stuffed her bag on one side of him and his on the other, then put his briefcase on his lap. "Here, you can write your report on the way," she laughed. "Just don't try to fly the plane."

"Are you kidding? I can't even move."

Louise climbed in front, started the engine, and closed the canopy. In a few minutes, they were climbing smoothly into the blue sky and Tom felt a little better. As they reached cruising altitude, Louise looked back and pointed to her headphones. Tom picked up his and put them on.

"Welcome to SNAFU Airlines," she said. "We'll be cruising at 9,000 feet today, at an average ground speed of 145 mph. If you look off to our right, you'll be able to see the beautiful Arkansas lowlands. For those of you who have never crossed the Mississippi River, we'll be crossing it in about an hour at Memphis. You might see one of the barges carrying supplies to our fighting men overseas."

She looked back again and Tom waved, smiling. Louise flew along keeping track of progress on her charts, though she had flown this route before. Soon the big river was passing under them, and she knew that some of the water down there had passed by Sioux City in the Missouri. She wondered what she was going to do when they got to Nashville. She was already skirting the edge, and they might run into someone she knew. She thought about going on to a smaller field somewhere, but finally decided that they would attract the least attention at Nashville's municipal airport.

Louise made a few more attempts at humor as they flew over western Tennessee. About 4:30 p.m., she called the Nashville tower for permission to land. Switching back to Tom, she said, "We're heading down, Mr. Clark. Are you still alive?"

Tom waved again. Louise had to circle once to get a place in the landing pattern. She touched down at 90 mph, laughing as she thought about the landings she and Kate had made while practicing for the P-47. She taxied up to the service area and cut the engine, then got out as fast as she could to help Tom out of his seat.

"I don't think I can walk," he joked.

Louise jumped down from the wing and looked up. "Pass the stuff down to me." Then she steadied Tom as he climbed down. "I'll bet you could get a flight from here, Mr. Clark. Surely you don't want to do this all the way to Washington."

"I'll check on it. But really, it wasn't that bad, and the commentary was great."

Louise smiled. "I'm going to get this thing filled up for tomorrow. I'll meet you near the restrooms."

A half-hour later, Louise came out of the ladies' room and found Tom waiting for her. "Any luck?" she asked.

"Nothing very good. The best connection would get me to Washington at seven tomorrow evening."

"How about a train?"

"It would be the Southern to Cincinnati and the C & O from there. I'd have to leave tonight. If you don't mind, Miss Mitchell, I'd like to take my chances with you."

Louise did not want to show that she was pleased. "Well, we're all gassed up. We can get out of here at the crack of dawn."

"Let's find a hotel, then."

"I don't want to go to the usual WAFS hotel. I might run into somebody. Do you know one?"

"I know the Union Station on Broadway. Do you like staying in fortresses?"

"How expensive is it?"

"Not bad for us. They have a good rate for government employees. I'll get us a cab."

By six, they were checked into rooms in the rambling stone building, and Louise was steaming her uniform in the bathroom. She took longer than usual with her makeup and stood in front of the mirror trying to get her hair and cap looking just right. What am I doing, she thought? This guy works for the president. They'll have a good laugh about me in the White House.

Tom was sitting in the lounge sipping a Manhattan, wondering what to expect next from this ruddy-faced tomboy in the baggy flightsuit. Suddenly, he saw coming toward him a woman in gray-green slacks and belted jacket, with a matching overseas cap tilted above wavy brown hair. Silver wings gleamed over her jacket pocket. Tom sprung to his feet. "Miss Mitchell, you look great. I feel like I'm underdressed."

"It was this or the coveralls. I didn't want to embarrass you."

"I'm famished. Shall we find some dinner?"

They found a Cajun restaurant nearby and settled into a corner table. "What are you going to have, Mr. Clark?" asked Louise.

"It's between the jambalaya and the blackened catfish," said Tom.

"Let's get both and share."

"You're on. How about some Chardonnay with it? By the way, people call me Mr. Clark when they're annoyed at me. You're not annoyed at me, are you?"

"Does that mean I can be Louise?"

"It's a deal."

Tom gave their orders to the waiter and took a drink of water. "How many are there like you?"

"Close to a hundred now. We just started getting graduates from Jackie Cochran's school in Texas. I just delivered some planes there."

"So you work for the infamous Mrs. Cochran. What's she like?"

"I work for Nancy Love at the Ferry Division. I've never met Jackie, but I've heard she's pretty abrasive."

"Well, Mrs. Roosevelt likes her, I can tell you that."

The waiter brought their wine and poured a little in Tom's glass for tasting, then poured some for Louise.

"Would you like some of this bread?" asked Tom. "I haven't heard of Nancy Love. What's she like?"

"Nancy is a marvelous pilot. She works quietly, behind the scenes. She's kind of a mystery. I used to be afraid of her, but I hardly ever see her now. Nancy flew a P-51, three months ago."

"A Mustang? She must be an Amazon."

"She's not. She's one of the most beautiful, feminine women I've ever seen."

Tom held his glass out to touch Louise's. "To women pilots, may they always land safely."

Louise's face turned serious and she looked down at the table. "They don't always land safely," she said quietly. Both were silent for a moment, as a tear made its way down Louise's cheek. "Did you ever hear of Cornelia Fort?" she asked.

"It sounds familiar."

"Cornelia was the instructor who had a student up in Hawaii on December 7. She was right in the middle of the Japanese planes."

"I remember that now."

"She joined the WAFS. She was on a flight with several male pilots, and one of them had to show off. He buzzed Cornelia's plane and hit her. She went straight into the ground." After a pause, she added, "This was her hometown."

Tom could think of nothing to say. He sat silently, boiling inside with anger at men like that. Going through his mind as well was the irrepressible thought that both Anne and Louise lived with danger every day.

Louise broke the ice. "I'm sorry. I didn't mean to spoil our evening."

"Please don't apologize. I'm glad you told me."

The waiter brought their dinners, with an extra bowl and plate, and they set about dividing their food. As he looked at Louise, Tom tried to resist comparing her to Anne. She was not the polished, classic beauty that Anne was, but she had a very appealing face. She had expressive eyes, and she seemed like a very genuine human being.

As they finished eating, a band began playing waltzes and two-steps. Louise had never heard Cajun music, and soon she was tapping her feet to the infectious rhythm. They sat with their wine while the band played through its first set.

"We've got a long day ahead of us," said Tom. "Please let me take this check as a token of appreciation."

They walked back talking about different kinds of music, and as they reached her room, she turned to look at him.

"Louise," he said calmly, "I enjoyed the evening. I'll see you in the lobby at 5:30."

Louise smiled. "Good night."

By 6 a.m., they were at the airport canteen ordering breakfast. Louise was back in her flight suit with her hair in a ponytail behind her. As crimson lit up the scattered clouds over Nashville, she warmed up the Texan and called the tower for permission to taxi. Before long, they were cruising over the rolling hills and lakes of central Tennessee. This time, Louise had shown Tom how to use his mike, and they chatted off and on about the country passing below them. As they approached Bluefield, West Virginia, she asked if he would like a little break. She took the AT-6 down and got it refueled while they had a snack in the little canteen.

At noon, they took off for a run to Washington's National Airport, where Louise stopped as near to the terminal as she could. She helped Tom get his things down, and reached out to shake his hand. "You're on your own now, Tom. Say hello to FDR for me."

"Thanks for the ride, Louise, it really was fun."

"Actually, please don't tell anybody you rode with a woman. Promise me."

"I promise. Look, here's my card. If you ever get to Washington, please call me."

Louise climbed back up and, in a few minutes, was picking up speed on the runway. As the monuments of Washington disappeared behind her, she wiped away a tear.

"Don't expect anything, Louise," she murmured, "life doesn't happen this way."

30

Louise spent the next several weeks flying P-47s, mostly on the Newark shuttle service but with a few trips to Evansville. On a Sunday in late June, a P-39 Airacobra landed at New Castle, and out came the tall woman who had led Louise's first mission to Georgia. That evening, Betty called together the WAFS pilots who were on base.

As they crowded into her room, she began, "Ladies, there's a backlog of P-39 deliveries to the Russians in Alaska. Our former colleague Myra Tanner is here from Romulus, and she needs two volunteers to help get them as far as Great Falls, Montana. Men take them from there to Fairbanks. She'll give you two days of training and you go to Niagara Falls on Wednesday."

"Why don't we take them to Fairbanks?" asked one of the women.

"Our esteemed commander in Romulus doesn't trust the men in Alaska," said Myra. "He's trying to protect us."

The room rocked with groans and laughter. When order returned, Louise raised her hand. "I'll go."

Kate looked surprised. She was not used to having Louise take the initiative, but she was not going to be shown up. "Can you spare me, Betty?"

"You can both go if you really want to," said Betty. "You know the reputation the P-39 has. A lot of men don't want to fly it."

"Well, I'd like to try it," said Louise.

Monday morning, Louise and Kate were listening carefully as Myra went over the tech manuals with them. She drummed into them the speeds they had to use for landings and takeoffs. The P-39 had a tricycle landing gear instead of a tail wheel, and the engine was mounted behind the pilot, giving it a completely different feel. Visibility was superb, however, and the sleek plane was highly maneuverable. Its nose cone held a 37mm cannon, making it an effective plane for supporting ground troops. Russian pilots liked it, and half of Bell's production went to the Russian front.

Kate and Louise watched as Myra took off and landed twice, demonstrating what she wanted them to do. This time, Louise was content to let Kate make the first flight. When it was Louise's turn, she buckled herself in with a little trepidation. She followed instructions to the letter, however, and soon she was climbing skyward. Compared to a Thunderbolt, this was like driving a sports car. The P-39 weighed barely more than three tons and had half the horsepower of a P-47, but Louise thought it was fun to fly. She took no chances on landing, though.

Tuesday they flew intensively from dawn to dusk, and on Wednesday morning, Myra took off for Niagara Falls in the P-39 while Kate and Louise followed in a BT-13. At the Bell factory, they met up with three women from the Romulus group and went over the charts for the first leg of their trip to Montana. As they took off, Myra led them over the famous waterfalls, and Louise was astonished at their beauty. She could not help wondering if she would see them someday with a lover.

Cruising at 250 mph, the flight refueled in Green Bay and landed for the night at Fargo. The next day was seven hours of flying over the dreary high plains of North Dakota and Montana. As they waited for their receipts in the late afternoon sun, Myra came up to the group with a sarcastic smile on her face.

"Guess what. The men for these planes are socked in at Seattle. Or at least they say they are. I hope they have to send us home tomorrow with no pilots. I hope these planes sit here for days."

Great Falls was not the liveliest place in the world, but the six women had a lot of fun swapping stories at dinner that evening. Louise was tempted to tell them about Tom, but thought better of it. At 10 a.m. the next day, they sat in the canteen drinking coffee, waiting for the C-47 that would bring the men from Seattle and take the WAFS pilots on to Romulus. Soon the twin-engine transport was parking outside, and four pilots climbed down the steps. As Myra stood watching, the C-47 pilot and copilot came down, nobody else.

"Where are the other two?" she asked one of ferry pilots.

"Infirmary. Food poisoning."

"Looks like you guys will have to come back for their planes," teased Myra.

"Not us. We've got orders to Australia. This is our last ferry job."

Myra went back in the canteen and told the story. "This commander is going to have everybody on his back, Bell, Ferry Command, and the Russians. Maybe he'll raise some hell with ours."

Louise noticed that Kate was not laughing. "You know," said Kate with mischief in her voice, "Louise and I aren't under any restrictions from New Castle. At least nobody's ever said anything to us."

Myra hesitated. "It isn't just Romulus. ATC went along with it."

"So you told us not to go, but the base commander overruled you."

"OK, but he hasn't overruled me."

"Let me go find him. Let's see what he says."

"Kate, this is a big base. You don't just waltz into the CO's office. Besides, that C-47 will be ready to go soon."

"Give me fifteen minutes."

"What the hell, go ahead."

Kate scampered off. Twenty minutes later, she was back with a big smile on her face. "I found the ops officer. He was thrilled with the idea and called the CO. They're willing to say they thought it was just your commander's policy."

Myra seemed annoyed. "Well, that's the damned Army for you. I get this thing going, and you two get to go to Alaska."

Kate was quick to respond. "Look, Myra, this might be the break that gets rid of another silly rule. We won't screw up, I promise. C'mon, Louise, we've got to find the flight leader."

Louise had not said a word the whole time. Gazing at Kate with disbelief, she rolled her eyes and got to her feet. "You're either going to get me killed or court-martialed, Kate Burns."

After lunch, Kate and Louise were back in flying gear and warming up the Airacobras they had flown in the day before. They were assigned the left positions in the formation, and took off right behind the flight leader. Taking no chances with his unlikely comrades, the leader did a radio check every ten minutes, updating their position on the charts. The WAFS pilots did not mind the attention, since cockpits can be lonely places over the Canadian plains, even with the jagged crests of the Rockies in view on the left.

The flight stopped overnight in Edmonton. That was well within range from Great Falls, but the next reliable gas station was a long way off. The next morning, they were in the air by 7 a.m. and an hour later, they were high over the Peace River. Crossing into British Columbia, they followed their leader to the small airstrip at Fort Nelson, hoping there would be enough high-octane fuel for their thirsty tanks. Up to then, they had kept the mountains to the west of them, but now they headed over rugged country to find the historic town of Whitehorse in the Yukon Territory. Louise was intrigued by the vast, empty country passing below. She wondered how much of it had never felt the footsteps of human beings.

Finishing a late lunch in Whitehorse, their leader reminded them that if anyone got separated, they should find the Alaska Highway and follow it in. The Army had recently cut this unpaved road though the wilderness, in case it had to mount a major defense of Alaska. The sun was now in the afternoon sky, and it seemed to hang there as the little formation worked its way northward. They followed the highway alongside the rugged and beautiful St. Elias Mountains, crossed the border, and stayed just northeast of the Alaska Range into Fairbanks. Louise marveled at the magnificent wilderness she was viewing from a first-class seat. It was way beyond anything she had seen before.

There was still plenty of daylight when they landed at Eielson Field near Fairbanks, so much that it hardly seemed like evening at all. Louise caught up with Kate at the operations office. "That was incredible! Thanks for getting us on the mission."

Kate laughed. "Stick with me, kid, it's a big world out there."

"Any ideas about where to stay tonight?"

"Well, these guys are staying at BOQ. Maybe we can find something in the nurses' quarters."

"Did you check on flights out?"

"Yeah, day after tomorrow is our best chance. A C-47 to Seattle."

"All right, a day in Alaska!" purred Louise.

Receipts in hand, they sent a telegram to New Castle.

NO RELAY PILOTS GREAT FALLS FOR TWO P-39S STOP CO BELIEVED POLICY ONLY FOR ROMULUS STOP BURNS MITCHELL ORDERED TO FAIRBANKS STOP EXPECT RIDE TO SEATTLE MONDAY STOP

Kate grinned. "That ought to do it."

They caught a ride to the nurses' quarters, where they found two spare bunks and sprawled out in their long underwear. "I'm too tired to look for food," said Kate.

"That's all right, that sandwich I had in Whitehorse was enough for two days. That sure was lean beef wasn't it?"

Kate let out one of her infectious laughs. "Honey, that was moose."

"Moose? Why didn't someone tell me?"

"We were waiting to see your reaction, but you didn't say anything at all. You just wolfed it down."

"Someday I'm going to get you on something, Burns."

"Fat chance. What shall we do with our day tomorrow?"

"Do you think we can get off base?"

"Yeah, things seem pretty casual here."

"I think I'd like to check out the local airport. See what goes on there."

"Boy, we have a lot of imagination, don't we?"

31

The next morning, Louise and Kate ate a hearty breakfast at the officers' mess and headed for the main gate to see if they could get a taxi. They had not brought their dress uniforms, so they were in their slacks and leather jackets. As they approached the guardhouse, Louise fretted, "I hope he doesn't object to these outfits."

The guard looked at their credentials and studied them curiously. "Women's Auxiliary Ferrying Squadron, what's that?"

"We're civilian employees, delivering planes for the Army," said Kate. For once, she was glad to call herself a civilian.

"How long are you going to be here, ladies?"

"We're out tomorrow," said Kate.

"But we might be back," added Louise.

Just then, two of their flight companions drove up in a jeep. "These gals came in with us, Corporal. They're top-notch pilots."

The young guard handed back their credentials and saluted. "Have a good day, ladies."

"Can we give you a ride?" asked one of the pilots.

Louise and Kate piled into the back of the jeep. As they started away, Louise leaned forward. "Thanks for what you said, Lieutenant."

"Don't mention it. You two can fly with me anytime."

The jeep dropped them off at the small municipal airport, near a modest building that looked like it might be the terminal. Inside, there was an unattended ticket counter, a lunch counter, and several benches. They approached the older man behind the lunch counter. "Morning, ladies, you looking to go somewhere?"

"Maybe," said Kate, "where can you go from here?"

"We've got service to Anchorage Monday, Wednesday, and Friday. We've also got mail runs to Nome, Barrow, and Kotzebue. Anything else is charter. I call the pilots from here."

"Who charters planes?" asked Louise.

"Mining companies, people with business in the villages, hunters, fishermen, surveyors. Anybody who doesn't mind carrying some cargo on their laps."

"You the only one here today?"

"Cam's probably here. His shack's out to the right, about fifty yards. He does a lot of sightseeing."

"Thanks," said Louise, "I think we'll go talk to him."

The two headed down a gravel path toward a corrugated steel hut. Over the door was a hand-lettered sign:

Mt. McKinley Aviation
Cameron James, Prop.

The door was open so Kate poked her head in. The walls were decorated with aerial photographs and hand-drawn maps, along with a few printed ones. There were a few wooden chairs and in one corner a rough desk. Behind it were photographs of various people beside a plane, apparently celebrities. Kate recognized Wiley Post and Will Rogers, who had perished when Post's plane went down near Barrow in 1935.

A bearded, middle-aged man in a baseball cap looked up from the book he was reading. "Can I help you, ma'am?" Louise followed

Kate inside, and their host took his feet off the desk. "Those look like flying jackets. Are you ladies married to pilots?"

"Not exactly," chirped Kate. "You must be Cam."

"I am. How'd you know?"

"We stopped in the terminal." Kate extended her hand. "I'm Kate Burns and this is Louise Mitchell. You give sightseeing trips?"

"Yes, ma'am. Up around the mountain."

"How much?"

"Ten dollars each up and back. Fifteen if you want to put down."

"What do you think, Louise? Can we afford it?"

"It's worth it to me," said Louise. "What do most people do?"

"Most just go up and back," replied Cam. "What are those jackets, anyway?"

"WAFS," said Louise. "We flew a couple of P-39s in yesterday."

Cam stared at them. "You two are fighter pilots?"

"Ferry pilots," said Louise, "you name it, we fly it."

"Well, bless my soul. Tell you what, ladies, for twenty dollars total I'll give you something special."

"You're on," said Kate, as she dug into her purse.

"We'll have to go down to the river and get the float plane."

They piled into Cam's old car and drove to a place where the Tanana River broadened into a small lake. Anchored at a dock was a rugged-looking plane on pontoons.

"What's that?" asked Kate.

"Norseman," said Cam, "Canadian plane. They do real well up here."

They settled in and Cam taxied to one end of the lake. He gunned the engine and they picked up speed as they consumed the available still water. Near the end, he pulled the nose up and they lifted off over small trees toward the blue Alaskan sky.

"Do you always cut it that close?" asked Kate.

Cam chuckled. "Closer if there's four of us." He banked south-ward and added, "Sky looks good down there. You might actually see the mountain."

As he leveled off at 12,000 feet, they could see a huge peak looming on the horizon. It seemed to be alone at first, but gradually other snowcapped peaks came into view.

"How high is that thing, anyway?" asked Kate with awe in her voice.

"Over 20,000 feet," replied Cam. "Those other peaks are fifteen to seventeen."

"It dwarfs them," said Louise. "How high are we going?"

"We'll take it to about 10,000. You'll have to look from there."

Cam followed a course to the eastern side of the mountain, then banked west and circled the north face. Below them were glaciers and ridges that snaked their way down the massive base of Mount McKinley. As a Christmas present to herself, Louise had bought a small camera at the PX, and now she put it to good use. Cam headed west and began descending over alpine meadows and great valleys. He pointed to a dark swarm in an open area ahead. "Caribou herd. I'll try to give you a closer look."

They dropped to 7,000 feet, where they could see hundreds of animals roaming though a broad valley. Cam continued west and soon a beautiful lake came into view. He went in on a straight run and kept the nose up a little as the pontoons settled on the water and slowed the plane. At the far end, he taxied up to a small dock with a cabin nearby. Just to the left, the lake let out into a rippling stream.

Cam pulled on some hip boots and climbed into the water. He unwound a line on the left pontoon, pulled the plane up to the dock, and held it while Louise and Kate got out. "Welcome to Wonder Lake," said Cam as he anchored the plane against old tires. "I have a park permit to use this cabin. Some of my customers stay overnight and I pick them up the next day."

"That was a great ride!" exclaimed Louise. "I wish I had one of these."

They went ashore and looked out over the lake. "Wow," said Kate, "look at that!"

Mt. McKinley loomed in the blue sky beyond the lake, and as the plane's wake settled, the reflection in the water became crystal clear. Louise and Kate took each other's pictures with Cam, and Louise took a shot of the lake and mountain alone. "I wish I were an artist," she said.

"Is anybody hungry?" asked Cam.

"Don't tell me you run a restaurant out here, too," laughed Kate.

"C'mon, I'll show you the cabin." He led them up a path to the rustic little building. Nearby were a weathered picnic table, a stone fire pit with an iron grate, and a small pile of firewood. Inside were four bunks, a table and chairs, some oil lamps, and three metal lockers. Cam unlocked one and took out a pot, some bowls, cups, spoons, cans, and a bottle of wine. "How does caribou stew and wine sound?"

"Great," said Kate. They helped him carry things outside and Cam set about building a fire while the women opened the wine and sat down to sample it. The sun was high in the sky and the temperature was moving above 70 degrees.

"I thought it would be colder than this," said Louise.

"This is a little warm for late June, but Fairbanks can get to 90 in July and August. It can also get to 40 below in the winter. Anchorage is more mild, being near the ocean."

"How long have you been doing this, Cam?" asked Kate.

"Three years. There wasn't much business before the war. Now I get quite a bit from the base."

"Is that when you came up here?"

"I came up here first in '35. Flew the mail for a while, but my wife couldn't take it and she went home. I went back down, but we split up and I decided I wanted to live in Alaska. I worked for the founder of this service and then took it over when he went back into the Navy."

"What do you do in the winter?"

"The pontoons come off and the skis go on. I take over some cargo runs from guys who go south for the winter."

"Where'd you start flying?"

"In the first war. I flew in the 94th squadron."

"The ninety-fourth?" echoed Louise. "Did you know Sam Crane?"

"Sam Crane? Sure I did. How do you know him?"

"He taught me to fly. I worked for him in Iowa."

"Sam taught you to fly, how about that. Well, you had a good teacher. What's he doing now?"

"Hanging around his little airfield, I guess. Taking people up if he can get gas. We were doing the CPT program in Sioux City, but they've shut that down now."

"Gas is a big problem. I'm hustling all the time to get some. Lucky for me I've got friends on the base who think I'm serving a good purpose. I figure if I can hang on till the war's over, I'll be in a good spot."

Cam had taken off his cap, revealing a head of gray hair to go with his neatly trimmed beard. Together they made him seem older than he really was, and Louise mused that he was actually rather good-looking. He was about six feet, with a solid, athletic build that fit nicely into his blue jeans and red flannel shirt.

He put two steaming bowls in front of them. "Is this really caribou?" asked Louise.

"It sure is. There's a little cannery in Fairbanks that specializes in caribou and moose. They're selling a lot of it to the base now."

"It's delicious," said Kate.

They finished eating and washed the dishes in the lake. "When do we have to head back?" asked Louise.

"We can stay for a while more if you want. I've got to scrounge up some firewood for this place."

"I'd like to take a walk along the stream down there. You want to come, Kate?"

"I think I'll stay here and help Cam."

The stream was about 25 feet wide, and it snaked westward accompanied by clusters of small trees and brush. Louise wandered along the bank watching the sparkling water and thinking about the ways her life had changed in less than a year. She was working hard, in conditions that were far from glamorous, but she had friends who were among the remarkable women of their age. She was having the time of her life, yet she knew it would end. So many pilots were being trained, and she worried that there would be few chances for women to fly after the war.

Louise wondered if she could go back to Sioux City, to Jennie and Rose. Even if she fell in love, she wondered if she could settle down to a life of family and children. She had been flying for 13 years and could hardly imagine life without it. Still, she felt that a part of her was empty. She had love that she wanted to give, if only she could find the right man. On the lonely nights in strange towns, she wished there were someone waiting for her to come home. Was it possible to have everything in life?

Louise realized that she was getting pretty far from the cabin, and Cam was probably anxious to get home. She started back along the bank, but as she stepped around some trees, she was suddenly about 40 yards from a burly, golden brown, lumbering mass of fur. Louise had heard stories about grizzly bears, but she was not prepared for the size of the animal that had stopped to gaze into the stream and was blocking her way. She froze, not out of tactical knowledge but out of simple fear. Landing P-47s and P-39s was dangerous, but at least she was in control. Now she was at the mercy of something totally unpredictable.

The bear, however, was paying her no notice. After a minute that seemed like an hour, the grizzly stepped down onto a sandbar and ambled into the water, heading for a pool on the other side. There, he began to take a leisurely bath. Her fear subsiding a little, Louise watched with a mixture of awe and amusement. She was thinking about trying to back away and circle him when she realized that the grizzly had stopped swimming around and was looking straight at her. Not moving a muscle, she stared back. Again, it seemed like time was standing still. Then the bear scrambled out on some rocks, shook himself mightily, and calmly climbed up the opposite bank. In seconds, he had disappeared over a knoll.

Louise began moving as quietly as she could toward the spot the bear had vacated. I hope he was alone, she thought. When she could see the lake again, it was like seeing runway lights at dusk. She hurried to the dock, where Kate and Cam were talking about the plane. "I'm sorry to be so late," she bubbled. "I ran into a friend back there and just couldn't get away."

"Grizzly," said Cam in a matter-of-fact way. "I guess you did the right thing."

"I was paralyzed, if that's what you mean. He was beautiful. I wish I could have taken a picture."

"It's a good thing you didn't try, not if he could see you. You gals ready to head back?"

"I would say we got our twenty dollars worth," said Louise.

"I didn't see any bears," said Kate.

"C'mon," said Cam, "I'll make it up to you. Get in the driver's seat."

"No kidding?" Kate did not wait for an answer. With Cam coaching her, she pointed the plane toward McKinley and revved the engine. Then they were picking up speed across the water and taking off to bank toward Fairbanks.

OK, thought Louise, how do we top this?

32

Before they returned to New Castle, Kate and Louise joined another P-39 mission to Great Falls. In mid-July, they learned that their Fairbanks caper had the opposite effect from what they hoped. ATC headquarters notified all its bases that women were not to fly missions to Alaska. Despite this setback, however, the WAFS pilots were getting more freedom as their services were more in demand. Like the men, they could now borrow a plane if they had a day off. Returning from Evansville on a Friday, Louise found that she would have a rare weekend without a mission. On Saturday morning, she went to see a friendly sergeant in the operations office.

"Anything available for tomorrow?" she asked.

"There's a PT-19 you could take," he replied.

"Will you put it aside for me?"

"Sure."

Louise had been thinking about Tom, wondering what he would say if she called him. Would she be making a fool of herself? If he had been interested, he could have easily tracked her down. Maybe he's already involved with someone else. She really wanted to settle her mind and get on with her life. Guessing that he was at his office, she summoned up her courage and dialed the number.

"Tom Clark."

"Hello, Tom, this is Louise Mitchell."

There was a slight pause. "Louise, are you in Washington?"

"No, I'm in New Castle." She was afraid her voice would break, so she decided to get right to the point. "Are you busy tomorrow?"

"Nothing I can't change. What's up?"

"It's supposed to be a beautiful day. May I take you for a ride?"

Tom laughed. "On a mission?"

"No, just a little sightseeing. A surprise."

"Now you've piqued my curiosity. Are you going to land on my street?"

"No, silly, can you meet me at National?"

"Sure, whereabouts?"

"The north end of the terminal, where I dropped you off. Can you be there by nine?"

"Should I bring my parachute?"

"I'm going to borrow one for you. I don't want you wearing that old thing again."

"OK, I'll be there."

Louise hung up and stood for a moment leaning against the wall. "I can't believe I just did that," she said aloud.

Tom called Jack Pierce and postponed their tennis match until the following Sunday. He sat thinking for a while about the dilemma he was allowing himself into. He had not thought about Louise for a month, but her call awakened the feelings that had lingered after their first encounter. He liked her. She was certainly different from Anne. She did not have Anne's glamour or sophistication, but in her own way, Louise was very attractive. There was something in her eyes and smile that he could only describe as good will. He had felt very comfortable in her presence, and he wondered if Louise could be a friend without being a lover.

In New Castle, Louise got a haircut and puzzled over her clothes. How could she look feminine and fly a damn plane, especially one with an open cockpit? Finally, she carefully pressed her white shirt, silk scarf, and tan slacks. She would have to wear her leather jacket, but she picked up her flight helmet and tossed it down again. "It's warm enough," she said to herself, "I'll just wear the headphones."

Coming back from lunch, she passed the PX and had an inspiration. Sure enough, they had some aviator's caps. She settled on the smallest one and dipped into her meager funds to pay for it. Well, she thought, I've always wanted one of these.

Just after 9:00 a.m., Louise taxied up to the general aviation end of the National Airport terminal and cut her engine. She climbed down and came around the wing to see Tom coming toward her, wearing his leather flight jacket and aviator's cap. They stopped and began laughing. "Don't tell me you're a pilot," said Louise.

"No, I wish I were. They gave me this when I was in the Philippines."

She helped Tom into his parachute, and soon they were climbing into a clear summer sky. "Pilot to navigator," Louise said as she leveled off, "come in please."

"Navigator here, but I have no idea where we're going."

"I am taking you to zee faterland, Mr. Clark. Ve have ways of making people talk."

"Ah, well, in that case, I'll have to pull the pin on this hand grenade in my pocket."

"You win, Mr. Clark. You Americans are so clever."

Louise set a course to the southwest, toward the Blue Ridge Mountains. She wondered why she was so witty around Tom and thought that maybe she was overdoing it. They passed over Charlottesville, and she asked, "Recognize that estate down there?"

"Looks like Monticello. I guess you're taking me to the mountains."

"White Sulphur Springs. Do you mind?"

"Not at all. Do they have an airport, or do you plan to land on the railroad tracks?"

"There's an airfield on my chart, let's hope it's right."

Louise climbed over the mountains and concentrated hard to find White Sulphur Springs. "There's the town, I can see the Greenbriar."

She circled and spotted a tiny airstrip on a green knoll. "PT-19 to White Sulphur Springs tower, come in please." She repeated the call, but there was no answer. "OK, they don't have a radio. We're going in for a look, watch for other aircraft."

They scanned the area as Louise turned into an approach to the field. Getting closer, she could see a green flag on a small building near the runway. A few Cubs were parked nearby. She brought the PT-19 in about as smoothly as possible on the grass strip and taxied back to the shed. As they climbed down, a man in overalls came out carrying a wrench.

"Howdy. What kind of plane is that?"

"Fairchild PT-19, army trainer," said Louise. "Mind if we park here for a while?"

"Help yourself."

"You got any gas here?"

"I got some. Ain't high octane, though. How much you need?"

"Can you sell me twenty gallons?"

"I reckon so."

"Will you be here this afternoon?"

"Yep."

"How far is it to the Greenbriar?"

"Bout a mile. Want a lift?"

"That's very kind of you."

He stuck his head back into the shed. "Willie, give these folks a ride."

Willie was about 13 years old, with freckles and no socks. He waved them toward a Model T Ford. "Just a minute, ma'am, I gotta get that door from inside."

He let Louise into the front seat and Tom pulled open the rumble seat. Willie cranked the engine and it coughed into action. Off they went down a dirt road, and a few minutes later, Willie delivered them to entrance to the stately Greenbriar resort. As the doorman eyed them sternly, Tom reached in his pocket and gave the young man two quarters. "Thank you, sir," said Willie, beaming.

They walked up the steps, and Tom grinned at Louise. "You're just full of surprises, aren't you?"

"I'm not done yet."

"By the way, what would we have done if he hadn't had any gas?"

"We could make it back to Charlottesville. I'm sure they'd have some."

They went to the front desk. "Which way to the dining room?" asked Louise.

"I'm sorry, madam, our dining room is for our guests only."

"Oh. Well, may I borrow a piece of paper?"

"Certainly, madam."

Louise wrote a note and handed it to the bellman. "Would you please give this to Janet Simmons?"

The bellman disappeared, and a minute later a woman in white apron and chef's hat came through a door. "Louise, I can't believe you're here!"

They collapsed into a hug. "I guess we can't eat in your dining room," said Louise.

"Nonsense, come on. By the way, who's this?"

"This is my friend Tom Clark, from Washington."

Tom extended his hand. "It's a pleasure, Miss Simmons."

Janet led them into a large dining room with chandeliers and white tablecloths. She took the Maitre d' by the arm. "These are my special friends. Give them that table by the window."

Louise and Tom ordered a bottle of white wine and sat looking east toward the Virginia mountains.

"Is Janet the head chef?" asked Tom.

"She sure is. I met her on the train when I came east."

"That reminds me. You haven't told me where you're from."

"Sioux City. Before I joined the WAFS, the Black Hills were the furthest I had been from home."

The waiter brought soup and bread and opened their wine.

"*Tortolini in brodo* and Italian bread. Your star is rising, Louise."

"Does this make up for the rumble seat?"

"I guess so," said Tom. "You know, I used to know someone from Sioux City when I worked in the Navy Department. Come to think of it, *her* name was Mitchell. Jennie Mitchell."

Louise stared at him with her mouth open. "You knew my sister Jennie?"

"So Jennie's your sister. Where is she now?"

"Back in Sioux City, with my sister Rose. Did you know Jennie well?"

"We used to have lunch sometimes. I remember that I loved talking with her. She knew so much about literature and music and art. We went to a few of the art galleries together."

"I can't believe you knew my sister. What a small world."

"Did Jennie ever marry?"

"No. Frankly, I think she was just too cultivated for the men in Sioux City. She should have stayed in Washington."

"She was still there when I left. When did she come home?"

"In 1921, I think."

"I left at the end of 1920. Went to Wall Street for a while. Lucky for me, I went back to work for Roosevelt in '28, before the big crash."

The waiter brought their dinner, pheasant with sautéed vegetables, followed by apple cobbler. As they ate, Louise told Tom about her trip to Alaska. Then Janet came out and sat down.

"This was delicious, Miss Simmons," said Tom.

"My pleasure. This is such a wonderful surprise. Louise, you look terrific."

"Thanks. How do you like it here?"

"I love it. It sure is different from Chicago. I hike in the mountains every chance I get. And I've learned to ride. We have some wonderful horses."

"Can you get away for a little while? I've got a promise to keep."

"Sure, let me show you the kitchen first."

They got up and headed across the dining room. Tom stopped by their waiter and asked for the check. "No, sir, you are guests of Miss Simmons."

Tom took a dollar from his pocket and offered it. "Please take this, at least."

"Thank you, sir."

After they toured the kitchen, Janet went to her room and changed into jeans. "I can get us a ride," she said.

They piled into the Greenbriar's limousine and headed back up the dirt road to the airfield. When they arrived, they saw four five-gallon cans sitting near their plane. Willie had gotten them filled at the local gas station.

"We'll gas up after this little excursion," said Louise. She helped Janet into the extra parachute, buckled her into the back seat, and adjusted her earphones.

"I'm surprised we can use that gas," said Tom.

"It'll be all right in this trainer. We'll just be a little slow."

Louise taxied to the very end of the little strip and revved the engine. As she accelerated into the slight wind, Tom worried that there would not be enough room. The wheels were barely off the ground when the land sloped away at the end of the runway, making it look like a carrier takeoff. As they climbed safely into the blue sky, Tom found their host and paid for the gas.

A half-hour later, the PT-19 floated in and landed smoothly. Tom went to help Janet off the wing. "How was it?"

"Beautiful! My first plane ride! I was so nervous when we took off, I was shaking. But once we got up there, I couldn't believe how beautiful it was."

"Sounds like another pilot in the making."

"Oh, I don't know if I could do that. Louise is fantastic."

"How are you going to get back?" asked Louise. "You want to see if there's a phone here?"

"I'm just going to walk. I love the smell of the woods along the road. Mr. Clark, I'm glad to have met you."

"Thank you again for the wonderful dinner. It was very gracious of you."

"You're welcome. Please come back some time."

Louise and Janet walked together to the road and stood talking for a few minutes. "So, is this something serious?" asked Janet.

"I don't know if it's anything at all. This is our second time together. I had to call him."

"Well, if he's got any sense, he'll call you next time. Thank you so much for coming, Louise."

They held each other for a long time, and then Janet headed down the road, turning back once to wave.

Louise was wiping a tear as she approached Tom. "I paid Mr. Overalls for the gas," he said. "I've got to contribute something today."

"Thanks. Ready to go?"

Late that afternoon, Louise parked again at the end of National Airport's terminal. She took off her parachute and climbed down, this time letting Tom help her. She was a little disappointed when he let her hand go, but she walked with him to the door.

"I've had a wonderful day, Louise. I'm very glad you called."

"Me, too. I've been wanting to visit Janet. I'm glad you could come."

"Back to P-47s tomorrow?"

"Back to Long Island, at least until Friday. By the way, here's the phone number of our barracks in New Castle."

Louise looked at him expectantly, but he put the paper in his pocket and held out his hand again. This time, at least, the handshake lasted a little longer.

"Take care, Louise," he said with a smile.

Back in the air, Louise was feeling discouraged. Well, I guess that settles that, she thought. I don't know what else I can do. How many women fly a man to the mountains for lunch? That evening, however, she did write to Jennie, telling her about the old friend of hers she had met.

33

When Tom did not call, Louise tried to put him out of her mind. She returned to base one day in early August and picked up her mail. There was a check for per diem expenses, very welcome, but no letters from Jennie or Rose. She looked at a small envelope addressed with a pencil, and saw an APO return address. The name above it was Fawcett. Louise hurried to her room and sat down to open the envelope.

Dear Miss Mitchell,

I found your note in my new P-47, and it was a very happy surprise. It brought back the pleasant memory of dancing with you. I was sorry that I had to leave New Castle without saying goodbye.

I am sure you are happy to be flying some real airplanes. I love this Thunderbolt. I feel much safer than I did in the P-40 I was flying in North Africa. I have been in England for two months now, escorting B-17s into Germany. The action is heavy, and I've brought back a few bullet holes, but the plane you sent me is really rugged.

If you have time, I would love to hear from you. Please say hello to Miss Burns and the others for me.

Your friend,

Terry Fawcett

Capt., USAAF

Louise read the letter several more times, then took out stationery and began a long response. She congratulated him on his promotion and told him about her first time in a P-47. She wrote four paragraphs about her trip to Alaska. As she finished her news, she could feel emotion rising in her chest. She tried to think of something romantic to say in closing. She wanted to tell him how good it had felt when he held her hand at the end of their last dance. Don't, Louise, she thought, he's a nice kid and you'll just embarrass him.

I know how busy you are, Captain, but if you have time to write again, I promise to answer.

Fondly,

Louise Mitchell

She read it again and put it in an envelope. Then she hurried back to the post office to get it in the mail.

"Did you have to run me all over the court?" puffed Jack Pierce as he wiped sweat from his face.

"I'll do anything to win," said Tom. "Besides, you can use a little running. You're spending too much time at that desk."

"No kidding. I wish I could get overseas."

"You're doing an important job. General Arnold needs you right where you are, and I need a tennis partner."

They got beers from the snack bar and sat at one of the umbrella tables on the club's deck.

"Are you going to tell me what was more important than our match last Sunday?"

"I guess so. I had a lunch invitation, to White Sulphur Springs."

"West Virginia? How the devil did you get there?"

"Jack, keep this just between us. I rode out there with a woman who flies for the Ferry Division."

"One of the WAFS? You know one of them?"

"I just met her recently. She has a friend who's the head chef at the Greenbriar, and we went out to visit her."

"What about Anne?"

"Nothing's changed with Anne. I still care about her."

"Care about her? I thought it was a little more than that."

"Look, Jack, Anne is wonderful. She's amazing. But how often do I see her? How often am I ever going to see her?"

"There's a war on. It won't last forever."

"I just wonder if Anne could ever settle in one place. Frankly, Jack, she takes so many chances, I think each time I see her may be the last."

"So the answer is to get involved with a pilot. Do you know how many pilots we lose in accidents?"

"I thought about that. Want to hear something else weird? I used to know her older sister when I was at the Navy Department. You might even say I dated her."

"Tom, old friend, you are getting in over your head. If you want my advice, you'll do your job and wait for Anne to come back. It'll be worth it."

"And leave it to you to date the rest of the women in Washington."

"Believe me, if I had someone like Anne, I wouldn't be out looking."

"Well, you're probably right. I do appreciate your advice."

Tom had had two more letters from Anne, but none since early June. From her dispatches, he knew she was in Sicily, tagging along somehow with one of Patton's tank battalions as it swept toward Palermo. As usual, her stories gave the best insight into what the war was like for the troops.

As August progressed, Tom busied himself preparing materials for the conference in Quebec that Churchill had requested. He tried not to think about Louise and Anne. On the second Friday of the month, he put the final touches on a briefing book for Roosevelt's trip and walked out into the summer evening to catch the trolley. Back at his place, he poured a glass of sherry and sat on the balcony watching as several couples strolled by under the gaslight. He took out his wallet and stared at the piece of paper on which Louise had written her number.

The phone rang in the hall of the WAFS barracks at New Castle. Soon there was a knock on Louise's open door, and she looked up from the letter she was writing. "Mitchell, you've got a phone call, from a gentlemen with a nice voice."

Louise did not want to assume that it was Tom. She was not even sure she wanted it to be. "Mitchell here," she said in a military tone.

"Mitchell, this is the White House calling."

"Tom? Hi."

"I hope I'm not calling at a bad time."

"No, I was just writing to Jennie. I've been in New York all week."

"P-47s?"

"Yeah. Up and down, up and down."

"Well, we need them, as many as you can deliver."

"I'm ready for something more exciting. I'm starting to talk to the Statue of Liberty."

Tom gave a little laugh. "Louise, is there any chance you could get away tomorrow?"

She took a deep breath. He could have called before this, what did she want to say now? "I don't know. Can you hold on for a few minutes?"

"Sure."

Louise went to the end of the hall and knocked on Betty's door. Soon she was back to the phone, having resolved her doubts. "OK, I've got permission."

"Great. Have you ever seen the sights of Washington?"

"Not from the ground."

"I'd like to take my turn as tour guide."

"That would be nice. Shall I take the train?"

"I'd like to pick you up, but I don't know if I can get enough gas."

"That's all right. I think I can get a train at eight-thirty and be there by ten."

"Then I'll meet you at Union Station."

Louise went to work pressing her uniform and picking out some extra clothes to take with her. Before long, Kate appeared at her door.

"Have you been holding out on me, Mitchell? Who is this?"

"Hi, Kate. It's just a friend. I met him on one of my trips. He lives in Washington."

"So you're off to Washington tomorrow. Well, I want a report this time."

"Oh? How many reports do you owe me?"

"A few, maybe, but none as interesting as this. Besides, you're not as nosy as I am."

"I'm not as pretty as you are, either. I'm keeping this one away from you."

"What's that supposed to mean? Are you talking about Cam and his floatplane? Believe me, Cam was more interested in you than he was in me. He asked me if you had a boyfriend."

"Are you putting me on?"

"No. It was very deflating."

Louise stared at Kate, then shrugged her shoulders. "Well, it hardly matters now, does it?"

Mother Nature had a pleasant surprise Saturday morning, as unseasonably cool weather moved into Washington. Louise had worried that she would melt in her uniform, but she wanted the confidence that it gave her. With a forecast high in the mid-70s, she would be reasonably comfortable. She got off the train carrying her purse and flight bag, and looked up the platform to see Tom coming toward her. He was looking very sporty in a sweater vest over an open shirt.

He greeted her with the inevitable handshake. "You even have the trains running on time, Louise. It's nice to see you again."

"I'm glad you called, Tom. I needed a break from that shuttle service."

"May I carry your bag?"

"Sure, you can spoil me a little. Where are we going?"

"I want to take you to a few of my favorite spots. But we can start with the Capitol if you want, it's definitely worth it."

As they arrived at Tom's car, Louise purred, "Well, this is impressive. What year is this?"

"It's a 1931 Roadster. I just can't give it up."

"Why would you want to? It's great."

"It runs like a top. Of course, I don't drive it much in the city."

They parked on the elliptical drive in front of the Capitol and took their tour. Afterwards, Tom headed away from town on New York Avenue. A few miles along, he pulled into a huge open area, passing a sign that read, "National Arboretum. U.S. Department of Agriculture."

In the next few hours, they walked through the National Herb Garden and the Grove of State Trees, taking turns snapping each other with Louise's camera. They stopped in the National Bonsai Collection and admired the carefully shaped miniature trees, some of which were nearly 300 years old.

"How can people who cultivate such a fine art be waging such a terrible war?" asked Louise.

"That's a good question," said Tom. "How can people as enlightened as the Germans be following a Hitler and persecuting the Jews? I don't have an answer. I guess we should ask how a country dedicated to human rights could practice slavery and segregation."

They went on to the rhododendron groves, which were beautiful even when not in bloom. As they stopped at a fork in the trail, Louise looked away down one of the lovely paths. She decided that she had been patient long enough. She did not want to spend another month wondering if it was all right to feel something.

Without turning, she said quietly, "I have a question, Tom Clark."

"What's that?"

"When are you going to kiss me?"

Tom smiled, turned her chin with his hand, and kissed her softly. "I was just thinking about it." He took her into his arms and gave her a real kiss, then held her head to his chest. "I'm sorry I waited so long."

Louise slipped her hand into Tom's and they followed the path back to the car. Her hand was strong, but soft and sensual at the same time. A woman can say a lot with her hand, thought Tom. They drove back to Capitol Hill and stopped at a pub with tables on the sidewalk.

"Here you must have a corned-beef sandwich and beer," said Tom.

"Yes, sir. You haven't been wrong yet."

They nursed their beers and chatted until mid-afternoon.

"Ready for another favorite spot?"

"Ready."

They drove to the banks of the Potomac and pulled into the parking area of the new Jefferson Memorial. Walking around the columns supporting the great dome, they stopped to look at the Tidal Basin surrounded by Japanese cherry trees. Blue sky and the gleaming Washington Monument reflected in the water. Louise saw an older couple seated on a bench and asked if they would take a picture of Tom and her. The couple smiled warmly, and the husband rose to take the camera. Louise put her arm inside Tom's and maneuvered him near the edge of the basin, with the great obelisk behind them.

The photography finished, they mounted the steps to look at Jefferson. "It's awesome," said Louise as she gazed at the towering bronze statue. She began reading aloud the words around the base of the dome. "I have sworn upon the altar of God eternal hostility against every form of tyranny over the mind of man."

She gripped Tom's hand more tightly and led him to the great tablet containing the words, "We hold these truths to be self-evident...." Silently, she read each of the quotations until they arrived again at the entrance and looked out on the water.

"This is a wonderful place, Tom."

"I come here to think," he said. "It's beautiful at night."

They descended the steps and began walking around the basin. As they approached the memorial again, Tom asked, "Do you think you'll keep flying after the war?"

"I hope so. I'm afraid there will be a lot of pilots looking for jobs. I'll probably have to go back and help my friend Sam in Iowa."

"Are there any other possibilities?"

"Well, I'd like to work for Republic or one of the other companies, testing and delivering their planes. But that's probably just a dream. If I could buy my own plane, I could start a little flying school. Another dream."

"It would be a shame if you couldn't find a job. I know what an excellent pilot you are."

She smiled and pulled him close for a lingering kiss. "Flattery will get you everywhere."

"It's not flattery, but I like the results."

"Do you think about the future?" asked Louise, as they started walking again.

"I've been thinking about it. I don't know if Roosevelt will run again next year. Anyway, I might be ready to do something else."

"I could teach you to fly."

Tom did not answer, and Louise suddenly felt she had overstepped. Damn, she thought, everything was going so well. After a moment, he said rather blankly, "Learn to fly at my age? I don't know." It was obvious he was thinking about something, and Louise remained silent.

They reached Tom's car and he opened the door for her. Settling into the driver's seat, he asked, "What time do you have to be back at the base?"

Louise hesitated and looked straight ahead. She had stuck her neck out a lot already today, and she was not sure she wanted to do it again. She folded her hands on her lap and looked down. "I have an overnight pass, Tom."

He leaned toward her and put his arm on her shoulders. As she turned, he kissed her on the forehead. "May I take you to dinner?"

Her lips met his and quivered. "I brought some clothes. May I press them at your place?"

34

Louise emerged from the guestroom wearing a light gray Shetland sweater, pearl necklace, charcoal gray wool skirt, and black heels. Tom had put on a sportcoat and tie.

"You look radiant, Louise."

"Thank you. This necklace belonged to my mother. It was her treasure."

Tom was smiling. "I'm thinking about the first time I saw you, in that oversized flying suit."

"Did I look funny?"

"You looked absolutely intriguing. I was disappointed when you left me sitting in the canteen."

"Were you surprised when I came back?"

"Yes, and you've been surprising me ever since. Nice surprises." He kissed her forehead. "Ready for dinner?"

They drove to the Willard Hotel, where the valet took Tom's car. Louise paused to look at the great columns and huge vases in the lobby. Then they made their way to the stately dining room, with its red and gold drapes and decorated ceiling.

"Is this where you have lunch?" she teased.

"Not very often."

They were seated at a small round table and given menus. "French cuisine," said Tom, "it's excellent. Would you like a Manhattan?"

"I'd love one. Back at the barracks we have to drink our bourbon straight."

"You must have made some good friends there."

"I have wonderful friends. I'm going to miss them so much when it's over."

"It's ironic, isn't it? War is so tragic, and yet it brings people together."

"It's given me an opportunity I could never have dreamed of. Sometimes I feel guilty that I've been so lucky."

"You don't need to feel guilty. You're doing a vital job."

"I know. But some young man is flying in deadly combat because I'm flying these missions instead of him. I have nightmares about it sometimes."

"Louise, you take chances every day. I'm the one who should feel guilty. I go around and meet with the generals."

"I'm sorry, I didn't mean to be morose. I really love what I'm doing. I feel blessed."

The waiter came and they both ordered fish, with a bottle of Chardonnay from the Ohio Valley. As they waited, Louise told Tom about her notes in the P-47s and her letter from Capt. Fawcett. She left out the part about dancing, however. Tom was delighted with the story.

"I'm sure that every pilot who gets a note is keeping it in his plane. Would you mind if told the president about this?"

"Oh, no, please don't do that. It might get out to my bosses."

"OK, but I think you're being too modest."

Tom watched Louise as she talked and smiled. He wondered how this woman, so vibrant, so genuine, so caring, could still be single. Had some deity saved her for him? Was that same deity amusing himself with Tom's dilemma? Was he the object of a wager among the gods over how he would resolve the situation? If so, some of them would soon be disappointed. He was falling very much in love with Louise Mitchell.

They parked in the driveway and Tom came around to open the door. Louise was feeling the effects of a large Manhattan and half a bottle of wine, and she held Tom's arm as they slowly climbed the steps. She stumbled into the bathroom while Tom laid his jacket and tie on a chair and turned on the radio. When she returned, Glenn Miller's orchestra was playing "Moonlight Serenade." Tom took her hand, put his right hand on her back, and began to dance slowly. Louise laid her head on his shoulder until the song ended, then looked into his eyes and their lips came together.

He led her to the bedroom, where he took off her necklace and laid it on the dresser. As the music and dim light drifted in, he rested his hands on her hips and gently began to raise her sweater. She trembled as his hands touched her slip and moved slowly through the curve of her waist toward her shoulders. He laid her sweater and skirt on a chair, and she began unbuttoning his shirt. As Tom finished undressing, Louise took off her slip, stepped out of her heels, and climbed into bed. He came in beside her and took her in his arms for a long kiss. His skin was warm and smooth and felt very sensuous next to hers.

He turned her on her side and kissed the back of her neck. Unhooking her bra, he pushed it slowly off her left shoulder, letting his hand continue to the edge of her breast. His fingertips moved lightly, and she whimpered as they touched her swelling nipple. She rolled on her back and he kissed her other breast. With tantalizing slowness, he slid her panties down over her stockings, and she felt herself getting wet.

Louise soon found herself enjoying pleasures she had never experienced. After they climaxed, she lay on him limp and exhausted, but Tom was still hard and she would not let him leave her. They dozed off briefly, then awoke and kissed before she finally rolled over and pulled up the sheet and blanket. She put her head on his shoulder and her hand across his chest. "I've never felt like that before."

"You were wonderful. No, you were sensational."

"I think we were sensational."

She thought about taking off her stockings, but she did not want to move. Tom awoke at dawn and lay there with Louise curled up against him. The radio was still playing in the living room. He wondered if he should write to Anne to tell her about Louise. He thought about a future with Louise, in which he could help her financially to continue her flying. He imagined starting and ending each day with this adorable woman at his side. It was a future that he could probably never have with Anne.

Louise stirred and moved her leg across him. She kissed the side of his neck and gradually moved on top of him. Feeling him harden against her thigh, she reached down and guided him into her. After a few minutes of kissing, she straightened up, let her arms fall to her side, and closed her eyes to concentrate on the movement inside her. I want to do this forever, she thought.

They made blueberry pancakes for breakfast and listened to the news. German and Italian troops were escaping from Sicily across the Strait of Messina, thanks to Montgomery's caution. Other German divisions were pouring over the Alps into northern Italy, with plenty of time to occupy key defensive positions in the country. The war intruded on the conversation.

"I'm not looking forward to this conference," said Tom.

"Why not?"

"We're still letting the British push us where we don't want to go. They're going to take us into Italy, and the Germans are going to love it."

"Where should we be going?"

"France, southern France first and then across the Channel. We should have started this summer."

"So why aren't we?"

"The British are clever. They realize that if they defer to us in the Far East, they can insist on their own approach in Europe. Churchill is very stubborn, and he uses all of his political skills to keep us from talking about France. Roosevelt respects him and doesn't want to just take over."

"Why are the British so reluctant to fight in France?"

"I think they just don't want to slug it out with Hitler. They would rather just bomb Germany and let the Russians wear him out. They're also very keen on keeping their influence in the Middle East. But I'm afraid this Italian campaign could really bog us down."

"So you think the conference is just going to be more maneuvering."

"That's exactly the word for it, Louise, two weeks of maneuvering. And then I can listen to the Navy trying to outmaneuver the Army in the Pacific. If we spent half as much effort outmaneuvering the enemy as we do each other, we could shorten the war by a year."

"Do I detect a note of cynicism, Mr. Clark?"

"We're trying to run a war by committee, so we miss our best opportunities. I guess the bright side is we don't do anything really crazy. Hitler's invasion of Russia, that was a piece of lunacy that only a dictator could pull off."

Louise got up and put her hand on his shoulder. "Tom, is there any chance of visiting the White House?"

"I think so. No harm in trying."

Louise bathed and put on her uniform. They drove to the west gate, where the guard knew Tom well. He vouched for Louise and they parked near the great columns on the south side. Tom took her through the historic rooms but not to the west wing, because he did not want to raise any eyebrows. Then they drove to Capitol Hill and walked along the townhouses south of the Capitol. By mid-afternoon, they were back at Union Station.

Louise put her head against his shoulder and pulled him tightly against her. "Will you call me when you're back from Canada?"

"When's the best time to reach you?"

"Friday night if I'm doing the Newark shuttle. Otherwise, it's hard to say. You'll have to leave a message. The girls are good about that."

"I'm going to worry about you."

"I'm very careful. I don't fool around."

"I'll still worry. But I'm very proud to know you."

They kissed and reluctantly let each other go. Louise boarded the train, and Tom watched until it was well out of the station. Another goodbye, he thought, will it always be this way?

35

Tom sat near the cockpit as Roosevelt and Hopkins chatted in the quieter tail section. The drone of the engines helped him forget the wrangling at Quebec, and he drifted off into his own thoughts. He resolved not to write to Anne. It had been almost three months since her last letter, and he felt no obligation to break the silence. If she was involved with someone else, then he was free to enjoy his relationship with Louise. He probably still loved Anne, but trying to hold on to her would mean long stretches of loneliness, and he was getting tired of loneliness. Louise was not far away. He could see her often during the war and be with her after the war.

It was Friday evening when he arrived home. He immediately called the barracks in New Castle, hoping Louise might pick up the phone. Instead, he heard a cheerful but unfamiliar voice. "Burns here."

"May I speak to Louise Mitchell?"

"Sorry, Louise isn't here. She's in Florida."

"Do you know when she'll be back?"

"I'd like to help you, but there's no telling. She could be hopping around the country for a while."

"May I leave a message?"

"Sure, go ahead."

"Tell her Tom called."

"From Washington?"

"Yes, how'd you know?"

"I'm her friend Kate."

"You're Kate. She must have told you about me."

"Not as much as I would like."

Tom chuckled. "Well, don't expect to get anything out of me."

"I don't give up easily."

"I know that from the stories I've heard. I hope to meet you sometime, Kate."

"Same here. I'll be sure Louise gets the message."

Saturday morning, Tom headed to the post office to pick up his mail. There, among the bills, was a letter in that familiar artistic hand. He went to a nearby bench and sat down to read. It had been written from Sicily two weeks earlier. Inside the letter was a picture of Anne in a brown Army uniform, combat boots, and helmet. She was standing in front of a jeep, holding the arms of two dusty GIs.

Dear Tom,

I'm sorry I haven't written for so long. I've been under fire so much that I go from fear to exhaustion. Things are finally quieting down here, and all I have to do is watch out for mines.

I was depressed for a week. My friend Jim Andersen (yes, he made it here, too) was killed by a mine 10 days ago. He was in a jeep right in front of me. I've just now been able to write about it. I almost left the front, but I hated to let down the young men I've been moving with. They've been so good to me, and they're all just as scared as I am.

I've seen Gen. Patton several times. He's not very good at disguising his opinions. He drives the press officers crazy. He's furious with Montgomery for letting the Germans escape, and he's mad at Eisenhower for letting Monty have his way. I have to admit, I have a better opinion of the men in the companies than I do of the generals. There's no doubt in my mind who's responsible for getting us this far.

You're probably shocked to hear me talk like this. I'm sure you could explain the big picture if you were here. But it's hard to see the big picture when you're looking for Germans through field glasses.

I do think about you. I wish this war could just go away and we could be together again. Please let me know if you're coming over here. The Post can help you get a message to me.

All my love,
Anne

Tom let his hand fall to his side, then raised it and read the letter again. He did not know how to feel. Everything was there— the courageous and caring woman he knew, the coincidence of Jim Andersen being in Sicily, the recklessness, the insights, the affection. Why was she writing now, after all this time? He thought about what Jack Pierce had said. Maybe he should have just been patient and waited for Anne. Now he had a real dilemma. He would have to disappoint someone, someone he cared a lot about. He sat for a long time before wandering back to his townhouse.

Over the next several days, Tom tried a few times to start a letter to Anne, but ended up throwing them away. On the Friday before Labor Day, he answered his phone late in the afternoon.

"Hi, Tom."

"Louise, are you back?"

"Finally. I've been all over the place."

"What happened?"

"There are just so many planes waiting to get somewhere, nobody would let me go home. I logged over 10,000 miles. I even rode shotgun in a B-24."

"Did you like that?"

"It was fun to have somebody to talk to, but I'd rather fly fighters. I just like the freedom."

Tom shook his head, wondering how he kept getting mixed up with these women. "Are you home for the weekend?"

"I certainly hope so. May I come down tomorrow?"

"Of course, how long can you stay?"

"I have to take care of some things in the morning, but I think I can get a pass for tomorrow night. I could be there around two."

"I'll be at the station at two, unless I hear differently."

"Tom?"

"Yes?"

"I missed you."

"I missed you, too."

A little after two on Saturday afternoon, Louise and Tom were sharing a long kiss on the platform at Union Station.

"What do you want to do?" he asked.

"Now, or later?"

Tom smiled. "Let's start with now."

"Can we go see Mr. Jefferson?"

"Sure."

They sat on the steps of the big memorial looking out at the familiar sight of the Washington Monument reflecting in the basin. "How was your conference?" asked Louise.

"Endless."

"Did you get anywhere?"

"Well, we talked about Italy, we talked about Norway, we talked about Burma. Anything to keep from talking about France."

"Mr. Churchill wouldn't talk about France?"

"Oh, he agrees we should invade it, sometime. Meanwhile, Stalin sent a message to let us know that he's pissed. So now I'm sure we'll have to meet again and include him."

"Tommy, are you getting disillusioned?"

Tom laughed and squeezed her hand. "Nobody's called me that since I was on the high school baseball team. I'm sorry, Louise, I guess I have been feeling a little down."

She pulled him tight against her. "I'm sorry I was gone so long."

He put his arm around her and leaned over to kiss her softly. "I've just had a lot on my mind. Let's go for a walk."

They walked along the Potomac for more than an hour. Back at the car, Tom proposed dinner at an outdoor café near Dupont Circle. As they dined, Louise entertained him with stories about her trip. Then they drove to a spot in the Northwest hills where they could see the lights on the monuments.

"It's beautiful," said Louise. "I hope we never have blackouts again."

"I guess that's what this is all about, isn't it."

"Are you feeling better?"

"Much better, thanks to you."

She put her arms around his neck. "Let's go home."

36

Autumn 1943 was an optimistic time for the Allies. They took the initiative with landings in Italy, New Guinea, and the Solomon and Gilbert Islands, while the Russians launched an offensive on a broad front. Names like Salerno, Bougainville, and Tarawa became household words in America. Japanese and German resistance was fierce, however, and the outcome of these offensives was by no means obvious. The one certainty was the relentless production and delivery of American planes, ships, tanks, and a host of other war materiel.

Louise and the growing corps of women pilots were in constant demand. Louise continued to ferry fighter and training aircraft, but graduates of Jacqueline Cochran's program were towing targets, moving personnel and cargo, and testing planes after repair. With their changing role came a new name, the Women's Airforce Service Pilots, or WASPs. When male pilots were trying to avoid the B-29 Superfortress, two WASPs made a tour in a one to overcome the men's reluctance to fly it.

Louise and Tom managed three more visits that autumn. The sexual chemistry between them was so compelling that they began going straight to Tom's place from Union Station. Afterwards, they would lie together and talk about the worlds they lived in. Louise's body was incredibly hard but her skin was soft as silk. Feeling her next to him, Tom enjoyed these conversations so much that he had to remind himself to be careful about classified information.

The question of Anne remained unresolved, however. Tom finally wrote in mid-September, but it was a newsy, neutral letter that would not raise any suspicions. With Anne in such a stressful situation, he simply could not bring himself to tell her about Louise. Sometime he would have to face his predicament, but not right now.

On a Friday evening in mid-November, his phone rang at home.

"Hi, Tom."

"Louise, where are you? This isn't a very good connection."

"I'm still on Long Island. Have you had a good week?"

"It's been interesting. I've been studying Russian history and geography, trying to prepare Roosevelt for what to expect from Stalin."

"When are you leaving?"

"Wednesday. I hope I can see you before I go."

"Tom, I'm not going to make it home this weekend."

"What's up?"

"I've got to take a P-47 to California, to an Army pursuit school."

"There's no one else to take it?" Tom immediately wished he had not said that.

Louise hesitated. "I could try to find someone."

"No, I'm sorry to sound selfish. We both have jobs to do."

"I thought it was a chance to stop and see Jennie and Rose."

"Great idea. We'll just have to wait a few more weeks. You'll be in real jeopardy when I see you."

"Oh, I hope so."

"Have you told Jennie about me?"

"I told her I met you."

"Well, tell her I have good memories of her."

"I will. Tom?"

"Yes?

"I love you."

"I love you, too. Please be careful."

Early Saturday morning, Louise stowed her flight bag in a shiny new Thunderbolt at the Republic factory. She had taken it up for a quick test flight the day before, and now she was ready to get out of New York for a while. She warmed up the powerful engine and signaled the ground crew to take away the wheel blocks. The crewmen knew her and her companions well, and they saluted as she began to pull away from the hangar. She taxied to the runway and called the tower.

"Mitchell to tower. Ready for takeoff."

"Roger, Mitchell. Cleared for takeoff. Try not to get sunburned in Palm Springs."

"Very funny, Dave."

Louise pushed the throttle hard, and 2,300 Pratt and Whitney horses galloped down the runway and into the autumn sky. She banked over the Statue of Liberty, where she would usually be throttling down. "See you later, baby. Behave yourself."

She leveled off at 10,000 feet as the Pocono Mountains passed below. She would have liked to fly nonstop to Sioux City, but that was at the end of the P-47's range and it was too risky. She would make a pit stop in Peoria. Cruising through the blue sky at 275 mph, Louise felt as if she were on top of the world. Could life be this good? Had she earned this happiness or was it somehow going to be taken away? Then she wondered if anything was wrong in Sioux City. Since she wrote about Tom, she had received only one short letter from Jennie.

She crossed into Ohio, and the farmlands of the Midwest began to stretch in front of her. It was barely 10 a.m. local time as she began a descent into Peoria. Some difference from the old days of limping along in PT-19s, she thought. In Peoria, she requisitioned fuel for her internal and auxiliary tanks and found a telephone. At the big house on Third Street, Rose accepted her collect call.

"Louise, where are you? Are you all right?"

"I'm fine. I'm in Peoria. Would you like a visit?"

"A visit? Of course, when?"

"I can be there for lunch."

"My goodness. I'd better get busy."

"Could you call Sam and see if he can come?"

"I'll try."

Just before noon, Louise called the tower at Sioux City and asked clearance to land. Before long, a familiar voice was on the radio.

"Louise, is that you?"

"It's me, Harry."

"What are you flying?"

"A P-47."

"Wow, we haven't had one of those here. Bring it in."

"On my way."

Louise pulled up to the terminal and the ground crewmen gathered around to look at the Thunderbolt. Harry came running out and shook her hand.

"I called Andy down at the paper. He wants a shot of you with the plane."

"Harry, my sisters are waiting lunch for me."

"He's on his way over. Can't you wait a few minutes?"

"OK, let me call home."

Andy arrived and took a couple of pictures. As people crowded around, he asked Louise where she had been and what planes she

had flown. She decided not to mention Alaska, just in case the
story found its way back to ATC. What was she going to do after
the war? She didn't know. Would she encourage young women to
fly? Yes.

Louise felt uncomfortable with all the attention. She also worried
about Harold reading the story and feeling badly again. "Could you
give me a ride home, Andy? We can talk more in the car."

"Sure."

"Harry," said Louise, "can we put this thing in the hangar? I
need to have it locked up overnight."

"Don't worry, we'll lock it up tighter than a drum. And I'll have
CAP volunteers here to watch it all night."

Louise stowed her helmet and coveralls in the plane. Wearing
her leather jacket and aviator's cap, she was soon watching Rose
come down the front steps to meet her.

"Louise, my, you look so military."

Louise embraced her sister. "How are you, Rose?"

"I'm very well. I've missed you."

"I've missed you, too. Where's Jennie?"

"She's upstairs. She'll be down."

"Is she all right, Rose?"

"Oh, yes. She's been a little moody lately, but it's probably just
change of life."

They went inside and saw that Rose had set the table beautifully for four.

"Is Sam coming?"

"He said he would try."

"Oh, I hope so. I want to show him my plane, well, the Army's
plane."

Jennie came down the stairs with a big smile and hugged her
sister. "Louise, this is such a wonderful surprise."

"I'm sorry I didn't give you more of a warning. I wasn't sure I could make it."

"Nonsense, we're just happy you're here. I'm sorry I haven't written more. I've been lazy."

"I bring you good wishes from Tom Clark. He says he has good memories of you."

The smile faded from Jennie's face. "Have you seen him lately?"

"I spoke to him on the phone yesterday. He was getting ready to go to the Middle East with the president."

"Yes," said Jennie distantly, "he liked Mr. Roosevelt."

There was a knock at the door and Louise ran to open it. "Sam! I'm so glad you're here!"

For the third time in her life, she felt Sam's arms around her. The first had been after her first solo flight, and had kindled romantic hopes in a young woman. The second was when she left for New Castle. This time, she held on as long as she could. As they went to the dining room arm-in-arm, Jennie seemed a little more cheerful again.

For an hour, they sat around the table listening to Louise tell stories. Finally, she was worn out. "I want to hear something about you folks. Are you still working at the Red Cross?"

"Three days a week," said Rose. "We roll bandages and pack food boxes and whatever they have."

"You remember the Lawrence boy, Jeremy?" asked Jennie quietly.

"Yes."

"He was killed in Sicily."

"Oh no. He couldn't have been more than twenty."

"We've lost several young men."

They were silent for a moment, then Sam spoke up, "I should be getting back soon."

"Are you able to fly much?" asked Louise.

"Maybe four hours a week. That's about all the gas I can get."

"How are you hanging on?"

"Mechanical work. I've got a few planes I work on, and I go around to people's houses and fix things. That's one thing about the war, people can't buy much so they have to keep things running."

"Can we go over and see my Thunderbolt?"

"Wouldn't miss it."

Sam had an old sedan now, and they all piled in and went out to the airport. He climbed into the cockpit and Louise went over the layout.

Gazing ahead, he said with unusual emotion, "You've gone way beyond me, Louise. I'm really proud of you."

"I'm sure you could fly this thing. It's just an airplane."

Sam laughed. "Spoken like a true pilot."

They took pictures all around, and Sam dropped them back at home. Louise spent the rest of the afternoon roaming around the big house and the neighborhood. She stopped to chat with several people and answered the questions of a group of curious kids playing with a football. After a few hours, however, she began to feel the limits of this environment. Had she lost forever her capacity to live here like Jennie and Rose? She had seen the sadness in Sam's eyes as he looked out over the engine of the P-47, and she reflected again that opportunities like hers were rare and fleeting. She had to live it as long as she could.

With a long day ahead of her, Louise went to bed early. At 6:30 a.m., she held each of her sisters a long time and said goodbye. Soon she was warming up the Thunderbolt's engine and getting ready to take off over the Missouri. As she set a course for Colorado Springs, she began to think about Jennie's shifting moods during her visit. Did this have something to do with Tom? Had he told her the whole story about Jennie? She shuddered at the thought, but then realized that she was letting her imagination run wild.

As lunchtime approached, Louise could see snow-capped Pike's Peak ahead of her, and she called the tower at Colorado Springs for permission to enter the landing pattern. She circled in and saw the trademark reddish-brown rocks of the Garden of the Gods. An hour later, with a full stomach and tanks full of high-octane fuel, she donned her oxygen mask and began climbing above the Rocky Mountains. Louise had never seen the Grand Canyon, so she crossed into southern Utah and banked gently southwest to follow the most spectacular part of it. The rim being at 7,500 feet, she dropped down to 10,000 to get a good look. The majestic canyon seemed to go on forever. None of the descriptions she had heard did it justice. Gaining time and daylight, Louise continued her course over the California desert into Palm Springs.

The operations officer was quite happy to see the P-47. "We need more of these. By the way, Miss Mitchell, have you flown a P-51 yet?"

Louise was surprised at the question. She was used to men being astonished when she climbed out of a Thunderbolt. "Not yet, why?" she asked tentatively.

"They're backed up at North American, waiting to go east. Mrs. Love and her squadron at Long Beach have taken some of them. Can you stay here a couple of days and check out?"

"I guess so. I should call my squadron leader and make sure."

After calling and leaving a message for Betty, Louise gathered her things and called a taxi. The driver laughed when she asked him to take her to something modestly priced, but he took her to a nice place and went in to speak to the desk clerk. She ended up with a lovely room at the high end of what she could afford. As she lounged under the poolside palms in the warm evening air, she thought about her encounter with the operations officer. He had practically begged her to check out in a Mustang, the hottest plane in the world. She remembered how she and Kate had to wile their way into P-47s. Things have certainly changed, she mused.

37

Tom sat at the small table in the back of the C-46, nursing a cup of tea. Roosevelt sat across from him, wrapped in his cloak, with Hopkins and Sumner Welles on either side.

"I liked your memo about Russia, Tom."

"Thank you, Mr. President."

"You seem to agree with Churchill that Stalin has designs on the Balkans."

"I think Stalin will try to dominate any area that his troops occupy. He's going to push his security line as far west as he can. Poland is at the top of his list, but he'll be opportunistic everywhere."

"You don't think he would allow freely-elected governments? What if we insist on it?"

"If there's a communist party capable of exercising power, Stalin's going to support it. He's going to do whatever the forces on the ground allow. I think he doubts our commitment to Europe, and he's never going to trust Germany again."

"So maybe Churchill's right that we should focus on southern Europe."

"I'm afraid that's where I part company with the PM. I think the answer is to defeat Germany as quickly as possible, before

Soviet troops start moving into Eastern Europe. I don't think we can do it in Italy or the Balkans."

"Are you suggesting we move up Overlord?" asked Hopkins. "That's exactly what Stalin wants us to do."

"We would give Churchill a heart attack if we proposed an earlier channel crossing," said Welles. "He's already trying to push it back to July."

Tom nodded and sipped his tea. "I know I'm swimming against the current, gentlemen, but I want to get this off my chest. I believe the route to Germany is through France, and every day that goes by, the Germans will be better fortified. I think we would surprise them if we moved early. I believe we could land in southern France and draw Rommel's panzer divisions into the battle. Then we could land in Normandy and start taking the ports. If we concentrated on controlling the air over France and the Low Countries, we could stop a lot of German supplies. The Resistance would help."

"What would we do with our forces in Italy?" asked Hopkins.

"Well, we've already got 12 German divisions committed in the South. We could help Montgomery keep them there with a minimal offensive effort. But I would recommend canceling the Anzio landings and throwing those resources into southern France. Besides being a better place to fight, it would complicate the German supply situation."

"Cancel Shingle, accelerate Anvil and Overlord," said Roosevelt. "You know, Marshall would probably agree with you, but I don't see how we could ever sell it to the British. They're still haunted by Dunkirk. And Eisenhower is reluctant to take any chances with the Channel weather. I think we'll be doing well if we can keep Overlord on schedule."

Tom felt he had made his pitch, and now it was time to go along with the consensus. Roosevelt, however, was pondering the smoke from his cigarette.

"I'm going to talk to Marshall about this again when we get to Cairo," said FDR.

Three days later, Tom stepped out onto his third-floor balcony and squinted in the Egyptian sunshine. The conference was in its final day, but the major discussions were over, and Roosevelt expected to rest and socialize with Churchill. Tom surveyed the palm-encircled fountain and the crescent drive that led to the hotel entrance. Suddenly, he heard a familiar voice.

"There you are. I've been looking for you."

He looked down to see Anne, in khaki shorts and pith helmet, knapsack on her back. "Anne, for God's sake, I'll be right down."

She met him in the lobby and gave him a long hug. "Why aren't you over at the villa? And why didn't you send me a message?"

"Slow down. I don't think they need me today. Were you at the press briefing this morning?"

"Yes, and I asked four people before I found out where you were."

"I'm sorry. I have to be careful when I travel with Roosevelt. I can't send messages ahead."

"Well, thank goodness the *Post* tipped me off. I got in last night."

They went out toward the fountain. "Did you get anything out of the briefing?"

"Not much. Only that we're going to liberate Rome by Christmas, and you're going to meet with Marshal Stalin."

"Rome by Christmas, eh? Did they say which year?"

"I figured that was for the Italians' benefit. Are you going to see Stalin?"

"Yes. I'm very much looking forward to it. I can't wait to see how he deals with Churchill."

"It's in Tehran, right?"

"Are you supposed to know that?"

"It's not much of a secret. Don't worry, I'm not going to follow you."

"I didn't mean that. Anyway, I guess it's safe enough. How did you get here? I thought you were slogging around in the mud with the Fifth Army."

"So you read my stories. I flew out of Naples to Tripoli. That's where my trunk is, at a hospital. Then I got a plane ride over here."

"How do you manage things like that?"

"I'm just a very good hitchhiker."

"I'll bet you are. Is that how some of these names get in your stories?"

"Now, Tom, don't be prying into my trade secrets. Are you really free for the day?"

"I am if I want to be."

"I have a great idea. Let's go to Giza."

"How?"

"I'm sure the man at the desk knows somebody with a car."

Anne was right, for ten dollars they could get a guided tour of the great pyramids outside Cairo. By mid-afternoon, after a harrowing ride in an open car with much horn blowing, they were gazing up at the incredibly massive structures.

"I just can't imagine what it took to set these blocks in place," said Anne.

"Maybe this was their version of the WPA," said Tom with a chuckle. "I wonder if FDR ever saw this."

A couple of camel drivers had sidled up to them. "Like to see Sphinx? Only five dollars."

"How about four?" countered Tom. Soon they were perched awkwardly on the strange beasts for the short ride over to the Sphinx.

"You look like T. E. Lawrence," teased Anne.

"I hope he rode better than this."

With the sun getting low in the sky, they set out on the dusty ride back to Cairo. "Mind if I use your bath?" asked Anne as they waved goodbye to their driver.

"Of course not."

While Tom shaved with a wash basin, Anne soaked for a while in the tub and put on the clean underwear she had in her pack. They went down to the dining room and ordered gin and tonics.

"I've seen your stories in other cities," said Tom.

"My editor says I'm in over a hundred papers."

"How many correspondents get as close to the action as you do?"

"A few. Most stay in the rear. Jim was always up there."

"I was very sorry to hear about that."

"I've accepted it now. Tom, I've seen so many broken bodies I'm numb."

"Why do you keep at it?"

"I don't know. The glory's gone, that's for sure. I just keep looking at these men who don't have any choice, and I feel like somebody should be telling their stories."

Their food arrived and Anne began to eat with uncharacteristic abandon.

"Is your dinner OK?" asked Tom with a grin.

"You can't imagine what a treat it is to have a good meal, and a hot bath."

"What do you carry with you?"

"Mostly food and water. My notebooks, extra underwear, my poncho, socks, as many as I can get my hands on."

As they ate, Tom was feeling very uneasy. He knew he should level with Anne, but he dreaded it. He hated the thought of letting her down. Anne did not seem to think of herself as a heroine, but she was to many people, including Tom. If anyone deserved loyalty, she did. As they sipped their wine, she looked at him quizzically.

"Tom, are you glad to see me?"

"Of course I am."

"You seem a little distracted."

"Do I? Maybe it's the conference. It's been pretty tense. Churchill has his heels dug in up to his ankles."

A minute passed in silence. "I haven't written very much, have I?" said Anne.

"Neither of us has. You have a better excuse than I do."

"Is there anything you want to tell me?"

Tom hesitated. He was tempted to take the easy way out and say nothing. "I guess I've been thinking a lot about our situation. It seems like we'll never be together."

"Never?"

"I think you'll always be on the move. I wouldn't ask you to change."

"Why not?"

She was not making this easy. He paused again, looking into his wineglass. "This is going to sound corny, I know. Journalism needs people like you. There's so much fluff out there. You set a standard."

"Thank you, Tom, I really appreciate that. But I'm a person, too. I want to have a life."

Tom was losing his nerve. He gazed across the room, at nothing in particular.

"You've met someone, haven't you?"

He could not answer.

"Is it serious?"

"Kind of. She's a pilot, for the Army."

"A pilot? And you think I live dangerously?" Anne paused and sipped her wine. "How often do you see her?"

"Once or twice a month."

"I see. Well, that explains a few things."

"I'm sorry, Anne."

She took a moment to compose herself. "I won't be angry. I knew it could happen. I half expected to get a Dear Anne letter."

"I feel lousy."

"Well, things happen during a war. Any day could be our last."

"That's not an excuse for me. I'm not in much danger."

"She must be a special woman."

"She is. I have the privilege of knowing two exceptional women. I feel very torn."

"You don't need to feel badly. I'll be all right."

They sat quietly for a several minutes, and Tom signed his room number for the check. "Would you like me to get you a cab?" he asked.

They went to the lobby, and Tom spoke to the desk clerk. Then they wandered out into the cool evening and stood looking up at the stars.

"I'm cold," said Anne.

Tom put his arm around her, and she pressed against him for warmth. He hated to just send her off in the dark. Would it hurt to spend one last night together?

A black English taxi came into the driveway and stopped. The driver opened the back door.

"Tom." She reached up to kiss him.

As their lips parted, he looked into her eyes. "Goodbye, Anne."

She lingered, fighting back tears. Then she got in and Tom gave the driver five dollars. He stood watching for a long time after the car had disappeared into the street.

38

Louise arrived back at the Palm Springs base at 8 a.m. and found the ops officer.

"Any messages for me from New Castle?" she asked.

"Nope, you want to get started?"

"Why not."

"I'll get you an instructor."

Louise spent the rest of the morning going over the tech manuals with a North American instructor. After lunch, she climbed into her first Mustang, went over the layout and pre-flight checks, and did some taxiing. Then she watched her instructor take off and land a few times. About 3 p.m., he jumped down and waved her over.

"What do you think?" he asked.

"I think I can do it."

Louise donned her parachute and climbed up. She taxied out, took a deep breath, put on her oxygen mask, and gave it power. In seconds, she was climbing steeply into the desert sky. Leveling off at 15,000 feet, she began to throttle down and suddenly realized she was going over 400 mph. She slowed to 350 and practiced some turns. Then she peeled off and dove to 7,000 feet before pulling up to head back to base.

"Wow!" she said aloud. "The boys are going to like this."

Her landing was a bit bumpy and unstable. "Sorry about that landing," she said as she came up to her instructor.

"You can practice some more tomorrow morning. As you can see, it's a very sensitive plane."

"You're not kidding. I'd like to go after a Messerschmidt with it."

The next morning Louise practiced takeoffs and landings for three hours.

"That'll do," said her instructor, "consider yourself checked out."

He signed her book. "What now?" asked Louise.

"Have some lunch. I'll get somebody to take you over to North American."

Louise was always nervous riding in the back seat with a young pilot, but the short ride was uneventful and soon she was introducing herself at the North American plant. Whatever they may have thought the first time Nancy Love showed up to fly a P-51, they were more than happy to see Louise now. A young man put her things in a car and took her to a nearby motel where North American had a corporate account.

"Just sign for everything," he said. "I'll pick you up at 0730 hours."

Well, this is more like it, thought Louise. She had bought a stylish swimsuit in Palm Springs, and now she had two hours of daylight to enjoy it.

At 8 a.m. the next day, Louise watched as ground crewmen wheeled out a shiny silver Mustang with an orange nose cone and black propeller. Six 50-caliber guns bristled on the wings, and underneath them were the rocket mounts. Her host held out a clipboard for her to sign.

"This one's yours, take it to Newark. You know the way?"

"I know the way," she laughed.

"Now remember with these tanks, burn off the center one first, then alternate the wing tanks every 20 minutes. If you don't, you'll get unbalanced."

"I won't forget."

"Good. We'd like you to come back."

Louise grinned. "I'd like to have this duty all winter."

Louise warmed the engine and went through her checks. She was feeling comfortable in her new toy as she went out to the runway. She revved it up, released the brakes, and took off smoothly. Her course would take her just south of Flagstaff, and she would refuel in Albuquerque, Kansas City, and Dayton. She would cruise at about 275 mph until the engine was well broken in, then push it to 350 for the last half of the trip. With the time changes, however, she would have to overnight somewhere, and it might as well be Kansas City.

The plane was purring like a kitten as she went through a series of tests on the equipment. Everything seemed fine. She crossed the Colorado River into Arizona and flipped on the right fuel tank. Then, as she headed over the mountainous country north of the old territorial capital of Prescott, she switched over to the left tank. The engine sputtered and quit. Her airspeed and altitude began to drop. She switched back to the right tank and got the engine restarted. Could it just be a sensitive switch?

She decided to try it again, carefully. Again the engine sputtered, and she quickly went back to the right tank. She grabbed her chart and located Flagstaff. It was not showing an airfield. She found Prescott, nothing showing. She could never make it to Albuquerque, but she thought she could make Phoenix, so she banked south. The plane was getting harder to hold on course, and she had a good 150 miles to the Phoenix airport. She gradually pushed down the opposing rudder pedal to counter the plane's drift to the left. By fifty miles out, her leg was starting to ache.

She got on the radio.

"Phoenix tower, this is P-51 pilot Louise Mitchell. I have an emergency."

"Copy P-51. What is your position?"

"Fifty miles north-northwest, headed your way."

"Copy P-51. What is your problem?"

"I've got a non-functioning left wing tank full of fuel. Right wing tank is low. I'm being dragged down to port side."

"Copy P-51. We are activating emergency crews. Have you landed here before?"

"Negative."

"Runways are east-west. Can you see the city yet?"

"Negative."

"We are clearing everything. Stay to the west. We'll get you in as fast as we can."

Louise strained to keep the Mustang on course as she continued her descent. She searched for Phoenix but all she could see was brown desert and scattered mountains. Sweat was dripping from her forehead into her eyes.

"We have you on radar, P-51. Begin a gradual 75-degree turn left."

Thank God I don't have to bank right, thought Louise.

"You're looking good, P-51. Are you able to hold it?"

"So far. Keep your equipment on the right side. If I spin out, I'll go off left."

"Roger, P-51, equipment is on right side. Your course looks good."

"I see the city."

"Copy P-51. We are south of downtown. Maintain your course."

"I see your tower. I'm on visual now."

"Copy, we see you, P-51. Good luck."

Louise was straining on the rudder and trying to control the stick and throttle. She could see the runway, but it looked like it was weaving back and forth. The left wing kept bobbing down every time she brought it up with the ailerons. She realized she could probably not bring the plane in level, but she had to keep the wing off the ground. If it hit, she might cartwheel, and either be killed on impact or incinerated by the left tank. She had to get a little bounce from the left wheel without hitting the wing and try to get the right wheel down. She could see fire trucks and ambulances ahead and she used them as a target to keep on the right side of the runway.

Twenty feet off the ground the plane dipped to the left and drifted toward the center line. She leaned on the stick and gave the rudder her last ounce of strength. The left wheel bounced and the Mustang veered left, but it came down on both wheels. It bounced again and Louise used the elevators to get the tail wheel down quickly. She settled on three wheels and straightened out just a few feet from the left edge of the runway. The plane rolled to a stop and she set the brakes. She sat there in a daze, wondering if she was still alive.

A fire truck pulled up beside and she waved meekly. She took off her helmet and earphones and wiped her brow. Slowly, she finished taxiing to the end of the runway and turned toward the tower. At least a hundred people had come out to watch the wavering Mustang try to hold the runway. As she stopped near the terminal, a ground crewman climbed on the wing and looked into the cockpit. "It's a girl!" he yelled.

There was a hush over the crowd. He gave Louise a hand getting out and she pulled the comb from the back of her hair, shaking it to her shoulders. Someone began to clap, and the entire crowd burst into cheers.

39

Louise was back at New Castle on Friday evening, her P-51 now awaiting shipment on the Newark docks. A fitting had not been tightened on the left fuel line, and the vibration had worked it loose. Louise refused to consider the possibility that it could have been deliberate. These planes were being turned out in record numbers, and such things could happen. She was just glad it happened to her and not to a pilot over Germany. Her friends crowded into her room to hear the tale, and she had to tell it several times. She realized that it got better after a couple of shots of Kate's bourbon. By 10 p.m., she was deep into her dreams.

The next morning, Louise barely made it to breakfast and then went by the post office to get her mail. She was handed a single envelope and started to walk away. Abruptly, she stopped and stared at the envelope, then dropped it and sank to the floor. As she sat there in a daze, a young sergeant knelt beside her.

"Ma'am, what's wrong?"

He picked up the letter and looked at it. It was addressed to Capt. Terry Fawcett, and stamped with red ink: "Undeliverable/MIA."

Louise spent the rest of the weekend in a fog. The war was no longer an abstraction. It was killing young men she knew in Sioux City, it had almost killed her, and now it had reached into her heart and torn something out. For the first time since she came to New Castle, she was weary. She could scarcely put one foot in front of the other as she went about her daily tasks.

Late Sunday evening, Kate came in to find Louise on her bunk, with her unpacked bag lying on the floor. She pulled the chair over and sat with her legs curled around the back.

"You could get some time off, you know, after what happened."

"And do what? Lay around here? Tom won't be back for a couple of weeks."

"Maybe you should just rest a little."

"They need us, Kate. They're counting on us."

"Louise, you've been going virtually nonstop for over a year. You've done everything they've asked of you. You don't have to win the war all by yourself."

"If I sit down, somebody else just has to work harder."

Kate stood up. "For Christ's sake, is everybody from Iowa as stubborn as you are? All right, go to Farmingdale if you want to, but let me tell you something. Twelve WASPs are dead already. When you get into a fighter plane, you damn well better have your wits about you. If your mind is someplace else, I've lost another friend."

She marched out of the room and down the hall. Louise sat up and let the speech sink in for a few minutes. Then she got up and began packing her bag for the next morning.

It was the week before Christmas when Louise and Tom finally connected on the phone. In the meantime, she had made another round trip to California, this time without incident.

"Are we ever going to see each other again?" he asked.

"I'm sorry, Tom, everybody wants his plane yesterday. But I've got two days off for Christmas."

"Let me pick you up. I know someplace we can go."

"You can get enough gas?"

"I've got a bunch of stamps saved up. Could you be ready by 10 a.m.?"

"You bet."

Louise did not make much money, but she had managed to save some for Christmas. That week, she and Kate took an afternoon train into Manhattan and did some shopping. There was not much time, so they headed straight for Macy's.

"Which one are you buying for?" asked Louise, as they browsed the men's department.

"Both," said Kate. "I can't make up my mind just now."

Louise finally settled on gifts for Tom, a cardigan sweater and a nice frame for the enlargement she had of their picture at the Jefferson Memorial. Then she wandered into the lingerie department. She looked longingly at a long, silver-colored silk gown, with a price tag beyond her means.

"Try it on," said Kate, coming up behind her, "just for the fun of it."

They went into the dressing room, where Louise slipped on the gown and looked in the mirror. "It feels wonderful. I've never worn anything like this."

"It fits you perfectly. It would drive him crazy."

"If I drive him any more crazy, I won't be able to walk."

"Let me pay half, as my present to you."

"Kate, I can't let you do that."

"Louise, you have got to have this gown. You can make it up to me. I'll find something."

Louise looked in the mirror again and embraced her friend. "That's enough," laughed Kate, "you're starting to drive me crazy."

Back at New Castle, Louise went about wrapping presents and getting ready to go with Tom the next day. Kate had stopped at the post office to pick up their mail, and she dropped off a brown package from Sioux City. Louise opened it eagerly. Two smaller packages were gift-wrapped inside, along with two front pages from the local newspaper. She looked at the first and saw herself beside the P-47, under the headline, "Sioux City's Own Louise Mitchell at the Controls." A nice two-column article followed.

The other page was more recent. It carried a small picture of Rose and an article about her being honored by the Parent-Teacher Association. As she finished reading it, Louise's eyes drifted to another story that began near the bottom. She remembered the author—Anne Wilson of the *Washington Post*.

They told us at Cairo that we would be in Rome for Christmas. Sitting in this muddy trench a couple of miles from the Gustav Line, trying to eat soggy rations with the scream of 88mm shells as dinner music, feeling the concussion of one that lands 50 yards away, hearing the agony of a man who's been hit, Rome might as well be at the North Pole.

Nearby, a dozen soldiers in their ponchos groan as they try to get a truck back on the road. Whoever named this 'sunny Italy' never tried to (Cont. on p. 5)

Louise shivered as she thought about this woman and these men coping with such conditions. She must be a saint, she thought. I don't think I could ever do that.

At 10 a.m., Louise was huddled in her overcoat, chatting with the young sentry at the main gate. She waved as she saw the elegant Packard turn in.

"Looks like you're goin' in style this time, Miss Mitchell."

"That's no jeep, is it Corporal? Have a nice Christmas dinner."

"You too, ma'am."

She melted into Tom's arms and they shared a long kiss. Then they piled her things into the trunk and climbed into the roadster. "Set a course due north," said Tom, "we're going to the Poconos."

Louise had decided not to tell Tom about her close call. She also did not want to talk about Terry Fawcett, nor about Jennie. The past was the past. After two hours of driving, they were climbing into snow-covered hills. They dropped into a narrow valley and pulled in at a rustic lodge. Inside, a huge fireplace dominated a spacious lounge, and wide windows looked out on a meadow and stream.

"What a wonderful place!" said Louise.

"Have you done any cross-country skiing?"

"No, but I've ice-skated. Does that count?"

"I'll bet you can do it."

They checked into a cozy room and Tom gave her an extra pullover he had brought. "Here's one of your presents," he said, as he handed her a stocking cap.

"Did you knit this yourself?"

"Not one of my talents, I'm afraid."

"Well," she said, as she kissed his cheek, "I'm not complaining."

In a back room of the lodge, they were outfitted with skis, poles, boots, and heavy gloves. They set out on a farm road that crossed a bridge and followed the edge of the woods on the other side of the valley. Louise plodded slowly at first, but soon she was getting the hang of it. Then came a short downslope. She bent her knees as she was told, but soon she was leaning too far forward. She pitched back, lost her balance, and went down in a heap. As Tom skied down toward her, she struggled like a turtle on its back.

"You think this is funny, don't you?"

"I didn't think it was funny when I used to do it. Get your skis crossways of the road and try to bring your knees under you."

Louise got herself back up and tried to brush off the snow. "Don't think I'm going to quit."

"I can't imagine you quitting."

She made it to the bottom, but on the next slope, she fell again. That, however, was the last time. On the return trip, she enjoyed each little rise and fall. As twilight fell, they went into the lounge and sat near the fire with cups of hot chocolate and brandy. Clouds had moved in and big snowflakes were falling outside.

"Oh, look," said Louise, going to a window. Deer were approaching the lodge looking for food. They watched for a while and went back to the fire.

"Tom, I love this!"

"Good, here's the *coup de grace*." He had found a book of poetry and began reading Robert Frost's "Stopping by Woods on a Snowy Evening."

As he finished, Louise put her head on his shoulder. "Did you plan all this? Is this all one big plot to seduce me?"

"Yes, all these people are working for me. Even the deer."

"Well," she said as her lips touched his, "against those odds, I don't think I can hold out much longer."

They had dinner around a long table with four other couples. Everyone was jovial, and no one mentioned the war. After a homemade dessert, they went up to their room. "When should we open our presents?" asked Louise.

"When did you do it at home?"

"Christmas Eve."

"Then let's do it."

Louise got to open the first one, a 3 x 5 authentic Persian rug, brought back from Tehran. "Tom, this is the real thing."

"I thought it would liven up your room a little. You can sit on it and meditate."

"Thank you so much. I don't have anything like that for you."

"Well, let's see what you've got." He opened the picture. "This is perfect. It will go on my desk."

Louise then opened a smaller package, and inside was a turquoise necklace from Egypt. Again, she was nearly speechless.

Tom opened the sweater. "Would you believe I don't have a cardigan. This is a great choice."

Finally, Louise opened a pair of earrings that matched the necklace. She modeled the jewelry and gave Tom a big kiss. "Would you mind if I took a bath?" she asked. "I won't be long."

"Leave the water and I'll rinse off, too."

Tom piled the presents to one side and turned down the covers. Before long, Louise came out wearing her robe. "Your turn."

When Tom emerged, he saw Louise curled up on the bed. She got up and let her robe fall to the floor, revealing a long, slender silk gown. She loosened Tom's robe and pushed it off his shoulders, then came against him slowly in a kiss.

Kate was right. They got very little sleep on Christmas Eve.

40

Tom and Louise managed to drag themselves out of bed in time to have brunch at the lodge. They dived ravenously into muffins, scrambled eggs, sausage, and fruit. Then they took their second cups of coffee to the fireplace and sat on the couch.

"Were you satisfied with the conferences?" asked Louise.

"No, but I guess Roosevelt was. It was pretty much a standoff. We ended up just about where we started."

"Why were you dissatisfied?"

"I'm afraid I'm a little out of step. I found myself agreeing with Stalin quite often. I think we should stop wasting resources in Italy and get on with the invasion of France."

"But Mr. Churchill says no."

"Mr. Churchill says no. It was fun watching Stalin, though. He knows a few colorful phrases in English, and he throws them out every so often."

Tom sipped his coffee. "Churchill started giving his reasons for delaying the invasion, and Stalin was getting more and more animated. Finally, he launched into a tirade to his interpreter, and the poor man got as red as a beet. He turned to Churchill and said, 'Mr. Prime Minister, Marshal Stalin believes I have not understood what you have been saying. He wants you to repeat it more slowly so I can get it right.' There was a Russian diplomat across

265

the table from me who understood English, and we were both trying desperately not to laugh."

Louise did laugh. "What did Churchill do?"

"He took a big puff on his cigar and began again, trying to say things as simply as he could. Halfway through, Stalin gets up, waves his hand, and says, 'The toilet is over there, yes?' Then he nonchalantly walks out."

Louise was laughing again. "Did Churchill get to finish his speech?"

"He never got to the end of it. Roosevelt wheeled over to him and said, 'Winston, why don't we forget about this. Let's just keep the invasion on schedule.' That was that."

"Tom, that's a great story." She leaned over and kissed him. "Will you always tell me stories?"

"I can't promise I'll have material like that."

When Louise returned that evening, there was an official-looking letter on her table. She opened it and sat down to read. The letterhead was that of U.S. Army Air Forces Headquarters.

Miss Mitchell:

Mrs. Nancy Love has given me a report of the incident at Phoenix earlier this month. I want to commend you for your brave and skillful action that saved both you and the aircraft. I am deeply sorry that a manufacturing defect placed you in this dangerous situation.

The press of business prevents me from writing letters to the many people who deserve them. I hope you will convey to your colleagues my deep appreciation for the service that they are performing. Please also give them my best wishes for the holiday season.

It is my hope that we will soon be able to convince the Congress to commission the WASP pilots in the Air Forces. That has always been my desire.
Sincerely,
Gen. H. H. Arnold, Commanding
U.S. Army Air Forces

She looked up to see Kate in the doorway. "I've been waiting since yesterday to know what's in that letter."

Louise handed it to her. "Whoa, the man himself, congratulations. And Nancy, when's the last time you heard from her?"

"Close to a year. Do you think they'll ever commission us, Kate?"

"I doubt it. We're too much of a bargain."

"It sure would be nice to have some benefits," said Louise. "Even a uniform allowance would help."

"Why don't we just commission ourselves? From now on, you are Captain Mitchell. I'll be Captain Burns."

"What happened to lieutenant?"

"That's for the new girls. We'll be captains, and Betty can be a major. Whenever you call a tower, it's Captain Mitchell."

"I don't know. Impersonating an officer is a serious offense."

"At the civilian fields, they'll never know the difference."

"Kate, sometimes I can't tell when you're kidding."

"I swear, I'm going to do it sometime."

"Well, don't do it at Republic. Dave will think it's funny, and he'll start calling us all captains. He'll get us in a peck of trouble."

"So, tell me, how did the gown work?"

"Like a charm. I really owe you."

"Do you think this is it? Theee one?"

"God, I hope so, Kate. I really hope so."

"How does he feel about your flying?"

"I know he worries about me. I didn't tell him about Phoenix. But he supports what I'm doing. I think I could keep flying."

"OK, I want to be maid of honor. That's the payback."

"Oh, Kate, I would have asked you anyway. You'll have to think of something else."

4 1

In late January 1944, Tom flew to Hawaii to observe a meeting of Pacific Fleet commanders. He was disturbed by the heavy casualties taken at Tarawa and wanted more first-hand information on what had happened. At Pearl Harbor, he found that almost nobody, not even Admiral Nimitz, was comfortable with the drive across the Central Pacific. They did not relish the planned assaults on the Marshall and Mariana Islands. Tom spent the trip home studying the reports and maps he had received at the conference. Back in Washington, he went to his scheduled meeting with Roosevelt and Hopkins.

"Good," said FDR, "now I can find out what's going on. The Chief of Naval Operations is fit to be tied."

"Admiral King is upset?" asked Tom.

"Upset?" said Hopkins. "Whoever said 'Hell hath no fury like a woman scorned' never met Ernest J. King."

"Well, I'm sorry to hear that. I thought it was an excellent conference. It was a sober reassessment after Tarawa. Here's my outline of the points they made."

He handed them each a sheet of paper. "Tarawa showed the unpredictability of Pacific tides and the difficulty of getting landing craft across the coral reefs. The Marianas will be very heavily defended, they have poor harbors, and they will be a long way from land-based air cover."

"King is saying we learned our lessons at Tarawa," said Hopkins, perusing the outline. "He says we won't take casualties like that in the Marshalls."

"Maybe not," said Tom. "The Japanese may sacrifice the troops in the Marshalls. There's good reason to believe that they are pulling back to make their stand in the Carolines and Marianas. I'm afraid Tarawa will look like a picnic compared to what we're going to see in the Marianas. Why hit the Japanese strong points if we can outflank them?"

"So the Pacific boys want to stay to the south and head for Mindanao," said Roosevelt, "and you agree with them."

"Yes. I've never liked the way we've divided our forces in the Pacific. We're much too scattered for what we've got out there. I think a coordinated drive in the South Pacific could take the Philippines much sooner. From there we could cut off supplies to Japanese garrisons and interrupt the flow of oil from the East Indies. B-29s could hit Japan from both the Philippines and China."

"King wants to draw the Japanese fleet out for a decisive battle," said Hopkins.

"I think we could have it in the Philippine Sea, when they try to stop the landings."

"Are you talking about a strictly naval campaign, or do you want MacArthur to keep going?"

"I think MacArthur should keep going and get more naval support. Beef up Halsey's forces as the southern wing of the naval thrust."

"So MacArthur gets to keep his pledge," said Hopkins.

"It's not just that. I think he knows now how to leapfrog the Japanese in New Guinea and put our air power to use. I think the two drives would put a real strain on the Japanese. If they try to move troops from the Marianas, their convoys would be sitting ducks."

"Tom, Tom," said Roosevelt, "why do you do this to me? You come in here after all the compromises have been made and you start with your analysis and put everything in question. What's worse is you're probably right. You were right about Chennault, and now I'm beginning to think you were right about Anzio."

"It's not too late to adjust our strategy in the Pacific, Mr. President."

Roosevelt wheeled back and looked out the window, drawing slowly on his cigarette holder. "You know, after Churchill and Stalin, the next biggest headache I have is keeping King and MacArthur from bolting the corral. If we overrule King on the Central Pacific, he'll resign. The Republicans will demand hearings and want to talk about the whole conduct of the war. It's an election year, they'll run with anything they can get their hands on."

"I'm afraid I agree, Mr. President," said Hopkins.

Tom sat silently as Roosevelt wheeled slowly back to his desk. "Tom, we've been together a long time. You're practically like a son. Don't think I don't value your reports. I think about them a lot."

"Thank you, Mr. President."

"We're going to win this thing. We're going to throw so much stuff at these people they'll drown in it. But as long as we're making progress, I'm going to let King and Marshall do it their way."

Tom got up to leave. "I understand, Mr. President."

"By the way, Tom, tell Anne Wilson that I read every one of her stories."

42

As spring progressed in 1944, Louise was in the air more than she was on the ground. Republic was sending planes to its Evansville plant for some key modifications, so Louise made a number of trips there, bringing back finished planes to the Newark docks. She would leave Farmingdale early in the morning, have lunch in Evansville, and be back to spend the night at her Long Island motel. Despite the repetition, she enjoyed these runs. She would put the Thunderbolts through a series of maneuvers, including climbs and dives, to make sure that there were no apparent defects. She loved the power of the engine, and in the last hour of each run, she would open it up several times to 400 mph.

Sometimes, she would take a P-47 from Evansville to Long Beach for shipment to the South Pacific and bring a Mustang back to Newark. She and Kate had a friendly competition to see who could log the most P-51 hours. The Army wanted to get as many Mustangs to Europe as possible for the long-awaited invasion of the continent.

Louise was finding it hard to get together with Tom. After a hiatus of several weeks, she was able to clear a weekend in late April.

"Hi, Tom."

"Who's this?"

"Silly boy, this is Captain Mitchell."

"Are you serious, have you been commissioned?"

"Kate commissioned me."

Tom laughed. "That's good enough for me, Captain."

"May I come down this weekend? I've got a surprise for you."

"It will be a surprise if you come down."

"I'm really sorry, Tom, I just haven't been able to get a break."

"I know. I've been working weekends myself, trying to get more landing craft on their way. Between us, we could do an amphibious landing."

"So, is it OK?"

"It's more than OK. It's a command performance."

Tom waited on the end of the platform for the train to come to a stop. He scanned the crowd emptying out of the cars, but could not pick out Louise. Suddenly he heard a familiar voice, and coming toward him was a lovely woman in a beret, belted blue wool jacket and skirt, and heels. On her jacket were silver wings and a shoulder patch.

"Louise, you've got a new uniform!"

"What do you think?"

"You look smashing. I've never seen a blue uniform in the services."

"It's called Santiago blue. Jackie Cochran designed it."

"Did you have to pay for it?"

"The Army issued us the uniforms, but I had to buy the shoes, shirt, and tie. We've also got duty uniforms with short jackets and slacks. We're supposed to get summerweight versions in a few months."

"It's about time. It seems like the least they can do for you. Are you allowed to kiss me in uniform?"

"Ooh, my first kiss in Santiago blue."

In the midst of people coming and going, he gave her a tender kiss. "Now I have a surprise for you. I have matinee tickets for *MacBeth* at the Folger."

"Really? I love Shakespeare."

"Best of all, we can walk there. I didn't even bring my car."

They had a light early lunch at Union Station, then strolled around the Supreme Court and Library of Congress, a roundabout but pleasant way to the Folger Library. Leaving the bright spring sunshine, they stepped into Renaissance England, with oak paneling and richly carved wood. They browsed through the beautiful manuscripts and editions of Shakespeare's works, then took their seats in the Elizabethan theater, with its classic railing across the stage balcony. As she sat listening to dialogue that she had only read before, Louise slipped her arm gently inside Tom's and touched her head to his shoulder. She resolved that she would not let this happiness escape.

At dinner that evening, Louise told Tom about an unpleasant incident she had during a refueling stop in Oklahoma City. "I started to leave the canteen and a man stopped me and said, 'Why don't you girls go home where you belong? We don't need you anymore.' He had a real bitter look in his eyes. It scared me."

"There are always going to be people like that. Don't let it upset you."

"I guess so. I told my squadron leader about it, and she said a lot of private instructors are out of work because the Army is closing down contract programs. She said they're starting to agitate."

"Well, I do know that our pilot losses have been considerably less than we expected."

"If I'm not needed, how come I can't get a day off? The guys at North American all say the WASPs are their best ferry pilots. They say we're the only ones that don't complain. At Republic, we're the only pilots they've got."

"I don't think you should worry about it. General Arnold knows how important the WASPs are. And with the track record you have, I think you'll be able to stay with Republic after the war."

"How would you feel about that, Tom?"

Tom hesitated, and Louise thought she might have done it again. He seemed so cautious about the future.

"I know how important flying is to you. I hope you can keep on."

Louise wanted to change the subject. "Well, spring is here and we're together. Can we go see the azaleas tomorrow?"

"You're thinking about tomorrow?"

She grinned and reached with her feet to touch his. "You're right. First things first."

On Sunday morning, they returned to the National Arboretum and reenacted their first kiss, this time among the overwhelming colors of the rhododendrons and azaleas in bloom. As he watched Louise's train disappear that afternoon, Tom felt that he had made the right choice. It still bothered him that he had put his own happiness ahead of Anne's, and he hoped that she would fall in love with someone who could accept and support her career. He still cared a lot about her.

43

The streets were dark and quiet as Tom drove to the White House on the morning of June 6, 1944. Hopkins was in his office pondering a draft of the president's radio broadcast, expected later in the day. The news from Italy first—Romans were celebrating the occupation of the eternal city by allied forces. The uncertain part was what Roosevelt would be able to say about the drama unfolding on the beaches of Normandy.

"Anything from Eisenhower?" asked Tom.

"Not yet," said Hopkins.

"They should have hit the beaches three hours ago. I hope they achieved maximum surprise."

"There's been nothing on German radio so far. That seems like a good sign."

"Is the president awake yet?"

"He called down half an hour ago. He should be here any moment."

Before long, the president's secretary called to say he was in the Oval Office, and the two of them went in. Roosevelt was wearing a polka-dotted bow tie, and despite the early hour, he looked energized. "Gentlemen, we are beginning an historic day."

"The waiting is finally over," said Hopkins. "Now we'll see if it was worth it."

"I wish I could have seen that flotilla," said Roosevelt, "the greatest in world history."

"Imagine what it must have looked like to the Germans on the shore," said Tom.

"They've been told to expect a diversionary action in Normandy," chuckled FDR. "I can just hear the commander trying to talk to Hitler, '*Mein Fuhrer*, this does not look like a diversion.'"

"We'd better not assume anything," said Hopkins. "If Hitler reacts quickly and throws his Panzer divisions into Normandy, we may not be strong enough to hold the beachhead."

The phone rang, and FDR answered. "Yes, George, what have you got?" There was a pause. "What about Omaha?...Hmm... OK, keep me posted."

"The British and Canadians got ashore with little difficulty. They're moving inland. We're in good shape at Utah Beach, but we're pinned down on Omaha. Heavy casualties."

"Well, I guess that's good news overall," said Hopkins. "We should probably wait on Omaha before making an announcement."

Later that day, with the Omaha beachhead finally established, Roosevelt went on the radio to inform the nation that the great crusade to liberate Europe was underway. During the next several days, Tom spent a great deal of time at the White House following the course of the campaign. Then he returned his attention to supply bottlenecks. Although several fierce battles ensued, such as those for Caen and St.-Lo, it was clear by mid-July that allied forces were poised to break out of Normandy.

One morning, Roosevelt called Tom over to talk about strategy in the Pacific. He was in a mischievous mood.

"Now, I want to see if I've got this straight. The Chief of Naval Operations wants to bypass the Philippines and invade Formosa. The commander of the Army Air Forces agrees with him."

"Yes," said Tom, "General Arnold would like to have Formosa as a B-29 base."

"General MacArthur, of course, wants to go straight for the Philippines and just bomb Formosa. Admiral Halsey agrees with him."

"Yes."

"Admiral Nimitz probably agrees with Halsey, but he doesn't want to go against King. General Marshall can't make up his mind."

"I think you've got it, Mr. President."

"So where do you weigh in, Tom."

"I agree with MacArthur and Halsey. If we go after Formosa, we'll have to assault heavy Japanese defenses head on. It will be Saipan multiplied several times." Tom was trying to avoid looking at Hopkins, whose son, a Marine, had recently been killed in the Marianas.

"The Philippines offer many alternatives for landings, and we can use our mobility to greater advantage. MacArthur can continue his strategy of cutting off Japanese garrisons. Once we control Luzon, we'll have excellent bases to cut off Japanese oil and bomb all of their strongholds."

"How can we get King to accept this? He still wants the big naval battle."

"The Japanese know the Philippines are critical to their empire. They'll send their entire fleet to try to stop the invasion. The key is to get there before they do. There are plenty of narrow waters where we could ambush them."

"I like this approach," said Roosevelt, "but I don't like just imposing it on King and Marshall."

"I think Nimitz is the key," said Tom. "If he would weigh in with MacArthur, Marshall would come along and King would have to give in."

"Maybe I should go out to Hawaii and meet with them," said Roosevelt. "Let them make their cases. If I leave the chiefs here, Nimitz can be a little more candid."

"Bring MacArthur to Hawaii?" asked Tom.

"Yes. I haven't seen him in years. I want to see if he's grown horns."

"Well, I can tell you one thing, Nimitz will have a hard time getting a word in."

"I'll make sure he gets his say. What do you think, Harry?"

"I think Admiral King will be suspicious as hell, but I like it. After all this 'MacArthur for President' business, we could use some good pictures of you with the General."

"MacArthur will see the politics in it," said Tom. "He'll go along if gets his way on the Philippines. If he doesn't, he could raise a lot of hell before the election."

"Well, I think your strategic analysis is sound," said Roosevelt, "and if we can get MacArthur back on board, it may clinch the election for us."

A few weeks later, Tom was aboard a cruiser accompanying the president to Pearl Harbor, where they had a two-day conference with Nimitz and MacArthur. He was back in Washington in early August and called New Castle on a Saturday. To his delight, the WASP who answered said Louise was there."

"Aloha, Tom. You're back from Hawaii."

"I'm back."

"I hope you didn't let any of those Hawaiian women put flowers around your neck."

"Well, we did have a luau on the last night."

"My, the things you do for your country."

"When can you get away?"

"Why, you're in luck, Mr. Clark. I can get away tomorrow."

Shortly before noon on Sunday, Louise stepped off the train in her crisp, blue, summerweight uniform. After a long embrace, they set off for lunch on the banks of the Potomac. As they sat finishing their wine, Louise shifted her seat closer to Tom and took his hand.

"So, how did it go with the General and the admirals?"

"I wish you could have seen it, Louise. We docked at Pearl, and all these admirals were lined up, decked out in white. The band started playing and they marched up the gangplank like a family of ducks. But no MacArthur."

"He wasn't there yet?"

"When everybody was on board, we hear sirens, and several police motorcycles appear, leading a huge open car. The thing circles around the area and finally stops at the ship. MacArthur gets out wearing his crumpled cap and leather jacket, smoking his corncob pipe. He strolls halfway up, stops and waves to the crowd, then comes on up and greets Roosevelt like they were old friends. It was a masterpiece."

"So did the General get what he wanted?"

"He and Roosevelt both got what they wanted. They did a tour of the hospitals and a motorcade in town. Lots of pictures."

"Did you do anything serious on this trip?"

"As a matter of fact, there were two long strategy sessions. The General outdid himself. It was the most impassioned performance I've ever seen. FDR needed aspirin afterwards."

"What about Nimitz?"

"Roosevelt quizzed him a lot. He just about conceded that MacArthur was right. King will have to come around before long."

"Are you happy with the outcome?"

"Yes, I think it's the right thing. I think it will reduce our casualties."

Louise squeezed his hand and kissed his cheek. "Well, I know just how to celebrate. What do you think, Mr. Clark?"

"I think you always know what to say, Captain Mitchell."

44

On a Friday in September, Tom came home and picked up his mail. To his surprise, there was a letter from Anne. He sat on the balcony, took a deep breath, and opened it. It was written more than two weeks earlier.

Dear Tom,

I'm writing this from a field hospital in a house on the Left Bank. After 2 ½ years of Japanese and Germans shooting at me, one of them finally got lucky. I took a sniper's bullet in the left shoulder. It's not serious, but it did glance off my collarbone and break it.

After what I've been through, I'm almost embarrassed to tell this story. I came into Paris with a Free French armored division. I was riding in a jeep with two officers in what we assumed was a secure area, and I asked them if they wanted to see where I used to live. So we went across the Pont Neuf and pulled up in front of my old building. As we got out, a sniper opened fire from just up the street. Thank God he was a poor shot; I'm the only one he managed to hit.

The force of it knocked me down, and my companions thought I was dead. I guess the sniper did too, because he didn't shoot me again. I lay as still as I could while one of the officers returned the fire. The other made his way into the sniper's building. After several minutes, there was a grenade blast inside and no more sniper.

So now I'm a casualty. The worst part is that I missed de Gaulle's march down the Champs Elyseés. I could hear the cheering but couldn't see a thing.

I hope you don't mind my writing to you. I was just sitting here feeling sorry for myself and wished I could talk to you. I know you're probably happy with your new love, and I don't mean to be a nuisance. I just want you to know that I'll never forget you.

I don't know what I'll do when they let me out of this little infirmary. It looks like the Germans are on the run, so I may go to England for a while. I may even head for home. There are plenty of correspondents here now.

I hope you are well and giving Mr. Roosevelt lots of good advice.

Best wishes,
Anne

Tom sat in the autumn sunlight and pondered the letter. His heart had jumped when he read the first paragraph. It was obvious that Anne still had an emotional effect on him. He was touched that she wanted to share her experience with him, but it was also unsettling. It had been a terribly painful experience to let her down in Cairo, and he never wanted to be in that position again. He could not imagine letting Louise down.

Still, he felt it would be hurtful if he just ignored Anne's gesture. Maybe if he wrote her a brotherly letter, she would understand that he cared about her but was committed to someone else. In the next few days, he tried several times to start one but could not get very far. The problem, he realized, was that he was trying to say something without really saying anything. Maybe he should just tell her the truth, tell her how he really felt. He began again.

Dear Anne,

I shuddered when I read the first paragraph of your letter. I have had nightmares after reading some of your stories and realizing how exposed to danger you have been. Thank heaven you were only hit in the shoulder and can recover fully.

I hope you will decide to avoid the front now. I still worry about you—I have always worried about you. My decision to end our relationship did not mean that I didn't love you and care about you. I just came to feel that we would always be separated for long periods of time. I have reached a point in my life when I want to be close to someone, to share common experiences.

I am in love with someone now who makes me very happy. It's true that we only see each other once or twice a month, but that will change when the war is over. She is a remarkable woman, and I know that under different circumstances you would like her a lot.

It was very difficult for me to say goodbye to you, Anne. I know that if I had asked you directly, you might have given up your international career for me. But I didn't want to take that responsibility. I admire your work greatly, and I believe you make a valuable contribution to our public life. I am not just saying this as an excuse—I truly believe it.

I hope you will forgive me for speaking frankly about where I am in my life. I would like very much to keep in touch with you, but I want to be sure it is not under false pretenses.

You have been and will always be a very special part of my life. I hope you will find love to match your achievements.
    As always,
    Tom

    This time he put the letter into an airmail envelope and sealed it. He called the *Post* and got her current address, then with a twinge in his heart, dropped it in the mail. He felt he had done the right thing. Now he could be more confident with Louise. He wanted to see her as soon as possible.

45

In early October, Louise descended from a C-47 at New Castle with four other tired WASPs and loaded her gear into a waiting jeep. The barracks were unusually quiet as they trudged in, and Louise noticed several groups of her colleagues sitting around in rooms but saying little. Kate had picked up her mail and left it on the table, and Louise noticed a letter from AAF headquarters. Could it be her commission at last?

She opened the envelope and found two letters, the first from Jacqueline Cochran.

To All WASP:
General Arnold has directed that the WASP program be deactivated on 20 December 1944. Attached is a letter from him to each of you and it explains the circumstances leading up to his decision.

Louise felt increasingly frustrated as she read the rest, the usual expressions of gratitude, etc. She had known this day would come, but why now? She and her friends were busier than ever. She curled up on her cot and began to cry. She wished she could burrow into Tom's arms and shut out the world.

She awoke at 10 p.m. and sat for several minutes in a daze, wondering if the letter had been part of a dream. It was still lying on the floor, however, and she decided to try calling Tom.

"Hi, Tom, it's me."

"Louise, you sound a little down."

"They're disbanding us."

"What do you mean, disbanding the WASPs?"

"We got the letters from General Arnold. December 20 is our last day."

"I can't believe it. Did he give a reason?"

"They've got enough pilots without us."

"Are these guys willing to do what you women have been doing?"

"Who knows? I wonder how many of them want to tow sheets for target practice, or chase around the country like I do. I don't think North American is going to be very happy, with the Mustangs they've got backed up out there."

"Well, maybe this is the time to line up a job, while you're still working with the companies."

"I guess so. I'm just feeling really let down. May I come see you tomorrow?"

"Of course. I wish you were here tonight."

"So do I."

As October and November ground along toward the WASP's D-day, Louise had little time to feel sorry for herself. Among other things, she started getting assignments to fly combat-weary planes to salvage centers. They included things she had not flown before, such as Dauntless A-24s, and some of the instruments had stopped working. For the first time, Louise did not feel comfortable in the air. Maybe, she thought, it was time to be getting out.

She had one more trip to California and took the occasion to talk to her friends at North American about a job. They were evasive.

Orders were winding down. They were not sure what they would do with their own pilots. Let them know how they could get in touch with her. As she sat in the canteen near the hangar, two men came in accompanied by a poised, lovely woman in a short blue jacket and slacks. The woman noticed her and excused herself from the men. Louise rose to shake hands with Nancy Love.

"Louise, it's been so long. I've missed you every time I came to New Castle."

"Hello, Nancy, how are you?"

"Trying to keep my chin up, like everybody else. May I join you for a while?"

"Please do."

Nancy got a cup of tea and sat down. "Are you here to pick up a Mustang?"

"Yes, it might be my last one. I sure will miss them."

"I know what you mean. It's my favorite plane."

"I talked to the people here about maybe getting on with them. They discouraged me."

"They discouraged me, too. I tried to interest them in some of our Long Beach pilots."

"I'm going to give it a try at Republic, but everything I hear from people is gloomy."

"I wish I could offer you some hope, Louise, but I'm not optimistic. It seems like the backlash is starting with us. I think we could have kept flying for a while if Jackie hadn't pushed so hard in Congress."

"What do you think you'll do, Nancy?"

"Probably go back into the aviation business with my husband. First, I've got to write a report for the Ferry Division." Then with a sly grin, she added, "I still have to wangle my way into a B-29."

"Have you flown everything else?"

"Just about everything the Army's got."

"It's going to be hard to go back to small planes, isn't it?" said Louise.

"It sure is."

"I really shouldn't feel sorry for myself. This has been a wonderful two years."

"Have you flown any twin-engine planes?"

"Just copilot once, in a B-24."

"There's one thing I can do for you. I'll cut you orders for three days at Palm Springs to check out in a P-38. That'll give you a twin-engine rating for your license."

"Nancy, I really appreciate that."

"You've earned it. I've got to run now. I'll call the ops officer at Palm Springs and he'll have your orders. Somebody here should be able to give you a ride."

Nancy offered her hand. "Good luck, Louise."

"Thank you."

Louise sat for a while and mused about what had just taken place. She had been chatting casually with the most accomplished woman flyer in American history. Not bad for a girl from Sioux City, she thought. She finished her tea and got to her feet. OK, I'm off to fly a Lightning.

46

MacArthur's troops landed on the beaches of Leyte on October 21, 1944, and the General himself waded ashore four hours later. Although he was annoyed about wading at the time, he soon realized that he had inadvertently starred in one of the most famous photographs of the war. As Tom expected, the Japanese gambled most of their remaining fleet in a desperate attempt to destroy the carriers and transports supporting the invasion. The battle of Leyte Gulf, full of confusion, misjudgments, and heroism, resulted in devastating losses for the Rising Sun.

The battle of the Philippines was far from over, but the enemy's naval losses made it possible to start thinking about plans for the final defeat of Japan. American pilots, now flying superior fighter planes, had eliminated most of their Japanese counterparts, but a new phenomenon made its appearance in Philippine waters. Young Japanese men with minimal flight training were loading planes with bombs and flying into American ships. Despite the large number of kamikazes sent crashing into the sea, some of them were getting through and either sinking or heavily damaging their targets.

With most of the supply issues resolved, Tom was spending a lot of time reading intelligence reports and studying the situation in the Pacific. In early December, he asked Hopkins to make time for a strategy session with Roosevelt. Entering the Oval Office in mid-afternoon, Tom was alarmed at the president's appearance. His face was pale and the dark circles under his eyes gave him almost a ghastly look. Tom felt uneasy about asking him to sit through a presentation, but FDR smiled and got things started on a humorous note.

"Ah, we've heard from all the Joint Chiefs, now we have the gospel according to General Clark. I hope you won't disappoint me by agreeing with someone."

"I won't disappoint you, Mr. President."

The president's secretary brought tea and cookies on a silver tray, and Hopkins poured for all of them.

"OK, I'm ready," said Roosevelt. "Let's hear your ideas."

"What concerns me is the kind of defensive strategy the Japanese used at Saipan. They didn't try to keep us off the beaches and they didn't throw banzai charges at us. They were dug into caves and bunkers in rugged country and they defended every yard of ground they held. Our bombardments didn't do much good. As you know, we took over 16,000 casualties there."

"So you think this is the way the Japanese are going to fight from now on," said Hopkins.

"Yes. I think they're going to be heavily dug in on Iwo Jima and Okinawa. I believe they will use those battles as a preview to an invasion of Japan and then try to negotiate an armistice."

"An armistice, not a surrender," said Hopkins for clarification.

"Right. The army still controls the political situation, and they're not going to think about surrender."

"We're committed to unconditional surrender," said Roosevelt, "are you suggesting we back off?"

"We can't have one policy in Europe and another in the Pacific," said Hopkins.

"I'm not suggesting we seek an armistice. I've been thinking about strategies for achieving a surrender without taking massive casualties."

"Well, I'm going to hear you out, Tom," said FDR, "but the Japanese are fanatical about not surrendering in the field. I doubt there's going to be any easy way to end this."

Tom went to the map rack and flipped to the Pacific Theater. "We now control the Marianas, and we will soon control the Philippines. With air and naval bases in those locations, we can deny the Japanese all of the oil and raw materials from the East Indies. We are also finally waging an effective submarine campaign. We are now capable of mounting a submarine blockade of the Japanese home islands and denying them materials from Malaya and Indochina. We can also prevent them from supplying their troops on Iwo and Okinawa."

Hopkins interrupted. "But as long as the Japanese hold those islands, their planes are a threat to our bombers and ships. Iwo is right on the route to Japan."

"I think the kamikaze attacks indicate that we have almost destroyed Japan's conventional air power. I think if we carry out continuous raids on Iwo, Okinawa, and Formosa, we'll be able to eliminate the air threat altogether."

"Without destroying the factories?"

"Planes aren't much good without pilots. The key is to keep our ships out of range of the kamikazes. If we try to take Iwo and Okinawa, our invasion fleets will be heavily exposed. I think that instead we should cut the supply lines with submarines and air attacks."

"So you think we can lay siege to Japan and force a surrender," said Roosevelt. "That could take a long time."

"It would take time, I agree. But it would reduce our manpower requirements and allow us to bring home the units that have been out there for two years. That would be a politically popular move."

"I just don't think a blockade alone could bring about a surrender," said Hopkins.

"I don't either," said Tom, "but combined with our B-29 campaign, I think it could. In my opinion, the Emperor is the key. We know he wants the war to end. We have to convince him that his country will be destroyed if he doesn't take control and overrule the army. It's also important to realize that the civilian population is just beginning to feel shortages. We can make that a lot worse."

"Our B-29s are not doing a very good job of hitting targets," said Hopkins.

"I know. I don't think precision bombing is going to work. But if we concentrate the raids on Tokyo, the Emperor will see the consequences of holding out. We could also drop millions of leaflets informing the population of the situation."

"I still don't see how we would deal with the Japanese army," said Hopkins. "It's largely intact."

"I've studied the reports we've had about Rabaul. The troops there were psyched up to fight a decisive battle for Dai Nippon. Instead, we just left them there and cut their supply line. Their morale eventually fell apart. We can deal with all the Japanese garrisons the same way. If the Emperor makes peace, we'll let their troops know they can come home without their weapons."

"So how would we deal with the Emperor?" asked Roosevelt in a hoarse voice.

"At the right time, you could send him a personal message spelling out the terms of a surrender. He would have to agree to an occupation force under General MacArthur's command, complete disarmament, and adoption of a democratic constitution subject to our approval."

"Leave the Emperor in place?" asked Hopkins.

"He would be our best ally. The Japanese people would cooperate if he instructed them to."

"You're really asking me to stick my political neck out, Tom," said FDR. "The popular notion is that Hirohito is a war criminal."

"If we could occupy Japan without another bloody battle, it would be a political victory. And one more thing, with this approach we could drop our request that Stalin join the war against Japan."

"After we badgered him to commit to it?"

"I believe we could do it without him."

"Well, you haven't disappointed me, Tom. What do you think of all this, Harry?"

"I think it's very speculative."

FDR reflected for a moment. "You're not completely out in left field, Tom. Admiral King seems to be leaning to a blockade. He's an old submariner, of course."

"It might be the first time I've agreed with King. Maybe I should rethink this."

They all laughed a little, then sat pondering and gazing at the map. Tom finally broke the ice. "Would you mind if I went out there and did some poking around? I'd like to talk to the intelligence people at Pearl and Guam. I'd also like to sound out Nimitz and his commanders informally."

"I guess there's no harm in that," said FDR. "Just be sure you don't raise a lot of eyebrows, and stay away from the press."

"Agreed. Thank you, Mr. President."

47

O ne day in early December, Louise went in for a talk with the test department at Republic. The response was so similar to North American's that she wondered if somebody had written it for all the companies. Her colleagues had all been scouting around, and nobody was encouraging them except the Civil Aeronautics Administration. It was looking for air controllers and communications people.

On December 19, Louise and Kate wandered from one office to another at New Castle, turning in their uniforms and flying gear, settling up accounts, doing paperwork, saying good-byes. It was a debilitating experience. They were allowed to keep one uniform, and Louise decided to keep her wool dress blues. She wished she could see Tom right away, but he was in the Far East. She had a key to his townhouse, and they had agreed that she would go there and wait for him. They would spend Christmas together and, Louise hoped, talk about the future.

That evening, Louise and Kate dressed in their best civilian clothes and went to a farewell banquet. It seemed strange to be in the officers' club without their uniforms. A lot of tears were shed, but as the evening went on, the women decided that their last night together was going to be fun. Jokes began to fly, mostly at the expense of male pilots. They told funny stories about what had happened to them as they traveled the country. As Louise and Kate walked back to the barracks, they had a warm feeling despite the uncertainties that lay ahead. They promised to keep in touch with each other and get together often.

The next day they were given a ride to the Wilmington train station. Kate was heading to Philadelphia for a connection to Pittsburgh. As the conductor gave his final call to board Kate's train, they shared a last embrace.

"Don't forget, I'm the maid of honor. Don't wait too long."

"You haven't even met him yet."

"That's all right, I'll take him sight unseen."

The train began to move, and Kate was gone. Louise felt as if the ground beneath her feet was falling away, piece by piece. She had checked her trunk with a porter, so she lugged her suitcase and flight bag to her platform. As her train clanked along toward Washington, she was oblivious to the people around her. She tried to imagine what the days would be like when Tom got home. Was he ready to accept her as a full-time companion? Should she stay until New Year's and then go back to Sioux City while he decided what he wanted? What would she do with herself if she stayed in Washington?

She let herself into the townhouse and tugged her trunk inside. Everything was neat and clean. On the dining room table was a set of keys and a note.

Dear Louise,

Please make yourself at home. I made room for your things in the guest room closet and the highboy.

Feel free to use the car. There is also a supply of trolley tokens and a line map in the top left drawer of my desk.

I hope to be home by the 23rd. I will call when I have an ETA.

In case you have any problems, I have left the office and home phone numbers of my friend Jack Pierce near the phone.

I love you very much,

Tom

Louise smiled and read the note a few more times. Then she began settling herself, thinking about what she could do for the next few days. She decided she would do some decorating for Christmas. A tree did not seem practical at this point, but perhaps she could find some pine boughs and candles. She needed to look for some presents for Tom. She also wanted to just get out and walk around the neighborhood, which was populated with lovely homes. It would give her time to adjust to the abrupt change in her life and think about what she really wanted at this crossroads.

Louise kept busy over the next few days, and the feeling of being adrift began to give way to the anticipation of hearing Tom's voice. She stayed up late on the 22nd hoping for a call, finally giving in to a fitful sleep. Awake at her usual early hour, she bathed and washed her hair, generally trying to make herself as attractive as she could. She laid out the sweater and skirt that she wore the first night they made love.

As noon approached, she became more and more anxious. Reluctantly, she opened Tom's address book near the phone and found the number for Roosevelt's secretary. She stared at it for a few minutes, then nervously picked up the phone and dialed.

"White House."

"Is this the president's secretary?"

"Yes, who's calling?"

"My name is Louise Mitchell. I'm a friend of Tom Clark. I've been expecting a call from him, and I wondered if you had heard something."

"We know he expected to be home for Christmas, that's all."

"OK. I'm sorry for disturbing you."

"That's all right, Miss."

Louise was sorry she had made the call. The president's secretary did not seem to have any idea who she was, and she hoped it would not cause Tom any embarrassment. She found a duster and began to poke around looking for surfaces that needed dusting. After a while, she sat down at Tom's desk and began looking at Jack Pierce's phone numbers. Hesitantly, she lifted her finger to dial the number.

"Col. Pierce here."

"Oh, Col. Pierce. My name is Louise Mitchell. I'm a friend of Tom Clark."

"Louise Mitchell the pilot?"

"That's me."

"Yes, Miss Mitchell, what can I do for you?"

"Colonel, I know I'm being silly. I've been expecting Tom to call and let me know when he would arrive back in Washington. He was supposed to get here today."

"Do you know where he was starting from?"

"I'm not sure, I think either Hawaii or Guam."

"Where are you now?"

"I'm at Tom's place. I'm really sorry to bother you. I just thought I should have heard from him by now."

"I understand. Listen, I know somebody at Hickam Field who might be able to help. It's early there, but I'll send a radio message and see what I can find out."

"I feel like I'm causing unnecessary trouble."

"Don't worry, I'd like to know myself. Call me if you hear anything."

"I will. Thank you so much, Colonel."

Louise felt a little better for having done something, and she tried to relax while waiting to get some news. As the sun moved toward the horizon in the winter sky, her nervousness was turning to worry. She tried to imagine reasons why Tom had not been able to call. He was probably delayed getting to California, and would call as soon as he could. The phone rang about 4 p.m., and Louise hurried over to it.

"Hello?"

"Miss Mitchell, Jack Pierce again."

"Yes, Colonel."

"My contact in Hawaii replied that Tom went to Guam a week ago and, as far as he knew, was still there. I sent another message to someone I know in Guam. It will be a while before I get a reply, but I'm going to stay here and wait for it."

"Colonel, I don't know how to thank you. I'm sure we'll hear that he's taking off from Guam today."

"I think you're right, but I'd like to pin things down. Are you all right, Miss Mitchell?"

"I'm OK, Colonel, just nervous. I'm sure we'll get some news."

"I'll be in touch."

Louise turned on the radio and settled down with a New Yorker magazine. Before long, she was reading words but they were not registering. She would go back to the top of a page and start again. Eventually, the evening news came on, and she found herself listening intently. American troops were surrounded at Bastogne and were desperately holding on while allied armored divisions maneuvered to break the surprise German attack. MacArthur's forces were mopping up on Leyte and securing airfields on the island of Mindoro, south of Luzon. Louise wondered what was involved in "mopping up," and how a mother would feel if told her son was killed while his unit was mopping up.

The news ended and music came back. Louise lay on the couch and drifted off to sleep. She awakened a few hours later to a knock on the door.

"Who is it?"

"It's Jack Pierce."

Louise quickly opened the door. "Colonel, come in. I dozed off. I must look a fright."

Jack took off his overcoat and sat at the other end of the couch from Louise. "I received a reply from Guam. Tom left there yesterday morning in a B-17."

"Yesterday? Where could they be? What's he doing in a B-17?"

"I don't know for sure. My guess is that they were flying one back for salvage, and he hitched a ride."

Louise was turning pale. "A crate? I flew some of those. God, I hope he didn't get in one."

"I sent a message to all of our stations between Guam and Hawaii. They may have made an emergency landing for repairs and didn't bother to let anyone know."

Louise got up and began to pace. "But why wouldn't Tom get a message to me?"

"I don't know. I don't have an answer. I'm hoping to have a report first thing in the morning."

She sank back onto the couch, her hands clutched together. "I'm sorry, Colonel. I know you're doing everything you can."

"Miss Mitchell, have you eaten anything today?"

"Just some breakfast. I haven't been very hungry."

"I know where we can get a late dinner if you're up to it."

"I don't want to leave, in case Tom calls. I made a pot of corned beef and cabbage yesterday. Would you like some?"

"Sounds delicious."

Louise began heating dinner while Jack sliced some bread and opened a bottle of burgundy. She could not bring herself to be cheerful, but she was grateful to have some company and a reason to talk about something else.

"How long have you known Tom?"

"Since the first war. We served on some committees together when he was in the Navy Department and I was in the War Department. We started playing tennis. When he came back to Washington in '33, he tracked me down."

"It's nice to have a close friend for so long."

"Tom means a lot to me. He's like an anchor in my life."

"That's such a nice way to put it."

"I understand you have a friend in West Virginia."

"Yes, at the Greenbriar, but I've only seen her twice. My best friend is Kate, my buddy in the WASPs. I'm going to miss her terribly."

They sat down to dinner. "I'm sorry about the WASPs," said Jack. "I work closely with General Arnold, and I know he wanted to keep you flying. He was just fighting too many battles in Congress and had to give in on something. His top priority is his B-29 program."

"Why was Congress upset with us?"

"It was mostly southerners with a lot of seniority. They just aren't ready for women to step outside their traditional roles. The civilian pilots gave them the ammunition they needed, and I'm afraid Mrs. Cochran was an easy target."

"It's hard for me to believe it's over. For two years, I've been flying around in wonderful airplanes."

"You've been in pursuits, haven't you?"

"Mostly 47s and 51s. I loved them."

"I envy you. The only flying time I get any more is in transports and a few bombers. I was born too soon."

"Do you think the Army will open up to women pilots again?"

"I wish I could say yes, but I doubt it. We'll be discharging a lot of pilots who would like to stay in."

"Well, I have Tom now. I'm not going to worry about flying. If something comes along, fine."

They finished dinner, and Jack prepared to leave. "I'll let you know what I find out in the morning. I think we'll have some good news."

Louise was feeling much better, and she relaxed enough to sleep soundly until 6 a.m. She bathed and had a light breakfast, then put on the clothes she had laid out the day before. As she sat listening to the morning news, she again heard a knock at the door. She opened it to see Jack Pierce, looking grim.

"Jack, what is it."

"I've had a report from Eniwetok, in the Marshall Islands. They got a distress signal from a B-17 two days ago. They sent out scout planes but couldn't find anything. Yesterday a carrier searched the area with 30 planes. Nothing."

Louise stared at him. "What are you saying?"

"They've given up the search. They consider the plane lost at sea."

"No!" she said angrily. Tears were welling up in her eyes. "No! It's not true! This is not happening!"

"I'm sorry." He took her in his arms.

"No, no, no." Louise was crying uncontrollably. Jack helped her slowly to the couch and sat with his arm around her. He let her cry for several minutes, then offered a handkerchief.

"They could still be out there, somewhere," she managed to say.

Jack was silent. A tear escaped slowly and trickled down his face. He did not want to prolong false hope. "I'm sorry, Louise, I wish I could believe it too."

She sank into his arms and closed her eyes. Finally, she sat up and wiped her face.

"Louise, you have my numbers. If there's anything I can do, please call me."

"Thank you, Jack. I need to be alone for a while."

Louise sat for hours staring out the living room window, not noticing the cars and pedestrians that occasionally passed by. Snow began falling and the trees and grass turned gradually white as Christmas Eve approached. She was numb. She felt as if she were trapped in a nightmare and could not wake up. She could not think about the future, not even about the next day. It was nothing but a blur.

She finally fell asleep on the couch, awaking in the early morning hours. She lay there for a while, then rose and changed into warm clothes. Putting on her overcoat and boots, she went out into the darkness and began wandering through the new snow. Eventually, colored lights began to come on in windows, a sign that children could wait no longer to open presents. Louise felt starkly alone. She knew she had to get out of Washington.

She went back to the townhouse and began to slowly pack her things. Mid-morning, the phone rang. It was the voice of an elderly woman.

"Oh, I must have the wrong number."

"This is Tom Clark's house."

"It is? I'm his mother. Is Tom there?"

Louise could barely answer. "I'm sorry, he's not here."

"Not there on Christmas day? To whom am I speaking?"

"This is Louise Mitchell, a friend of his."

"Oh, Miss Mitchell. Tom has told me about you. Where is he?"

"Mrs. Clark, I don't...I can't...." Louise was beginning to cry again.

"What is it, dear?"

"His plane is missing."

There was silence at the other end.

"Mrs. Clark?"

"Where is it missing?"

"In the Pacific."

"Since when?"

"Three days ago."

More silence. "Mrs. Clark?" There was a click, and the line went dead. Louise sat for several minutes, then dialed Jack Pierce at home.

"Jack, it's Louise. I just spoke to Tom's mother."

"What happened?"

"She couldn't continue. She had to hang up."

"Louise, I know Mrs. Clark. I'll call her back in a little while. How are you managing?"

"I'm trying to pack. I'm going back to Iowa."

"I think that's the best thing. I can take care of things here."

"I should give you the key I have."

"I'll come over this afternoon."

"Thank you, Jack."

Late that afternoon, Louise boarded a train at Union Station. No Pullman berths were available, so she settled into a coach seat by the window and tried to ignore the activity around her. As the train moved toward the Potomac, the Jefferson Memorial was silhouetted in the sunset. Louise fought back tears as it passed by. It would be a long trip.

48

The taxi pulled in front of the big house on Third Street, and the driver carried Louise's trunk to the front porch. Jennie and Rose heard the commotion.

"Louise, you're home," said Rose.

Louise said nothing, but somberly embraced her sisters.

"Let us help you get these things inside." Rose and Jennie carried the trunk into the living room.

"Louise, we had no idea," said Jennie. "What happened?"

Louise sank into one of the big chairs. "He's gone, Jennie."

Jennie stared at her and the color began to drain from her face. "Who's gone?"

"Tom's gone. His plane went down in the Pacific."

Rose went to her sister and put her arms around her. "Louise, I'm so sorry, I'm so sorry." They both started to cry.

Jennie was standing motionless. Suddenly she turned and went upstairs. Rose eventually helped Louise get her things to her room, and Louise lay down on the bed. Rose sat and took her hand.

"I'm tired, Rose. I'm so tired."

As 1944 drew to a close, Patton's Third Army was breaking the back of the German drive into the Ardennes, sealing the fate of the Third Reich. MacArthur was preparing to invade Luzon, the main island of the Philippines, while Nimitz and the Marines prepared to assault a small volcanic island named Iwo Jima.

In Pittsburgh, Kate Burns celebrated New Year's Eve with old friends from the local aviation community. She wondered when she would hear about wedding plans. In White Sulphur Springs, Janet Simmons prepared New Year's Eve dinner for guests of the Greenbriar. The manager told her that as long as he was there, she would be the head chef. Janet was happy, but she wondered why her Christmas card to Louise had come back, stamped "Discharged."

Anne Wilson left Europe to cover the final phase of the war against Japan. She spent Christmas with her parents at Asheville, then flew to Washington to renegotiate her contract with the *Post*. From National Airport, she took a taxi to Northwest Washington.

"Stop here," she said, a few doors beyond Tom's house. "Could you wait a few minutes?"

She walked back and stood on the sidewalk. Tom's car was in the driveway, but there was no sign of life inside. As snow collected on her head and shoulders, she thought about going to the door. What will I say if his new girlfriend is there? Do I want to meet her? I could just be an old friend wishing them a Happy New Year.

She heard a gruff voice down the street. "How much longer, lady?"

Anne looked at the driver, then back at the townhouse. Slowly, she walked away and got into the cab.

A few days later, President Franklin Roosevelt bundled himself up against a chill wind and attended a memorial service at the old Fort Myer chapel in Arlington Cemetery. He and Jack Pierce sat next to a silver-haired woman, trying to console her. Finally, the president left to spend New Year's at his retreat in Warm Springs, Georgia. No one noticed a woman in a black coat who had entered during the service and sat in the back, her face covered with a veil.

In Sioux City, Louise Mitchell stumbled through endless days, saying and doing no more than life absolutely required. She occasionally went out and wandered the neighborhood, barely acknowledging the greetings of those who saw her. She ate little and soon began to look thin. Her only interest seemed to be splitting firewood.

Rose and Jennie tried to engage her in conversation or games or cooking, but without success. They would come home from work and find her wrapped in a blanket in front of the fireplace, staring at the fire as if she were hypnotized. As December gave way to January, they became more and more alarmed. One Sunday, there was a knock at the front door, and Jennie went to open it. She let Sam Crane into the living room and quietly left them alone.

Sam went to Louise's side and touched her shoulder. Without looking, she reached across and laid her hand on his. "Jennie told me what happened. I'm truly sorry, Louise."

She said nothing, continuing to stare into the fire. After a few minutes, Sam moved away and sat at the other end of the couch. They remained in silence for a while.

Finally, he said softly, "Louise, I never told you this, but I was married once."

Louise glanced at him, then back to the fire. "I loved her as much as anyone could. She left me for another man while I was in France. I was so despondent I quit the Army after the war. I've always regretted it."

Louise glanced at him and pulled her knees up under the blanket. She gazed into the fire again, as if looking away would break her spell. "Why have you never told me this?" she said with an air of suspicion.

Sam reached in his pocket and took out his wallet. From somewhere inside it, he produced a small, worn photograph. It showed a young man in a flying jacket and a lovely young woman. Louise took it and looked at intently.

"I've never spoken of her to anyone. There was too much pain."

Louise remained silent. "Life has to go on, Louise. You've come too far to just give up."

Sam got up to rearrange the fire, then returned and sat quietly for a few more minutes.

"I was in Omaha yesterday, and they have some Army surplus planes for sale at the field there. Real cheap. I'm thinking about trying to get a loan to buy one."

He waited for some response, but none came. He did not seem to be getting anywhere.

"I saw an AT-6 that was in very good condition. I thought it would be fun to take people up in it."

Sam waited again, but Louise did not move. He leaned back and crossed his legs, letting his own gaze drift to the fire.

Suddenly, Louise stirred and shifted her position. "Did they have any four-seaters?"

Sam sat up and looked at her. "They had some nice liaison planes. I saw a Fairchild and a Stinson Sentinel. And a beautiful Beech staggerwing."

Louise was still looking at the fire, but a faint smile had appeared on her face.

"Do you think any of them could be fitted with pontoons?"

*   *   *

Franklin D. Roosevelt met with Churchill and Stalin at Yalta in February 1945, where Stalin renewed his promise to declare war on Japan after the defeat of Germany. Roosevelt died in Warm Springs on April 12, 1945, less than a month before the German surrender.

His successor, Harry S. Truman, was appalled by the 75,000 casualties that Americans suffered in taking Iwo Jima and Okinawa. In August, he authorized the use of atomic bombs on the cities of Hiroshima and Nagasaki, leading to the surrender of Japan without an invasion. Russian forces had just entered the war against Japan and proceeded to occupy Manchuria and northern Korea.

Douglas MacArthur accepted the Japanese surrender and became for six years the most powerful person in that country. Because of the reforms he dictated for Japanese society, he could legitimately be considered the father of modern Japan.

In 1945, Nancy Harkness Love became the first woman to fly a military aircraft around the world. She soon retired from aviation and gave birth to three daughters. A private person, she never lived in the limelight like Amelia Earhart and Jacqueline Cochran. She died of cancer in 1976 at the age of 64, one year before Congress finally recognized the wartime service of women pilots.

The women of the Ferry Division delivered over 12,000 aircraft for the Army during a two-year period. Their WASP colleagues flew a variety of missions, including many that male pilots tried to avoid. In all, nearly one thousand women flew in the WAFS and WASP. Thirty-seven lost their lives in the line of duty.

You can read more about women pilots of World War II in the following sources:

Sally Van Wagenen Keil, **Those Wonderful Women in their Flying Machines: the Unknown Heroines of World War II**. New York: Four Directions Press, 1990.

Adela Riek Scharr, **Sisters in the Sky** (2 vols.). Gerald, Mo.: Patrice Press, 1986-88.

Marianne Verges, **On Silver Wings**. New York: Ballantine Books, 1991.